PRAISE FOR KYLE MUNTZ

"Playful and painful and surreally real, and great fun to read."

BRIAN EVENSON, AUTHOR OF *SONG FOR THE UNRAVELING OF THE WORLD*

"There's a melodic beat to Muntz's writing, terse descriptions of events interspersed with sudden bursts of graphic visuals, often macabre in its evocations. It's a delicate balance, but one he masterfully navigates."

PETER TIERYAS, AUTHOR OF *MECHA SAMURAI EMPIRE*

"What if the horror boom of the 1980s had instead exploded during the era of emo? Everybody you know would be reading and re-reading *The Pain Eater*. A dark slow burn of a novel."

NICK MAMATAS, AUTHOR OF *THE SECOND SHOOTER* AND *I AM PROVIDENCE*

"Absurd, grim, and wonderfully unique, Kyle Muntz's *The Pain Eater* is an exceptional read from a new and distinct voice in horror."

ERIC LAROCCA, AUTHOR OF *THINGS HAVE GOTTEN WORSE SINCE WE LAST SPOKE*

"One of the strangest, most original things I've read this summer... a work of radical, subversive innocence."

JAMES PATE, AUTHOR OF *THE FASSBENDER DIARIES*

THE PAIN EATER

KYLE MUNTZ

Copyright © 2022 by Kyle Muntz

ISBN: 978-1955904065

Cover by Matthew Revert

CLASH Books

Troy, NY

THE PAIN EATER

THE OLD HOUSE

THE FUNERAL

IT WAS Michael who found dad's body, but Steven didn't see it until the funeral. He'd been home a few days already, but part of him still believed dad was somewhere else, maybe off on a trip (though dad hadn't taken trips). Lee Hanson had been a man who planned carefully for the future even if he didn't quite know how to live in the present, and it wasn't like him to go off like this. Of course, Steven wasn't the first person to think that. The strangest thing any father can do is die.

It was a small funeral, almost embarrassingly small—sixteen of them, barely enough to fill half the room. Mom sat in the front row, without Ben. Michael didn't want Ben there, and Steven hadn't cared enough to intervene. Anyway, it seemed weird to bring Ben to dad's funeral... so Michael had won that one. But he still wouldn't talk to her. Steven had seen mom keep trying all day without any luck. Though at least Michael wouldn't yell in public, like he did when mom came around the house.

Steven sat with Michael in the opposite aisle. That left mom alone with grandma Granger: a thin, corpselike woman Steven had never known very well, her voice gnarled and raspy from lung cancer. Mom always told stories about grandma Granger, how nice and supportive she was. But neither brother had ever felt like part of mom's family, and it had been a relief, after the divorce, to not have to see them anymore. They were nice, normal Christians who had big parties every Christmas and seemed to actually enjoy spending time with each other; and for as long as Steven could remember, he'd hated being in the same room with them.

Mom started crying early on—and Steven was surprised how, even now, any sign she was unhappy made him feel good. Michael gave her the same, almost triumphant look. Steven knew it wasn't fair, that really they were never fair to mom, but he didn't care. He hoped she felt like it was her fault. That was half of what Steven talked about with Michael: things mom did wrong. Michael's list got longer every time Steven came home; and each time it made Steven angry at her again, even when he'd told himself he'd be a bit nicer this time. At least a little.

Steven hardly listened during the eulogy. It was the pastor from mom's church, a large, almost leonine man who did his best to appear very cool and worldly and not like a religious person. Steven had never seen him start out so somber. Years ago, when she'd dragged them to church (something Steven had never forgiven her for), the pastor always started out with a joke. But it seemed weird to have him at dad's funeral. Dad hadn't been religious. He'd never believed in much of anything, except for *doing what needed to be done.*

Steven could still hear dad's voice in his head, the exact tone of him saying those words. Dad had said them so much over the years it was sort of annoying—except now there was nothing else left of him.

The truth hit Steven as they stood up, forming a line towards the casket. Every step forward brought a deeper, sinking feeling— a sort of tilting weightlessness, like flying someplace he'd never wanted to go; starting behind his throat, tracing a line down his stomach, and settling in some secret, hidden node behind his balls. [p1] It was fucking with his center of gravity; worse the closer he got to the casket, amidst the strained, respectful looks on everyone's faces.

They all looked down like there was something to see, like there was some significance to the gesture—but no. It was a ritual: staring at a corpse. Mom cried harder when she got there, so hard Steven almost felt embarrassed—the same way everything she did embarrassed him. But it was okay, because it kept him from looking at dad.

Instead, he watched Michael step forward. But Michael had seen dad already. He didn't stop, or even turn towards the coffin. He just kept his eyes down and walked past.

Steven had been to funerals before, his great-grandparents on both sides. As a little kid, when someone that old died it was still sad, at least theoretically, but at the same time something felt very right about it. Old people were meant to die. It seemed very normal for them to settle into their proper place in the universe, weighed down by those lines on their faces, their unsteady, shaking limbs and their turgid, brittle bodies. But it didn't seem right to look at dad.

The skin was strained and firm and almost waxy—a delicate, pellucid transformation that gave dad a kind of terrifying youth. One detail in particular stood out. Dad always used to have a mustache before the divorce. After that it became a beard, not a big one but enough to cover the way a man's throat sags when he hits fifty. When Steven was young, dad's mustache had seemed like the ultimate symbol of adulthood: some terrible remnant of the eighties dad would always wear on his face. Having a mustache marked you as grown up, as an adult who lived in the real world—until the mustache disappeared. Dad had changed forever. But now he was dead and he had a mustache again.

It was difficult, strangely difficult, for Steven to believe this body had once belonged to the man who raised him. Some details were right—the broad face with its wide cheeks and solid, almost oaken skin, just barely showing the jowls. But he seemed too small beneath the suit. Diminished. Dad had never been very tall, but that belly made him seem large: a robust, adult fullness... only maybe there was more to it. He'd pushed two-twenty at his heaviest, but it had gone down, way down, since the divorce. Going on five years now. A few more and dad might even have been thin.

Steven leaned down, like he'd seen everyone else do. The feeling surprised him—curiosity. But even that was odd. Wasn't he supposed to feel something, some terrible sadness? He almost felt proud of himself, and then a bit bothered. It must be in the details somewhere, the sadness. That's why he looked so close at the black wave of dad's hair, just now thinning at the front; those quiet, peaceful eyes that never rested when he was alive; even the hands folded delicately across his stomach. Shouldn't a normal person feel something more when he looked at the dead body of his father?

But then, there it was, the shimmer of something far in the distance—that lilting, sinking feeling in his pelvis. It had been there the whole time, only he didn't want to notice it. Was that what grief felt like? Was that real pain? He felt very curious, almost excited, as the sensation made its way up from his stomach, towards his throat, sharpening to a faint hint of discomfort. But he only turned his head at the last second, when he realized what was going to happen.

Any longer, and he would have vomited on the corpse.

———

Even while it happened, part of him barely noticed. Steven always made the same sound when he threw up—this heavy, lurching wretch. It was so loud, not a sound a human should make. He watched distantly as vomit flecked back onto his shoes: the nice, sharp Dockers he'd bought a few days ago from a shop out near the mall. Was it this loud when everyone vomited, this terrible roar churning in his ears?... or was it like part of him had always wondered, always secretly believed? (He was strange, different, somehow more grotesque—no one else made that sound. No one else was so terribly, brutally physical.)

Three sprays, he counted. The first came in a heavy, sharp blast —someone would have to clean that carpet, but at least it wouldn't be him. The second hit along with the smell: a harsh, acidic fire, reeking so much like it tasted. There were pieces of hot dog in it. (That was even worse, how something tasted when it went in you then came out.) The third convulsion struck hard, but the fourth conjured only a few bits of white foam—and after that, just pain as Steven wrenched a few more times, the sense of scraping at the bottom of an already empty barrel.

Steven looked up to a still and silent room. Part of him wanted to wipe his mouth on his arm, but he couldn't, because this was an expensive tuxedo and they were renting it. He wondered the same thing—shouldn't he be embarrassed? Again, it almost made him proud not to be. Everything used to embarrass him a little.

When he met people from high school, or took too long to order food at a restaurant. But now he'd vomited in front of a crowd and hardly felt a thing.

"I'm alright," he said, looking from face, to face, to face. Most of them he recognized. Older—dad's friends, men with very plain, American names like Dave, and Rich, and Buzz, and Cliff. So many wide eyes. Some of them frowning; others with their mouths hanging open. Mom was walking towards him—but Michael was backing up. And Steven could tell when his mom put her hand on his shoulder that she felt good being the okay one for once: the one giving advice, instead of receiving it.

"Don't worry, Steven," she said. "It's normal to be sad."

"I just got a little sick." He glanced, counted—six, no seven flecks on his shoes. Two tiny dots on the pants. He needed to clean them soon or else they'd stain. Someone else would have to deal with the puddle, warm enough to give off a faint mist of steam.

He started, but didn't finish, counting the pieces of hot dog. Rustling and footsteps—probably they stepped back because of the smell.

"Wow." Steven wanted some sign of disapproval, of transgression, from the pastor, but didn't get it. "I made a mess, didn't I?"

"It's okay, son." The pastor even sounded like he meant the words. But none of them understood. Steven wanted to explain. It wasn't because he was sad, though he was. It was simpler than that.

"I was just a little sick. It's over now."

"It better be," Michael said—and it must have surprised everyone when Steven started to laugh. Maybe that made it ok, which is why one, then a few more people laughed too.

"It's okay, hon." Mom rubbed him on the arm: soft, then harder. There was something very comforting and maternal in the gesture. Which was weird because she wasn't so good at being maternal—and seeing her like that, like such a mom, sort of annoyed him. "I miss him too. We all do."

Steven pushed her hand away, and it made him feel good to see her face fall. It always felt good to remind her they wouldn't let her be the mom she wanted to be.

"I should go clean up, shouldn't it?"

"Lick it up," Michael said. "That should do the trick."

"Shut up, Michael." Steven glanced up, around. Everyone was still staring at him—but now it didn't feel natural. Now his face burned, and he felt more pressure behind his pelvis uncomfortably like he needed to take a shit.

"I need to go," he said. "I'll be back."

"We'll be here," mom said.

The embarrassment finally hit as Steven walked past everyone on the way to the door. If dad was still alive, probably this would have made him angry. Dad would have done his best to stay composed in front of everyone, then he would have blown up at Steven in the car. *What's wrong with you?* he would have asked. But no answer was ever good enough.

For so many years, when something went wrong—even once, as a teenager, when Steven had gotten in a car accident—the hardest part had always been telling dad. For something small he would get a stern, disapproving look, and another lecture about *doing what had to be done*. For something big, especially something embarrassing, dad would call him an idiot. Sometimes dad got furious, so angry everyone knew to leave him alone for the rest of the day when he went into another room to watch TV... and when he came out once before bed, you knew to be still, to be quiet; and if his gaze passed over you, just one word could bring the wrath of the giant.

But now Steven was an idiot and there was no one to tell him, because dad was dead. So he went into the bathroom, cleaned off his shoes with a big handful of paper towels, and went into the stalls to take a shit. It took a long time: pushing, and pushing, and pushing. Except no matter how long he did it, that feeling in his stomach didn't go away.

When he got the call from mom with the news, a week ago today, the first impression had been an absence somewhere in himself: a space he'd thought would always stay filled, some force or solidity underlying the universe. No matter what happened, dad would always be there: to give advice that was never quite as useful as he thought it was; a looming authority even now, when he no longer told Steven what to do; to help out with money and taxes because Steven still didn't understand any of that stuff. But now there was nothing, and it left a hole: the shadow of a thing that ought to be there but wasn't.

That was what sadness felt like, he'd decided—but no, Steven realized as he was sitting in that stall, gritting his teeth and pushing. It felt like needing to take a shit; except even afterwards, you didn't feel any better.

TOGETHER IN DAYLIGHT

THEY WERE all waiting for Steven when he got out—a big crowd near the door. The casket had been shut into a big black car at the head of the procession. Seven cars in total. It had been an even smaller funeral when grandpa killed himself. This is what a Hanson had waiting for him when he died. But at least dad had a few friends. There had been no one for grandpa, so few it had made his funeral feel like a weird parody of a real funeral.

"I'm okay," Steven said again as they got into the car. They all sat in the back: Steven on one side, mom in the middle, and Michael on the other side. "I told you, mom. Just leave it alone."

"I'm here for you, bud." Her hand closed on Steven's knee this time; too warm on a hot day. Steven pushed it away, but that didn't keep her from saying: "We all love you."

"Stop, mom. I don't want to hear this right now."

"Yeah, he's just being a bitch," Michael said.

"Michael!" Mom was no good at sounding in control—hearing her try and fail made it almost funny. "That's not appropriate."

Steven couldn't see past her, so he leaned out first before saying, "Fuck you, Michael."

"Steven!" Mom's voice verging on shrill. "You're supposed to be the mature one."

"I didn't realize it was going to happen," Steven said. "I swear, I'm okay now."

A weird little awkward silence, the kind they always had with

11

mom. It had been a while since all three of them were in the same room.

"I didn't mean anything by it," Michael said.

Steven said, "It's cool."

"I couldn't help it. It's kind of funny."

"It's not right to make jokes at a funeral," mom said.

"Stop, mom," Michael said. "We know."

"We're not kids," Steven said.

Another pause. Steven felt her shrinking in the seat between them. And yeah, especially now, it felt good.

"I was just saying," she said.

"We know," Michael said. "You're always telling us things we already know."

"I don't mean to nag," she said. "It's just—"

"We know," Steven said. "It's better now. Michael misses dad too, mom."

"I miss him more than she does," Michael said.

There was the spear—Michael had been waiting to throw it, and it hit right in her weak spot. Four years ago, before Steven left, he would have leapt at the chance. He would have grabbed the handle of the spear, and twisted hard. Now it made him feel very mature and grown up and adult to bring the conversation back on track. (Though not so grown up he hadn't enjoyed it.)

"We're fine," Steven said. "Michael and I always get along."

"Well, at least it's good to have you here," mom said. "It's been a long time since we've been together as a family."

Michael said, "Stop being weird, mom."

MOM'S FRIEND

IT WAS A SHORT, quick burial, an awkward gathering in the grass—and Steven couldn't wait for it to be over. For Christ sakes, did they have to keep looking at him so much? He was okay, he kept saying, but no one seemed to believe him. And everyone kept coming up to him at the reception. They would put their hands on his arm, and offer their condolences; and he would lower his head and say he was alright, really. None of them believed him. It made him a bit angry every time, that disbelief, so eventually he felt claustrophobic and annoyed and he sort of wanted to punch someone in the face.

The reception was as quick and awkward as the funeral. Mom had decided to have it at the old house since there were so few people, and it was strange to see all those familiar faces in the front room, but older. Dad's friends had always come to play poker. His poker games had been an intermittent ritual throughout Steven's childhood, every six months or so when 'the guys' would crowd around the table and eat bean soup and burp and fart and shout at the end of each hand, and Steven would stay in bed listening to them in the front room. Afterwards there always used to be a mountain of beer bottles on the table, but the mountain got smaller as time passed. The guys were getting old, dad had said, and left it at that. Dad had gotten older too.

The worst part was the food. Steven was in a bad mood, and at least there should have been something good to eat—but instead they had Papa Johns, and potato salad and coleslaw from Walmart, and a tray of vegetables with ranch, and mom had made Rice Krispies. Back in Niles, a little pimple on the southwestern asscheek of Michigan, and goddam if they didn't eat like this was a small town. Four years in Chicago and Steven felt like he was basically the same, but he'd gotten a taste for real food. And there was a part of him that felt smug and couldn't believe mom had ordered pizza at a funeral.

It was a short reception—only an hour and dad's friends were gone. That left just mom, grandma Granger, and one of her friends—Tiffany. Michael had slipped away at some point, like he always did. Both of them had always hated mom's friends, especially the ones from church. Michael had told her that he didn't want all of those church women at dad's funeral, and Steven had agreed, so she'd only invited Tiffany, her oldest friend from high school.

Tiffany was mostly okay, but Steven still kept his distance. She was mom's friend, after all. Mom was careful to give him space at first, but he knew she would call him over eventually. He couldn't even pretend to be eating more because the food wasn't good enough to eat.

"Steven—" mom's voice was warm and almost tinkly in the way it only was when she was talking to friends. "Could you come over here for a minute?"

"Just for a minute. I'm about to go out."

"Where?"

"To find Michael." Or, really, anywhere.

"Yeah, you ought to bring him back—it's not right him for to disappear while people are still here. But come talk for a while! It's been so long since I've seen you."

"Right, okay."

Mom put her hand on Steven's shoulder and squeezed. She was always so *proud* of him—she couldn't talk to someone about him without showing off. He made her happy, so much it showed in her eyes. But yeah, it still annoyed him. Especially the way she asked questions she already knew the answer to.

"Steven's just graduated. Four years in Chicago—and for free! I'm so proud of my boy, going to school for free. Could you tell Tiffany what you majored in again?"

"Just general studies, mom."

"You know, Lee and I, we only did two years. It's what everyone did back then. But Steven's the first one in our family to get to a degree from a big school."

"Yeah mom, I know."

"When I heard—gosh, when I heard. 'My son's going to school for free!' I'm so proud of him. And it's good to have him back."

"Stop, mom. You're being weird."

"Hey, I'm a happy mom—I can't help it." She smiled and squeezed Steven's arm, and this time Steven didn't push her hand away but he sort of wanted to. "I always tell you how proud of you I am. And you have a job lined up, right?"

"Not yet." He wanted to lie and say yes, he did have a job and he could get one easily, one that would let him be an adult and stay in Chicago and be the person he'd always wanted to be. He wanted to lie but he couldn't, so he settled for a half-lie. "I think I can get one though."

"You hear that? Gosh. He's going to make enough to take care of me when I'm an old lady, he really will."

"You got it, mom." Steven smiled—and yes, he let her have it for now. It was much easier to be her son when Michael wasn't around. He always felt it whenever Michael was in the room—Michael didn't quite but sort of hated her. He blamed her for so much, probably even blamed her for dad dying. Without Michael, Steven could forget about that for a while, and instead he could just blame himself.

"It's impressive, Marie." Tiffany nodded in the encouraging, patient, vaguely absent way that everyone did when they talked to mom. Everyone found Marie Hanson a bit ridiculous, a bit too much. Steven had succeeded as describing her, once, as a very nice person that nobody liked very much—and it had never been more apparent than when you talked to her friends and heard what they said about her. It always made Steven angry, even if he and Michael said worse things about her. She was their mom and they were free to think she was ridiculous. It was different when it was some stupid lady from church.

"He's handsome, too," said grandma Granger, with a corpse's voice: hard and raspy, like someone who suffered as she spoke. "He lost weight."

"I did my best." Steven was legitimately proud this time. "It's because I was cooking for myself." And, he didn't add, because he wasn't eating out of packages like he'd done here his whole life; because he'd stopped eating Taco Bell and McDonalds, even though sometimes (a lot of the times) he still wanted them. "I think it's important to eat good food."

"I've seen him cook," Marie said. "It's amazing. You know he taught me how he makes eggs yesterday? Get that—a son teaching his mom how to cook."

"The trick is to go slow," Steven said. "Or they don't taste right."

"He made me breakfast, too. He knows I've always liked omelets. He wouldn't even use any cheese and it was still good."

"It's cause all you had was that stuff from the package. Not worth it."

Mom had been looking thinner ever since the divorce—thinner than she'd ever been when she'd still been his mother. She'd bought newer clothes, straightened her hair, and stopped looking, as Michael used to say, like an eighties soccer mom… which was a strange thing to say, because neither Steven or Michael had ever played soccer. But they'd always teased about how she hadn't changed her hair since high school; until eventually she did. It was the only thing about her that had ever changed.

"I'm just proud of him, you know."

"You're repeating yourself, mom." But Steven smiled—weirdly he was a bit happy, and this was actually making him feel good, which it usually didn't but it must be he was in a strange mood.

"My son is going places," she said, "but for now he's home."

"Sure, mom," he said—and wished, as he said it, that it hadn't felt so much like a lie.

CLEANING UP

MICHAEL STAYED DISAPPEARED for about an hour, but he came back as Tiffany was getting ready to leave. Grandma Granger—her head tilted back on the couch, her jaws gaping like some whispy ghost—had fallen asleep, but anyway mom would take her back when they were done cleaning. It wasn't much of a mess, but Stephen knew she couldn't clean it herself, so he needed to be out there. Mom had always had difficulty doing very simple things; even doing the dishes could take her an hour and a half when it would take him ten minutes.

It had been a problem, a huge problem, when she was with dad—the constant, endless frustration of a very efficient person unable to understand how someone, *anyone*, could take two days to clean a room or be forty-five minutes late for everything. At times he'd seemed like a boss at work, scolding her for doing badly at her job; but more often it became a subdued, cool anger, hovering just beneath the surface. That had been such an important part of dad: this hidden, frosty anger at the world, in its endless stupidity, its unwillingness to work right or make sense.

It didn't creep to the surface often, but sometimes it did. Steven had dealt with it himself so often as a child: this patient, brutal anger whenever he or Michael forgot to do their chores. In some families it might be a small thing, but not with dad. Until the divorce, dad had cared about the house more than anything. All mom cared about was her friends at church, he said; and the boys, hell, they only did what they were told sometimes, and they didn't want to do it.

But this was their livelihood, this old house on a dirt road in a little, nice corner of Michigan. Grandpa Hanson had built it, and he'd given it to dad. Wasn't it all of their responsibility to keep it clean? Shouldn't they *want* to contribute—shouldn't they offer to do more? Dad had always thought so, until the divorce. He didn't show it often, but everyone in the house felt it. That immense, cold fury, like an iceberg barely visible above the surface of the water. They didn't see it very often—but sometimes they did.

And when they did, well. It was best just to be somewhere else.

Mom had OCD, or something along those lines. It was a weird and awkward thing, watching her clean—the way she made throwing trash away something very complex. Every part of her life was like that. She couldn't work on a schedule. And the worst part was the more important something became, the less likely she was to finish. Steven could even see the beginnings of it now, cleaning the pizza boxes. It would take him about fifteen minutes, but if he left her there she'd be there all night.

Steven was sixteen before mom managed to hold down the same job for more than two years. The same thing happened no matter where she went: teacher at a daycare; aide at a hospital; even a clerk at a store. The complaints would start to come in immediately, the sense she was falling behind and couldn't keep up—hints she wasn't good at her job, maybe even was dragging everybody down. And the worse it got, the worse she would get: until, when the stress hit a certain point, she would go into a sort of fugue, and she wouldn't be able to work at all.

Dad had held the same job as an accountant going on twenty years. But, though he was always angry at mom for not cleaning the house, he took special care not to mention the jobs. You could see it: pride. Dad thought of himself as a noble, suffering beacon of responsibility in the family, and he wanted to remind everyone of it with his silence. Silence was so important to him. He was careful not to say anything, but he wanted everyone to know.

And it was okay. Dad was a rock and he'd always be there. Until the recession hit, the stock market collapse or whatever—Steven still didn't understand what had happened, and maybe nobody did. But he knew one thing for sure. That dad, the pillar of the family, the iceberg, had lost his job. And that had changed everything.

But no, this was too much thinking about dad. It came back every time Steven cleaned with mom. Funny how that worked. She took twenty minutes cleaning up the table and Steven would think of think of how dad, going out to the den to watch TV, would look over with cold eyes, and those eyes would say: *why can't you just do something right for a change?* That's why it was so hard to be a Hanson. No one else lived in a way that made sense, not the wife, or kids, and especially not that dumbfuck world where nobody cared about doing the job right anymore.

Dad had had it hard, but he was like everyone—he made it hard for himself. Mom made it hard for herself. And Steven made it hard for himself too. Before he came back he'd told himself he would get along with her better. That's what he told himself. Except the first chance he got, the first thing she said, he was jumping on her. She told him so many times how she loved him. But if only her love wasn't so obnoxious.

"Michael," mom said, as Michael passed through the room— staring intently forward, not meeting her eyes. "Shouldn't you help clean? Steven and I are working so hard out here."

"The cat," he said. "I need to go take care of the cat."

Steven said, "There's a cat?"

"The cat can wait," mom said.

"Hell yeah it can," Steven said. "Don't be a douchebag."

"Steven," mom said. "I don't know when you started to think you could cuss in front of your mother."

"I didn't say anything," Steven said.

Michael didn't stop, just said, "I'll be back. I need to check on the cat."

Then he was gone, leaving a sort of hovering film of frustration at his back. Steven had half a mind to go out and get him, but it wasn't worth it. Michael was never much help. If Steven went after him, it would be for the principle of the thing. And that wasn't like him. That was like dad.

"He won't be back," Steven said.

"Maybe he will." Mom shrugged and picked up one of those red plastic cups. She had talked about washing some and using them another day, but that was stupid. They're red plastic cups. You throw plastic cups away.

"Has he ever?"

"That's what I'm worried about." Mom set down the cups and turned towards him. "Michael can't take care of himself."

"Sure he can." Steven picked up the cups mom had sat down. "He'll figure it out."

"Have you thought about it? Michael, here by himself?"

"Mom, I don't worry about Michael. He can take care of himself."

Mom's voice got firmer, rigid. She was about to do that thing again, where she tried to show some sense of authority. She didn't do it that often. Partially because it didn't work. But when she did, it was at least worth paying attention.

"He's seventeen. You're twenty-three."

"I'm aware, mom."

"You're a man. You can take care of yourself—you know what it means to have responsibility. Michael doesn't."

"Stop it mom, you're talking like dad."

"He always said it. Michael's so messy, he doesn't pay attention to anything. Can you imagine him shopping for groceries?"

Even if Michael did, he would just eat cereal, ramen noodles, and plain white bread. Steven had seen him do it for years, and this was before Chicago, so sometimes he'd done it too, but even then, it had seemed weird and unhealthy.

Steven said, "Umm."

"I have a point, right?" Mom raised her arms in the air, obviously frustrated. "You boys don't listen to anything I say but sometimes I have a point."

"We listen to you, mom. It's just sometimes."

"And I'm right about Michael. Your dad, he gave this house to you two. To both of you. But Michael thinks he's going to live in it alone. He doesn't even have a job!"

"There's money from dad," Steven said. But that didn't sound right. A few thousand, maybe—dad hadn't had much money near the end. Two thousand nine and still nobody was sure if the recession was over, but it definitely wasn't over for dad, not after that shitty job he'd finally gotten. And held onto, because he was Lee Hanson, and he was too proud to let a job go, even one that punched him in the balls every day when he showed up for work.

"Not much," Mom said, and left it at that. "I've already talked to Ben about it. We'll be paying his bills. Food too."

"Michael would hate the idea of taking money from Ben."

"It's my money too. He'll be taking it from me."

"Shit, mom. You never gave money to me before."

"You didn't need it," she said—that same pride lighting up behind her eyes. A light that gave him that same sinking feeling in his stomach. "You still don't."

"Mom—"

"That's not it, Steven. Wait for me to finish."

She took a deep breath. This was a big deal, when she had to prepare to say something. Steven associated that pause, mostly, with the silence at dinner before she told the family she'd lost another job. He thought he'd always known what it meant—until, one day (this time dad wasn't there, he'd been out of the house all day) she told them she'd found another man.

"It's not just the bills," she said. "He's going to be living with me."

"The fuck, mom?"

"Language, Steven."

"Mom, there's no way. Michael didn't want to live with you after the divorce—there's no way he'd be okay with it now. And Ben—"

"Here, we're going to be living here, in the old house."

"So Ben—"

"Ben isn't coming with me."

"You're splitting up?"

"No, of course not." Mom got that weird, glowy smile she got whenever she talked about Ben—the one that had been there at first, even when she gave them the talk at the dinner table. Steven hated it and it gave him another of those sinking feelings in his stomach, and he wished she would just get on with it and not be so much like herself.

"It's just for a year," she said.

"Until Michael's eighteen? A year isn't going to change him."

"But it'll make me feel better." Another shift, a sound almost like a cough, and hell if she wasn't about to cry. Steven saw the beginning of it, and he stepped forward and put his hand on her shoulder.

"Mom, come on. It'll be ok."

"No," her voice cracking. "No it won't. I know, I know how he feels about me but I still love him."

"He still loves you too, mom." But to fill the lingering silence afterwards, Steven said, "He only hates Ben."

"I know, I know. But I miss my boys."

"We're here, mom."

"No." Real tears now, but she was still talking okay. "No, you're off living your own life. That's good but I don't have any boys."

And she couldn't, not anymore. That was the problem with Ben—as far as Steven could tell, his only problem. Ben couldn't have children. Steven had always found that sort of satisfying. The idea bothered him, of mom just trying again and having more children. The real reason, he sometimes thought, is that this time maybe it would work better—maybe those new Christian children would love her more, appreciate her more. Probably they would. Even Michael was still a Hanson—he didn't have much love in him.

"I miss him," she said, in a smaller voice. "Maybe if we live together—"

"No," Steven said. "He's like dad that way. Maybe he'll get over it someday, but he needs time. Probably years."

"But what am I supposed to do, Steven? I don't have children anymore. And the thought of my boy here alone—"

"Mom, wait." The idea had hit him hard, but he needed a second to think about it. Because once he said it he couldn't unsay it. Maybe he'd regret it. But also, a part of him didn't want to seem too eager.

"What?"

"I'll stay here, mom. Until he's eighteen."

"You mean... I thought you had—"

"Not yet, I don't. It can be a goodbye. A job can wait—I can even apply while I'm here. Michael will be okay with it."

"I thought you didn't want to come back. You're a city boy now."

"Well mom, I mean—home is home."

"Aww, bud." Her voice cracked again, from happiness this time. "You've always been the sweet one."

She came forward and hugged him and it didn't make him sick to his stomach this time. Steven had always found hugging sort of awkward.

"It just seems like the right thing to do," he said.

THE CAT

STEVEN FOUND Michael out on the deck, facing the dark forest behind the house, drinking a beer and smoking a cigarette. It was weird to see someone out here alone. Dad had built this deck himself when they were little kids, and it was where he did manly things like grill and drink beer. Before the divorce, he and mom had liked to sit together and watch the animals at the edge of the forest. They would set out food for deer, or spend hours waiting just to see a squirrel. It had always seemed super boring to Steven but well, you know, old people.

Alone, though, that was weird, since Michael wasn't just out here for the cigarette—it had been at least an hour. He looked sort of pensive sitting there, his long, straight hair falling over his eyes. Both like and unlike himself. The night was still and cool and sometimes the wind blew, the stars were pained and cold, and it seemed wrong as hell to be out on this deck knowing dad couldn't come out and catch Michael smoking.

"Where's my beer?" Steven asked. "I didn't see any in the fridge.""Under dad's work bench." Michael tipped his bottle in what Steven assumed was the right direction. "Warm though. I put them there to keep mom from throwing them away."

"Good call." Steven made his way back into the garage. Even in the dark, after all these years, he knew his way around. The garage had been dad's workspace, full of things he'd owned going on twenty years. In the end, he'd finally given up building stuff and let most of it sit there.

Steven reached blindly to find the beer beneath the workbench —a big, solid hunk of wood level with his chest, covered with tools and little things Steven hardly recognized. The work bench was big enough that (as a very small child) he remembered sitting on it and crawling from side to side, thinking how giant and powerful his dad seemed, how amazing it was that he could build things with his hands. But Steven still knew exactly where to find the bottle opener mounted on the end.

The cap clinked down into the darkness, but Steven didn't pick it up. He made his way back outside, and sat down next to Michael, facing the woods.

Steven asked, "So you're emo now, right?"

A quick turn of Michael's head. The hint of a scowl. "What? No."

"I mean, like, the hair. The tight pants. Looks pretty emo to me."

"I just like dressing this way."

"If you say so." It seemed to be mostly a high school thing, though a few of them still made it up to university: these thin, pale kids, some of them with brightly colored hair, wearing too-tight clothes and their hair down covering one eye. Steven thought they looked sort of like elves—delicate, fey. He'd always wanted to fuck one of the girls (a kind of idle, itching curiosity that he didn't think about often, but sometimes struck quickly and sharply), but never managed to do it. They looked sort of like weird, pretend people from another world, which made it funny to remember they were mostly just angry kids from small towns— like his brother.

"I say so," Michael said.

"I looked at your MySpace the other day. Emo as fuck."

"Shut up, bro."

Steven laughed and took a drink of his beer and thought how nasty Bud Light tasted when it was warm. Or ever. It was what dad had always drank—Bud Light, year in, year out. But not very much, only one or two. It was a man's drink, Steven had always thought as kid; he remembered, the first time he tried it, how disgusting a man's drink had seemed. There were two bottles sitting next to Michael already, and a few cigarettes spitting their ash onto the deck.

"So what is this shit about a cat?" Steven said.

"Hmm?" Michael's face just tilted a little. Distracted, watching for something.

"A cat. Mom said you were taking care of a cat."

"I found it a few months ago. Dad wouldn't let me keep in it the house, but he said it was fine if I fed it. He even seemed to like it quite a bit."

"Dad? But he's allergic to cats." He *was*, Steven didn't correct himself. It was easier that way.

"Yeah, well, it's fine when they stay a few feet away. He liked to sit out and watch. It was kind of ridiculous."

"Like with the animals, you mean? Like how he'd seen a squirrel and suddenly freaked out and stopped what he was doing to say how cute it was?"

"Yeah, like that." Michael closed his eyes, then opened them. "I really like this cat."

Steven said, "I hate animals."

"Good for you."

"It means I've never had to clean up any cat shit."

"Me neither." A frown, almost a grimace. "It makes me feel good. Taking care of something."

"Like a dad?"

"I guess so."

"Weird." Michael opened his mouth to respond—until all of a sudden Steven remembered why he'd come out here in the first place. "Oh wait, I have news."

"Yeah?"

"I'm going to be staying at the house for a while. Probably a year."

A long, not exactly awkward instant of Michael being surprised—and another where he immediately got used to it.

"Cool," he said.

"Yeah, I thought it would be pretty alright."

"Just don't, like, be a dick, and it'll be okay."

"Me? Never?" Steven laughed, though he could be a dick sometimes and both of them knew it. "I figured why not. I need some time to relax anyway. College, man."

"Seems fun. Parties. Girls. All that."

"Yeah," Steven said—and felt that pit in his stomach, the one he felt whenever there was something he didn't want to say. "Yeah, it was nice. But there was work too. It's all a bit tiring."

"For sure. So you're bringing all your stuff back here?"

"I'll drive up again next weekend. I got some things to work out, but—

"Wait!" A harsh whisper; Michael lifted one hand. "There it is."

"What, where?"

"The cat!"

Michael kept pointing with his beer hand. Steven didn't see anything, but he did hear a rustle in the grass. Also something he didn't recognize—this sort of harsh, grating moan. It reminded him a little of wind, but a cloudy, sick wind... one somehow gasping for air. Though that didn't make sense. How could air need to take a breath?

Steven looked at Michael.

"What's that sound?" he asked.

"The cat. It's sick."

"Since when?"

Another rustle in the grass. Michael stood. He took one step and sat back down.

"Here boy." Michael reached down to one side—a tin. Steven hadn't seen it in the darkness. "I've got food for you."

"Gross," Steven said.

"It's the kind he likes best. Here little guy."

Michael held his hand down, shaking it from side to side; and the cat stepped out of the darkness.

Its fur might have been brown once—maybe. Now it was streaked and matted with something very dark that wasn't mud; so thin Steven swore he could see the bone through it. Its eyes were huge and shadowed and crusted red, the mouth hanging open beneath these hideous yellow eyes. The thing couldn't even stand. The back legs hung stupid and slack, so it just crawled forward on the front two, every lurch taking it a little closer to collapse.

The torso and tail dragged along the ground, the head leaning forward on a too-thin neck.

"Jesus Christ," Steven said. "Is it alive?"

"There boy," Michael called. "Come here."

"Man, don't touch it. It'll make you sick."

"It's a cat. It doesn't work that way." Michael lowered his hand —the dead thing dragged itself forward and pressed its nose into the mush. Steven wasn't sure how much it managed to eat.

"It smells!" Steven stood up, stepped back. "And listen to the fucker breathe!"

"He's sick."

"You've been taking care of it? How long?"

"I told you, a few months."

Steven shook his head—silly, since Michael was facing the other way and couldn't see. "No, I mean how long has it been sick? Was it only half dead when you found it instead of all the way?"

"No." Michael shook his head, but at least Steven was in the right place to see. "Just a week, maybe a little more."

"It's nasty." Steven stepped back again. He could still hear its breath in his ears—somewhere between a gasp and a moan. Pain filled each of those breaths, a ringing echo in his ears. And hell if he wasn't getting that same sinking feeling in his stomach, watching that crusted nose press into Michael's hand.

"It's tough," Michael said, "staying with the ones we love when they get sick. But I decided to do it."

"There are other cats in the world."

"I know." Michael sounded very sad—and Steven realized that they hadn't talked about dad yet. They'd joked around a lot since Steven came back, but they hadn't said a word about dad. Michael had been close to dad—closer than Steven, which was surprising. Since dad had understood Steven fine, and Michael, with his video games and his anime (and now those jeans so tight they must be choking his balls) probably seemed like an alien to him.

But they'd been close, probably even more after Steven went to college. That's why Michael always took dad's side—why he blamed mom for everything. Why once, he'd even told her he hated her. Because he'd been close to dad… he'd been dad's boy in a way none of them really understood. Maybe not even him.

At college, Steven had talked to dad on the phone once every month or two, and that had been fine. He was grown up, moved on with his own life, and that was good and fine and it seemed okay—all that, and he'd been the one to throw up at dad's funeral. Michael hadn't shown much of how he felt. Instead, he'd just been taking care of that cat. But the cat was about to die too.

Steven hadn't asked yet, and he didn't know when he would, about what it had been like to find dad after his heart attack. Dead in his sleep. But Steven had heard the story from mom... how Michael hadn't even known at first, since dad always woke up early to go to work. He didn't come home the first night, which seemed strange, but Michael didn't think about it much—until the second day, when Michael got a call on the landline from dad's work.

Lee Hanson had barely missed a day of work in twenty-five years. Not that he liked to work. He got three weeks of vacation a year, and he'd hoarded them like a starving man, planning very carefully what he was going to do as a reward for all this. But more than anything he'd been setting aside for his retirement—or he had, until the recession hit and all of it went away. Someday, Steven remembered dad saying, he'd get the reward for waking up so damn early every morning. Someday.

Even after the call, Michael didn't check the bedroom. He said he would keep an eye open, and left it at that. At first he thought dad had gotten in a car accident. A small part of him even wondered if dad had run away, left to go somewhere, but that didn't make sense. Lee Hanson loved his house, his property. It was what he'd worked for all this time. A part of him had probably been happier alone with it, without a wife.

But eventually Michael had checked the bedroom—though a part of Steven wondered if anything he'd seen there could have been worse than this fucking cat.

"Man, if you really cared, you would shoot the thing and get it over with."

"No way."

"But I'm serious." Steven kept stepping back further every time the smell reached him again. "I'll get dad's gun. It should still be inside somewhere."

"I said no."

Steven chanced one more glance over Michael's shoulder. He was afraid he might meet its eyes. Instead he only saw a patch of stiff, matted fur. "Goddamn, a thing like that. It's not meant to be alive."

Then the cat jerked. Steven looked back without meaning to—had it bitten Michael?

No, it had turned it head away. And just like Steven earlier, it was vomiting.

Blood. It was vomiting blood.

A DEAD THING

BLOOD SPAT wildly from the corners of its mouth. A little flecked onto Michael's hand; more might have pooled under his shoes. It wasn't a little blood, either. It didn't stop after the first spray, or the second, or the third. Steven didn't understand—how could there be so much blood in such a little body? Gallons. Like somebody had turned on a faucet and it just wouldn't stop.

The sound it made reminded Steven of himself earlier today. It was a monstrous, dying sound: like the little thing was pushing out some of its life each time, more and more, until soon there would be nothing left. Each of these wretched, shaking heaves like a ladle scooping somewhere deeper inside it, amongst the sick, fetid organs, until soon those would come out too: its stomach, and its liver, and its heart, and maybe even its skeleton.

What made it worse, somehow, was that the cat was so small. Seeing so much pain in something so little—something that was supposed to be cute. (Steven knew, in an abstract way, that the cat had probably been cute once. Humans only loved animals that were cute. Anything else they killed; or at least, they didn't touch it.) But now it was nothing but this ridiculous mass of blood and coughing, hacking up so hard except there wasn't any fur ball coming.

"It's better off dead," Steven said.

"No." Michael's voice was firmer this time. "It's my cat. I decide what to do with it."

It wasn't easy for him to watch either though. Steven heard the shaking in his voice. He even saw Michael pull back. He probably felt all the same things as Steven—he just didn't want to admit it, because he loved this nasty little thing.

"And besides," Michael said. "Do you really think you could kill it?"

"Of course," Steven said. But the words just hung there. Hollow. Why hollow? Oh yeah—because he didn't mean them.

Funny, how that works.

"You see?" Michael said. "All we can do is wait."

It was done now, at least. The cat shook. It turned up at them, as if asking for reassurance—then it collapsed into the puddle of its own blood.

"Shit," Steven said. "That's not mud on its fur. You said it's been sick a week?"

"Vomiting three days," Michael said. "That's when I saw it the first time."

"And it keeps coming back here to do it? Why?"

"I don't know. Maybe it loves me too."

"Maybe." Steven coughed, and spat onto the deck. "But probably not."

"Why?"

"It's just an animal."

"So are you, fuckhead."

"Right, point taken."

Movement again—the cat was crawling away. Even weaker now. The torso dragged weakly through the pooled blood. Once it twitched, sharply and powerfully like a fish... but then just laid there, exhausted.

Steven took another step forward, curious in spite of himself.

"It is going to make it?"

"I hope so," Michael said. "But it's not an 'it.' It's a 'he'."

"No reason to linger on semantics."

Another rustle. It was further away, and Steven was sort of used to the smell, so now he was almost standing over Michael's shoulders."

"What?"

"You'll figure it out in college."

Michael's eyes had still hardly moved from the cat, but he

talked in a pretty normal tone of voice as he said, "I'm not going to college."

"Really? Have you told mom?"

"Why would I tell mom anything?"

"I mean, it's up to you, just—oh shit."

A liquid sound: not like rain; more robust, something with strength behind it. But Steven didn't react until the stench of it hit: newer, sharper, a different level of rancid. Only watched as a sharp, spurting stream of black tore out of the thing's asshole.

"No." Steven turned around, but nothing would be enough to erase the lingering image of the cat shitting blood. "I'm done, I'm out of here, I'll see when you when you get inside."

"Sure." But Michael hadn't moved. How could he stand the smell?

Steven paused at the sliding door to the garage and called back, "Man, tomorrow clean this shit up with the hose. It's disgusting."

"Sure." Michael waved once with the back of his hand. "The hose."

THE BACK YARD

STEVEN HAD LEFT HIS BEER, Michael noticed later, so he chugged his quick and reached over to pick it up. Three beers in and he was feeling sort of thick and liquid in his stomach—a feeling he associated with drinking, since he hardly ever ate enough to feel it—but maybe that would go away once he took a piss. There was a tree on the far side of the yard, next to a swing set dad had built when they were kids, where all the men in the family had pissed for almost twenty years.

Michael remembered standing there, a little kid with a little nub of a dick, going over to pee once in broad daylight when dad's friends were over, and dad had seen but not gotten angry for once. It rose to the surface, but unlike with everyone else—when it was Michael, the anger surged, but then it went back down. He knew in a kind of abstract way that didn't happen with Steven... and when it was mom, well, sometimes the anger welled up for no reason at all. But it was Michael and so it went down; and Michael learned for the first time, at four years old, how important it was to be alone when you pissed.

The beers had made him tired too, even if they were light. Michael remembered the first time he'd ever gotten drunk—in that shed over there, on another side of the yard. The one that smelled musty and good, where dad kept the wheelbarrow (bits of dirt still crusted to the bottom from all the times he'd used it); the rakes and the leaf blower; a big spray bottle of weed poison, and another to kill bugs. There were bags of seeds, and big sheers for cutting leaves (but not branches, dad always reminded him—you used the smaller clippers for that), and a huge axe; and other, older tools whose use Michael barely understood.

So many weekends when he was young, early on Saturday morning, Michael remembered getting in dad's truck to go shopping at Menard's—sometimes Lowe's or even Meijer's, but mostly Menard's, the cheapest hardware store in South Bend—to buy a new tool to put in that shed. Dad would wake up brisk and early every weekend (that's how he said it, 'brisk and early'), excited to work on some new project. Maybe they were going to plant trees; or built a fence; or redo the gutters. It didn't matter. Every weekend there was something new, and dad believed, with a firm conviction, in the importance of all of those things—believed it religiously, the way mom believed in god.

It was boring as hell and all of them had always thought so, but especially Steven. Every weekend, dad had wanted help with his projects—it was their responsibility as part of the family, he said. A Hanson tradition. And it was: all the men in the family, they liked to work with their hands. Or they had, until now. Neither Steven or Michael liked it at all, but it was Steven who had complained the most. Every Saturday, starting when he was ten, Steven would throw a fit, the same fit he threw on Sunday when mom tried to take him to church.

It was bullshit, Steven always said—spend all week at school, then mom and dad wanted to take the weekends from them. Though Michael had only caught the end of it. Sometimes, with a strange feeling of pride, Steven would talk about how he'd won both of those battles: one against mom (and especially against her God, who Steven still seemed to hate with a brutal, righteous intensity, because of all the Sundays he wasted), and another, more slowly, against their dad.

When Michael was very young, maybe six or seven, both of them had gone out with dad every Saturday morning. But then eventually it was only Michael. Dad told him once, only once, that if he wanted he didn't have to go to the store—but Michael had gone anyway. And, though it was still a little boring, he'd kept on with dad's Saturday projects until dad gave them up a few years later.

And the real reason, he thought of it now, as he looked at that shed and thought about taking that piss, probably had something to do with those early morning drives. There was a feeling of freshness, of possibility, to dad on all those mornings—a sense, which you didn't see very often from him, that life was good and worth living. Dad would take his very simple pleasures every Saturday morning with a sense he'd earned them: a bacon, egg and cheese biscuit from McDonalds, one for each them, with two hash browns apiece (but no ketchup, because they always ate in the car); black coffee for dad, and orange juice for Michael.

The coffee was bitter and unpleasant, a grown-up, manly taste; and even now, Michael couldn't stand the taste of coffee. There are things that belong to a father, to the man that raises you, in a way nothing else can: the hissing sound when a father opens a bottle of beer, the same Bud Light Michael was drinking now; the robust, manly scent of gas when he fired up the grill on the deck; the satisfied, unusually relaxed way he would laugh on those mornings when he took Michael golfing with him, sometimes fishing. It didn't happen often, but dad could laugh and enjoy himself too, even though he was a Hanson. It was rare, rarer the older dad got; and maybe Michael had seen it more than anyone else. Maybe that was why dad was so sad.

Nobody else saw dad like that—like he wanted to live. Michael had seen him in the morning when he got ready for work, and he seemed very tired: like a rusty, robotic kind of man, refueling himself with a grapefruit and the same bowl of cereal, every morning. Dad had a morning ritual: twenty minutes in the laundry room bathroom, then he would come out, dressed, cheeks freshly shaven with his mustache trimmed, smelling of Old Spice: a fatherly scent, something else that belonged only to dad, so much Michael could hardly believe that thousands of other fathers wore the same scent every morning.

Everyone knew dad's morning ritual was not to be disturbed; and sometimes, on those weekends when Michael would stay up all night watching anime (or maybe he just wouldn't sleep, because sleep had always been very hard for him), when Michael was still awake during the ritual, dad would give him sad, disapproving eyes: the look he reserved for the unfortunate people who didn't understand the benefits of proper sleep, the inarguable truth that everything has its proper place, and someone awake at five in the morning wasn't in his.

But if it was Michael, dad would sit and talk as he drank his black coffee—and once, dad had taken him to eat breakfast at Plaza, the best diner in Niles, which had been open twenty-four hours until just a few years ago. It had been a quick meal. A breakfast special for Michael, the same one he'd always eaten there: bacon, eggs, toast, and hash browns cooked in butter, which seemed to taste better than food from anywhere (including McDonalds). And for dad, biscuits and gravy—the best anywhere, he claimed. And he'd know, since he ordered biscuits and gravy everywhere he went... but nowhere was as good as Plaza.

It wasn't that late yet, maybe pushing nine, and a part of Michael suddenly wanted to go find Steven and get him to drive them somewhere to eat, somewhere that served breakfast food, the kind dad liked, even though his stomach was full and bloated from the beer, and he was a bit sick from smoking so many ciga-rettes. Steven would say no at first, but he would give in eventu-ally. Both of them had always liked going to eat with dad. Steven would understand. Michael was sure he would.

But for now he had to piss—and there was no point sitting here, watching for the cat. Maybe he was even dozing a bit, he couldn't tell; but it wouldn't be back for a few hours at least. Michael made a note to himself that he couldn't fall asleep, not yet, because he needed to come check on the cat again. Sometimes it came back two, three times a night, and he might not have another chance.

He was careful, as he stood up, to walk around the fresh blood. He hadn't given it much thought, but yeah, it was kind of gross to have all of that sitting there, one layer caked over the next. The cat had vomited in the same spot every day, and it hadn't rained since. There must be at least an inch of blood and shit caked there in the grass.

Dad would have thrown a fit—a mess like that in his yard! But he'd loved this cat, loved it ('him', Michael corrected himself, the cat was a 'him') in the strange, counterintuitive way a large man can love a small animal, and it would have torn him up to see it so sick like this. But he never got the chance. It was just a coinci-dence, of course, but the cat had only gotten sick after dad died. It had started a few days before, but finally got worse the day Michael found him in the bedroom.

It really did smell bad, didn't it? Michael couldn't see the exact marks in the grass, but he did his best as he walked around it, towards the tree. He paused again in the grass, halfway between the swing set, the tree, and the deck, circled in by the black mouth of the forest, looking at the tool shed. It seemed so tragic that dad had given up years ago—that he'd never put another tool in there. He had the chance for a good five years, but Steven had won his battle in the end, or maybe dad just got old and gave up his projects and never bought another tool for the shed. And now no one would.

Michael wanted to smell it, the warm, musty smell of the old wood, so he went over to the shed, painted white enough to see it in the darkness, and set his hand against the rickety lock that wasn't actually a lock. But he stopped. He wanted to open it but he couldn't, because that smell reminded of him of dad. This was dad's place, and if he smelled it that would be too much—and it was hard to say for sure, but this is probably when he started to cry.

Time to piss, he reminded himself, as he wiped his eyes. He had to take that piss. Four beers really was quite a bit; and wasn't he sort of a lightweight, being drunk already with four beers? Michael was no good at being drunk, he didn't do it often enough —especially the first time in that shed, drunk as hell on vodka, and when dad came home Michael had vomited all evening (thin, watery puke that still smelled like alcohol) and told dad he was sick.

It took a lot of focus, pissing drunk, and really Michael was pretty tired too, and weirdly out of it, and he just didn't feel great. He seemed to piss forever, and that felt good; but, as it turned out, he'd forgotten that first lesson, the one he'd learned so many years ago... since he never heard the footsteps of the person behind him.

THE BOX SET

"MICHAEL," she said. "Catch!"

He turned in the middle of zipping his jeans—but a little too late. Everything about it was a little too late: how he reached up, but his dick was still hanging out a little (maybe hidden in the darkness, but probably not). Also not quick enough to catch the thing—whatever it was—Halie had thrown at him. She was a thin, small shape in the night, outlined by the garage light at her back, though not enough to see her face.

Michael didn't need to. She'd have that mischievous, sort of annoying smile—especially as the DVD case she'd thrown slipped between his hands and hit him in the face; and harder when he reached down to zip his fly.

"Halie, goddamn it."

"Hey there." She bent down, still laughing, to pick up the case she'd thrown. It was hefty, which was good news. "This just came in today."

"I better like it."

"The *Cowboy Bebop* box set. Do you believe it was a hundred dollars?"

"That's pretty bad," Michael said. Though, of course, there had been a time when he'd spent that much to add a new show to his collection. They'd seen most of this one on Adult Swim already, but not all of it—and it was something different to own one of your favorite anime series. Fortunately, it had gotten much easier when Halie started stealing them from Best Buy.

"Their loss." She turned around, gesturing towards the puddle of blood on the ground. Michael leaned on her, because he was drunk and because he wanted to. At first she seemed too thin, too small to support his weight, but (Michael had always known) there was strength there... enough for make up for what he didn't have right now.

"So the cat was here again?" she asked.

"Yeah, and worse this time."

"That reminds me. I saw your brother on the way in."

"Yeah?"

"But he was being weird. He said he was going to get the gun and put it on the table. He told me to tell you it was there, in case you needed it."

Michael shook his head. "For the cat. He wants me to use it on the cat."

"Hmm." She reached up towards her chin, then said, "I'll do it if you want."

"Goddamnit, nobody is killing the cat."

"Okay, okay." She glanced over towards the woods. "There must be a trail of blood leading off here. Maybe we should check tomorrow."

"Tonight. I'm coming back out to check tonight, in case the cat comes back."

"Not me. I'm tired."

"Yeah," Michael said. "Well, me too."

The light was still on when they got inside, which was sort of surprising since Steven had always gone to bed a little early. But they went right to Michael's room and they didn't see Steven along the way. There was still some stuff from the party laying out: plates, forks, cups, a few cans of pop, which seemed to be half cleaned. The light was on in dad's room and Michael could hear Steven rummaging around in there.

Michael's room was the biggest in the house, the only bedroom on the second floor, which was good since it's where he spent most of his time. The centerpiece of the room was a big flatscreen TV, which dad had bought him for Christmas a few years ago. It had been expensive, but he'd managed to talk dad into it. Dad (who spent most of each day in the den watching TV, and hardly left it after the divorce) still used a little standard definition thing. Michael had tried to talk him into changing it, but dad always said the same thing—if it ain't broken, don't fix it.

At least, Michael had told him, he would get his use out of it, since he spent so much time playing video games and watching anime. Opposite the TV (across the film of discarded DVD cases, empty boxes from the store, random CDs, old plates, and whatever the hell else) was a queen-sized bed with a bunch of pillows lined against the wall, which also served as a couch, a table, and pretty much anything Michael wanted it to be. Against the far wall were a couple of beanbags for playing PS2.

The first thing anyone would notice when they stepped inside was the library of anime DVD's along the wall—the only part of the room that wasn't messy. Once every few months, he would even go and put them back in alphabetical order, though maybe he was falling behind now. He didn't know for sure, but he felt like it was probably the biggest anime collection for a hundred miles… which was basically South Bend and a bunch of fucking cornfields. But still.

Halie, walking a few steps ahead, tossed Cowboy Bebop onto the bed and leapt face first behind it. As always when she did this, which was most of the time, Michael was careful to note the sudden press of her ass in her jeans, and the way her shirt lifted up a little when she raised her arms. (He'd always, distantly and casually, wondered if it would be soft if he touched it, or firm and bony—he wasn't sure, probably firm and bony.) But she was taking up the whole bed and he wanted to sit down too, so first he pushed her leg aside, but didn't sit down.

She turned around onto her back and asked, "So how was the funeral?"

"It was okay," he said. "But mom was obnoxious."

"I've always liked your mom. She's nice."

"Just because she's always saying how pretty you are. It's the worst."

They'd had this particular conversation many, many times, and Michael could already feel it wouldn't go far tonight. Michael was pretty casual about most things, but not his mom—and even when Halie pushed, usually she was just playing around. Like a game: sometimes she liked to do weird shit, just to see what would happen. And even after so many years it still surprised him when she did it.

She laughed and said, "So I saw your dick earlier. And just for your information: small."

"Good enough for you." Michael said it casually, reaching down to brush some candy wrappers near his feet under the bed. He picked up the remote, turned on the TV, and the PS2 screen came up. He didn't want to play video games.

"You wish." Michael heard the beep on her little, boxy trac-phone as she got a text, and the faint (barely audible) press of buttons as she replied. Then a rustle as she looked over and said, "So what are we watching tonight?"

"The question should probably be what will you stay awake for?"

"You said you're in the middle of rewatching *Evangelion*, right?"

"Yeah."

"Well, not that. Maybe *Cowboy Bebop*?"

"Sure." It took a minute for Michael to open the box with his fingernails, and felt his shirt ride up as he knelt to put the disk in the PS2—a feeling that was still sort of unfamiliar, since he'd only started wearing shirts this tight last year. When it was done, he balled up the plastic wrapping in one hand and tossed it over towards the window, without checking where it landed.

"Some thanks are in order," Halie said as the disk booted. "You know I almost got caught?"

"Yeah?" Michael watched the screen, distantly aware of her telling the story afterwards—but something had occurred to him, red and sharp. Weirdly it bothered him much more now than it had before.

"The gun," he said.

"What?"

"That's why Steven was in dad's room. He was looking for the gun, like you said."

More rustling as Halie sat up. Good, since that would make room for him. "I wouldn't worry about it. He's just, well. He's Steven. He was always weird before too."

There was a brief (very brief) instant where Michael wanted to go yell at Steven, but it passed right as the DVD menu opened up, and mellowed even more when the theme song—punchy energetic jazz, with tall, shadowy figures running around against a multicolored background—started to play.

"Fuck him," Michael said.

"I thought you mostly liked Steven?"

"Some of the time." Michael watched the figures running, running and running, but didn't press start yet. "Not always."

"What's he doing here?"

"He's staying here awhile."

"Cool."

Michael hit 'start episode 1' and set the controller to one side.

"He said something else funny when I walked in." Another rustle as Halie picked up a pillow and sat it on her lap, clasped in both hands. Michael had never understood why she did that exactly, only that she always did, whenever they watched anything. "He didn't even recognize me at first."

"Well it's been four years."

"Yeah, and then afterwards he was like, 'so you're married now right?' And I was like, 'not yet.'"

"Gross."

"That's what I said. Then he looked at me and just sort of laughed for a minute."

"Some people just don't get it," Michael said. "Especially my mo—"

"Wait!" Halie clasped his arm. "Shut up! It's starting."

THE HOSE

MICHAEL WASN'T sure when Halie fell asleep, somewhere in the second episode, third at best. And he was glad, since he fell asleep at some point too, and woke up with that opening song playing back at the DVD menu. It happened all the time—they'd be watching, talking sometimes except only a little, and he'd look over and see Halie was asleep. It sort of pissed him off, except today it was good since she hadn't seen him do it too.

Michael's body felt heavy and tired, as if he'd been running all day. He really wasn't cut out for this drinking business. At first he was happy just to sit there, nodding off, right on the rim of tiredness. It felt good, even if his neck hurt a bit, and he could hear the faint whistling sound of Halie snoring. It was almost always quiet, except for these rare, pronounced outbursts, where all the snot caught and she sounded like a pig clearing its throat.

He was right there, right on the rim of good sleep, when he remembered his promise to himself. He didn't have to keep it, not really. But the memory of it was a sharp prodding along his backbone, and the more he tried to lay there the less comfortable he felt. Until eventually he stood up (without much thought, since he knew he wouldn't wake Halie), put on his shoes, and went outside.

There were a few more beers beneath the workbench, and he grabbed one on his way out. The night was just how he'd left it: clear, still, a bit cold. Maybe colder, because he'd been asleep.

He'd come out every night for the last few days, when the cat had stopped showing up during the day. Not that Michael minded—it was easier not to see it in full daylight.

His hair, when he pushed it aside to smoke, was oily again. He hadn't taken a shower today, and it was okay because he didn't smell, but he would have to take one tomorrow morning or his head would start to itch. His hair was almost as long as Halie's, though hers reached her shoulders, and sometimes she'd let him borrow her pants though they were a little too tight.

Michael finished the first cigarette, noting the crisp pain in his throat as he started the second. Mostly, when he waited for the cat, he would stare out towards the forest, searching for a sign of movement. But tonight he couldn't look away from the blood. It had become a sort of hardened pool, with a few blades of grass showing over the surface—the core, somewhere beneath, might still be wet—and Michael decided that yeah, maybe he should clean it up with the hose after all.

He tossed the second cigarette aside (it smoldered briefly, but went out on the cool, dewy grass) and walked along one side of the house for the hose. He could just barely see it in the dark, but it wasn't far from the pool. He unrolled the hose maybe ten feet to drag it out, but had to kneel and grasp blindly for the handle. The sound of the water, when it turned on, reminded him uncomfortably of the cat.

Maybe he hadn't thought this through enough. He'd imagined the blood would just dissolve when he hit it with the hose (he remembered as a kid when Steven had sprayed him with it, and it had hit as hard as a Super Soaker, or harder), but mostly it just flecked off into a cold little blood-mist. But it must be doing something. Michael stood on the concrete near the base of the deck, and when he'd sprayed long enough, thin, red pools of water trailed over to one side.

But it brought the smell back too, and that was worse. It was a terrible, brutal smell when it was fresh—but there was something wrong, almost evil, about the raw, caked over stink that rose when he hit it with the water. It wasn't as strong, but it was so much worse. He trailed the hose from side to side (the stream whipped and coiled, like piss, if he brought it over fast enough), and thought of the smell of a rotten lettuce he'd seen in the trash once

—the horror that something you'd eat could become like that, a stench that was familiar but transformed.

Only this was so much worse, and the second time Michael keeled over—close to vomiting, but not quite—it was time to give it up. So he tossed the hose into the grass (realizing, a second too late, that it might be sitting in the watery blood), then went to turn the hose off. It was always hard to make the water stop completely, and for a long time there was still a slow trickle in the grass.

Michael stood and listened to it, feeling half tired, and half stupid. That was when he heard the rustle in the grass. Or was it a cough? Michael recognized that sound; he'd listened for it every night this week. And it wasn't far away. Only there, a little to the left. Except it was too dark.

Michael realized he was scared—scared for the first time since all of this started. Part of him, a very small part, wanted to walk out onto the grass and search for the cat. But it didn't seem right to do it, especially without any light. This was a strange, unfamiliar feeling, one that reached far back into his childhood, one that believed there was something dangerous in the dark, something that wanted to eat him.

There was a flashlight in the garage on dad's workbench, and he knew where it was—but if he wanted it he'd have to move. Right now even that seemed hard. Something was watching him, it felt like; and if he moved, who knows. Maybe that would set it off. Maybe he wouldn't make it to the garage.

"Hey, little guy," Michael said, feeling stupid and cold as he talked into the dark. "You there?"

No answer—but then, yes, another rustle in the grass.

THE GUN

THE SOUND CAME CLOSER, but slow. At first the cat was a little wriggling lump at the edge of the light, and it couldn't even look at him. Michael's own head felt heavy on his neck, but what would it be like not to be able to lift it?

A long stillness, after that—except then it twitched. Once, twice. The cat staggered to its feet, fell forward.

"There you are boy," Michael said. But even now, without the fear, he couldn't walk towards the cat. Instead he stepped over towards the edge of the deck, and sat down. The cat's head followed him as he did it (too dark still to see the eyes), and a part of him almost felt he should help it over, but no. That wasn't possible. It was too much.

"Don't worry," Michael said. "Just take your time."

Which it did. There was no struggle forward. Just the head falling gradually, setting down its weight. The slow rise and fall of the small body, just barely breathing.

"It's hard," Michael said. "I get it. You know, Steven wanted me to shoot you? That's crazy, isn't it? Who shoots a cat? I mean, really."

A part of Michael had almost expected a reply. And when it didn't come, another part had to suppress its feeling of disappointment.

"Dad might have done it though," Michael said. "You know, he told me a story once about grandpa. He had this twelve gauge

—he was grandpa so he had all those guns, right? And one day when he was outside, right in the driveway, he saw a rabbit. It didn't move, just stayed there a while. And so grandpa went inside, and got his twelve gauge. And you know what happened?"

Michael shrugged—again, expecting a reply that didn't come.

"That's right. One second there was a rabbit, the next there was a smear of blood in the grass. And there's a moral to this story, right? You want to know the moral?"

The cat was still breathing.

"Well," Michael said, "the moral for me. It means that things die. They can die right in this house. You, me, mom, Steven. Dad told me this story a long time ago—I was still really young. But I thought about it for years. I thought I'd learned my lesson."

That same pinprick behind his eyes. But no, he wouldn't reach up, even if he was crying. Maybe he was, and maybe he wasn't. But he didn't care anymore. He didn't care.

"I was wrong though," he said. "Because when I found dad, I didn't believe it. Part of me still doesn't, probably. And all of this, it's taught me another lesson. Want to know what it is?"

The cat's ear twitched a little.

"I learned that it hurts." Michael thumped one hand against the hollow of his chest. "It's pain, right here. I think about dad and I'm full of pain. Sometimes it seems far enough, but sometimes it doesn't, and that's when—"

Not a twitch this time; the whole body flexed. The cat's front legs went rigid beneath it, nearly enough to bring it to feet: dragging forward once, then twice.

And it didn't fall. Instead it just vomited again, or tried, so that the throat wrenched and the body shook and a sound came out that vibrated awfully in Michael's stomach. But it was different this time, because nothing came out. The cat hacked, and coughed, and spat, and it went on for almost a minute but nothing came out. Nothing came out, nothing but pain.

It was in pain. It must be in so much pain—more than Michael had ever felt. And for a week, too. Waking must be agony for it, and when it slept, even then the pain probably just receded to a dull throb. But now it was at its crescendo. What did it have to look forward to, this sad, dying thing? What was it living for, if not just to die?

In spite of himself, Michael thought of the gun. It would be right on the table, Halie had said—part of Michael was still a bit angry at Steven, but the other part thought Steven had it right. This couldn't go on. And in just a second, Michael would go in, and he would get that gun, and all of this would be over.

Because it was selfish, really, and probably he was the bad guy here. It was selfish, and basically he was torturing it, to keep the cat alive just because it reminded him of his dad.

A few seconds longer, too, and he would have done it. A few seconds of the cat flailing and wrenching and suffering in a way nothing was meant to suffer, living a life that was all pain, working just to die. He would have, really he would have, even if it wasn't like him, and even the thought of it sort of made him sick to his stomach, and that would mean Steven would win and he didn't want to win. He would have.

Except, right when he took the first step, something finally came out.

A MATTER OF PROPRIETY

MOM HAD SAID she would drop by around eleven the next morning, but she got there late, as usual—even with Ben. Steven felt a faint, ancient twinge of annoyance at the back of his neck. (Even if he was doing something; even if he didn't mind waiting). Getting angry at mom had always been a family ritual. He could already feel himself making a list of complaints to hold against her; to sort of bubble and ferment in the back of his head even when he didn't bring them up.

But it was different now. Of course it was. Because when they were kids, mom being late or forgetting about something important would put dad in a bad mood. Michael and Steven had always held it against her, since they had deal with dad afterwards. Mom had ruined so many days for them. Except now dad was gone, and there was no one left to get angry. Only Steven.

Ben's sedan pulled in near noon, but Steven felt the cold incriminating electricity most in the four minutes it took them to knock on the door. They were sluggish and stupid, like mom had always been, just sitting there and taking their time and wasting Steven's. Like they didn't know everybody else had things to do.

They stepped through the door like people having a nice day. Probably they'd had a relaxing morning—a few hours in bed before a nice breakfast, careful to pray first before they ate their toast and grapefruit. Maybe next they went for a walk. (Ben ran when he was alone, but always walked with mom.). Afterwards, worst of all, maybe they just sat around and talked for a while. A perfectly decent Saturday morning. And Steven resented them for it.

"There's my boy!" Mom threw her arms around Steven's neck. A quick, alarming embrace. Steven returned it slowly and reluctantly. His arms wrapped around mom's back for just a second, but fell away while mom still was hugging. Steven had to step back before she let go.

"Ben," Steven said. "Mom."

Ben smiled and held out his hand. Ben's grip was cool and dry —not too tight, like dad's had been. Ben wore nice clothes like always: a button up that managed to look casual even though it was tucked in, and nice trim, crisp slacks. Ben must be at least fifty by now, like mom, but he didn't look it. Even his hair was full and thick and long enough to fall across his forehead—a younger man's hair. But at least there was a little sagging around Ben's jaws: faint, but there.

Ben's voice was bright—dad had referred to him once as 'that chipper asshole'—as he said, "Good to see you, Steven."

"It's been a hell of a week." Ben cringed a little at the word 'hell', his pert mouth falling down at the corners, and Steven felt good about himself. But a second later the smile was back.

"Steven's been so much help," Mom said. Steven already knew that. "Once he got back he practically handled the funeral on his own. Didn't you, Steven?"

"Until I nearly threw up on dad, yeah." Both mom and Ben visibly flinched. Maybe it surprised them Steven would bring it up—he was a bit surprised. But he didn't actually want to talk about it, not right now, so instead he said:

"I wanted to go shopping, mom."

"Now?"

"I need to go to Shelton's for lunch. There's nothing left to eat here."

Ben said, "Your mother told me you'd started cooking. Maybe we could team up for lunch someday."

Ben had seen a chance, and he'd lunged for it. He was a good cook, even if he was vegetarian. Steven actually was a bit curious, but he didn't want to seem too interested, so he said:

"Maybe sometime."

"You'd love Ben's recipes," Mom said. "He does this thing with mushrooms, whole mushrooms—what are they called? I forget?"

"Portobellos." Ben said it patiently and kindly. That was the difference between Ben and dad, right there. Even though it was a stupid little thing that didn't matter, dad would have gotten annoyed at mom for forgetting—he would have added it to the list of the things mom didn't do quite right. Except it was such a long list no one was reading it anymore.

"It's amazing," mom said. "He takes these huge mushrooms and bakes them with—butter, Ben?"

"Olive oil." Ben rubbed her arm. "It's healthier."

"Of course." Mom laughed, but it seemed like too much, an overcompensation. "He buys it on the internet because we can't get it around here. These thirty dollar bottles of olive oil. I still can't believe it."

Steven said, "There's a difference, mom." Only he realized, after he'd said it, that he'd drifted towards Ben a little—accepting him or embracing him or maybe even liking him—and that made him uncomfortable, and he hoped they dropped it soon because he didn't want to admit his moment of weakness. Already he wanted to take it back.

"I'm hungry," he said. "I wanted to go earlier."

Mom shrugged. "Sorry for the wait, hon. Hopefully you slept okay?"

"Good enough."

Ben kept that same chipper, approving look even though he didn't say anything this time.

Steven said: "Do you have the money?"

"Of course." Mom nodded and reached into her purse to rummage. "Right here. It should be…"

"Two hundred dollars," Ben said.

"Enough for two weeks. Maybe more." Mom pulled something out, but it was a wad of old receipts, not the money.

"Marie said she'll stop by to give you more when you need it. It's very kind of her."

"And that way I'll be able to see you." Mom pulled out her hand and let out a small whoop of excitement, followed by a larger one. "Oh yeah, go mom! Here it is."

"Thanks mom." Steven felt small, almost ashamed as he took it —but it also felt good. It had been a long, long time since someone handed him money for no reason. Dad didn't have any, and wouldn't have given it even if he had. A real man, dad would have said, works for himself, and he's proud of it. Steven had—all through college. A little shitty job he still resented. But here was a paycheck just for existing.

"Make sure you take care of Michael," mom said. "Make sure he eats. Maybe even cleans up after himself."

"I know, mom."

"And where is he anyway?"

"Probably still asleep."

Mom stepped towards Michael's room, but stopped halfway and shouted, "Michael! Your mom's here! Come out and see me before I leave."

Steven said, "Mom, Michael is still—"

Michael was just coming down the stairs, his long hair twisted and sort of greasy from sleep. Just far enough to say, "Yeah?"

Mom said, "Come here, I want to give you a hug."

"Not with Ben here."

He took another step, stopping near the base of the stairs.

"Be an adult, Michael," mom said. "Your mother is here and she wants to give you a hug."

Another voice as Halie came down behind him, also messy from sleep. "I was just leaving, anyway. You can talk to your mom for a bit."

Steven saw the corner of Ben's mouth droop—like when Steven said the word 'hell' only much stronger—but it would take a few seconds to become a full frown. His eyes locked on Halie, wide with alarm.

Mom said, "Halie, I hope you're doing well."

"Great." Halie stretched as she walked—a bone cracked some-where in her back. "Still tired though."

"How is your dad?"

Halie cringed. "He's okay."

"Mom," Michael said, "leave her alone!"

Ben stepped forward with a pinched, tight face. "Did this girl stay the night here last night?"

Halie said, "It's okay, Michael. Your mom is just being nice."

"No Halie, she's just being my mom and she should go away."

Ben cleared his throat loud enough everyone looked at him this time. "Did this girl sleep here yesterday?"

"Sure I did," Halie said. "I sleep here like half the time."

"I'm not sure that's appropriate." Ben's eyes fixed on Steven's. "You're supposed to be the adult here, and I think it's only right that—"

"Fuck you, Ben."

Michael's voice was clear and strong as he said it. But there was silence in the room afterward. The uncomfortable knowledge of many heads turning all at once—and just as many mouths not knowing what to say.

"This isn't your family," Michael said.

A second later he was gone. Ben, who seemed incapable of getting angry, just stared after him, then sort of deflated.

"It's okay, Ben." Mom's voice was soft, her arm around his shoulder. "I'm sorry for that. He's—"

"Just being Michael," Steven said. "You know how he is."

Ben blinked half a dozen times, still staring at the hallway.

Halie reached down to put on her shoes.

"Nice seeing you," she said on her way to the door. "You too, Steven."

"Sure, Halie."

Mom was too busy taking care of Ben to speak. It took a while, but his eyes went from the hallway to the door, and he said:

"Maybe we should go too."

"Thanks for dropping by," Steven said.

A NICE MAN

BUT STEVEN COULDN'T STOP THINKING about it, even as he drove to the store—Ben's face, the way he'd looked before he left. Steven's secret (and it really was a secret, since he couldn't tell anyone) was that he basically did like Ben. It had always seemed so important, a family obligation, to hate him. He was mom's boyfriend, yeah; except that wasn't all. He was so nice, so Christian, and handsome and healthy and put together in a way no Hanson had ever been.

But Michael had it easy. Michael could just hate him. Steven also had to feel guilty, and that made it so much more complicated. Ben had been Steven's English teacher in high school, and they'd gotten along just fine. Steven didn't especially like reading, but neither did anyone; and, as they read books like *Animal Farm, The Giver, Great Expectations,* or even Shakespeare, Steven had enjoyed listening to this happy, energetic man, who seemed not to understand some of the things he talked about. There was a dark side to everything that Ben seemed blissfully, even ignorantly unaware of, which even Steven couldn't help but see—but Ben was better than some droning old man, so it was okay, and he didn't think much about it.

Ben had met Steven's mom at a student teacher conference. They went to the same church, it turned out... they'd seen each other there, had mutual friends, but had never talked, imagine that? And at first it wasn't a big deal. Steven could imagine how it went—they talked sometimes at church, but not too often, off and on for years. Then one day mom lost her job (again) and told Ben about it. Ben worked at the school, but also part time at the church... and, as it turns out, he was able to offer her a spot in the church's community outreach.

Mom was good at the job, and he told her so—which must have been a big deal. No one else ever told mom she was good at anything. It was the first job Steven had seen her keep for more than a few years, and as much as he hated church and everything to do with it, she had the right personality for it: being the person at those weird, obnoxious bake-sales, or leading children's events, or helping design their procession for the community parade. She loved all that stuff, but she couldn't talk to anyone at home about it. Dad didn't care. Michael and Steven just got mean whenever she mentioned church.

That left Ben—who mom saw more and more, now that they worked together. Steven would always remember how she referred to him: the same way, every time.

"A nice man," mom would say. "He's such a nice man."

Later on, mom had referred to him as her 'special friend'. That's what she called him for years as they spent more and more time together, and mom spent more and more time at church. Mom and dad spent time together too, but dad would just get angry whenever church was mentioned, especially about how much time she spent there. And other times, well, dad was just angry.

They were such obnoxious, good Christians that at least, according to mom, it took years before they slept together. Years. And it wasn't some kind of long, secret affair. Mom immediately felt bad and told dad about it. He was furious at first, yelling and almost breaking things; but not for long. Soon he just fell back into that cold, incriminating silence, and wouldn't talk to mom at all. Even then, mom hadn't wanted to leave; but after two weeks of dad's brooding, lurking quiet (a kind Steven knew well, a thing that made everyone around him feel awful and in danger) mom moved in with Ben. And she'd been there ever since.

Shelton's was the only organic market in Niles—not a hippy kind of place, but an old-person store full of grandmothers buying big hunks of meat to make roasts and mashed potatoes with boiled carrots: real old proper dinners. Steven was the youngest person in the store, enough that he felt weird being there; but it was much better than, say, Walmart. There was even a decent-sized section for ethnic food and specialty items. In particular, he lingered to buy a few six-packs of cane-sugar sodas, and couple heavy, robust hunks of cheese.

Steven had always enjoyed shopping, he really did—and he resented Ben and mom for coming over and ruining his mood. He couldn't get them out of his head: as he picked up a bunch of fresh vegetables (more than had been in the house in years), as he waited for meat. He was angry, yeah, even if he was about to spend their money. Even if he kind of felt bad about what had happened. But he couldn't say anything, because that would be showing weakness. And that annoyed him too.

Being in a bad mood made him want good food. So when he went home, he seared two huge patties of ground beef (eighty percent meat, twenty percent fat: the perfect ratio for a good crust) in a cast-iron skillet. He put the patties on toasted brioche buns—more expensive, but worth it—with lettuce and tomato (beneath the burger, to keep the grease from wetting the bun), sautéed onions, muenster (a good melting cheese), and mixed a little sriracha mayo to put on top.

It was cooking, so he enjoyed it… but at the same time he did it resentfully; feeling, as everything slid into place, a slow, steady sense of wrongness, which this food better make go away. Michael passed through the kitchen once on his way to the back yard, but Steven didn't look up. He wanted these burgers to be good, even wanted them to look right. So he got two of the nicest plates in the house, and served the burgers next to a small pile—not too big— of vinegar and oil potato chips.

Michael came back in right as Steven finished, the screen door falling shut behind him.

"Smells good." He was still staring at the plates. "That's one hell of a burger."

"Good timing," Steven said. "I was just about to come get you."

"Great."

"About earlier. I was thinking—"

"Fucking Ben. Man, it's pissed me off all day."

"Just, maybe—"

"Really though, like he has any idea how we should live our lives?"

"Sure," Steven said. "It gets on my nerves too."

"I meant to tell you." A pause, enough to seem absentminded and weird. "The cat died."

"Did you do it?"

"Nah." Michael blinked very slowly, enough that it might have been better just to say he closed his eyes. "It just happened."

"Well good. But wait, why did you go outside?"

A visible flinch as Michael collected his thoughts. He shrugged. "I don't know. I just did."

So he'd been smoking weed. Steven couldn't smell it, probably because of the open air. No redeye yet either. But that must be it. It annoyed Steven a little that Michael hadn't offered. Not that Steven wanted it—this early in the day, it would just make him tired and sluggish and probably he would fall asleep and be angry about it later. But Michael should have offered.

"Okay," Steven said. "Did you at least clean it up?"

"Ah." Another pause. Those same absentminded eyes. "I tried."

"You tried?"

"It's caked on there pretty thick."

"You just spray it with the hose until it comes off."

"I tried." As Steven was about to speak, Michael grabbed a potato chip and put it in his mouth and cringed. "Ugh. What is that?"

"Vinegar and oil."

Michael stared; shook his head. "I can't eat that."

"Just give it time. It'll grow on you."

Michael didn't reply; just shook his head and walked to the counter. He picked up one plate and poured his chips back in the bag. But the plate looked sort of empty and naked without the chips, so Michael poured out animal crackers from a bag sitting on the counter.

The same brand they'd eaten years ago as kids—that pairing was just all wrong. But Steven didn't say anything even as Michael picked one up and took a bite.

"Hmm," he said. "Stale."

But that didn't stop him. He nodded, ate another, and began to walk away. And finally Steven had to say something.

"Wait. Where are you going?"

"I'm just going to eat in my room."

Steven clenched his fist. "I spent like an hour making that. You can eat it out here."

"Why would I do that?" Mild surprise; it passed quickly. Michael gave Steven another absentminded look, a little confused. Like he didn't know why Steven would suggest such a strange thing.

"I'm busy," Michael said. Not aggressively; more like he was explaining something very simple, very basic. Something he was surprised anyone would need to know. "I'll just take it to my room."

"Whatever," Steven said.

He watched, feeling even more annoyed, as Michael turned and walked away. Then he sat down, alone; but he was still pissed off, even as he ate. Not just an hour. He'd gone to the store for that, and made it fresh, and that burger was worth ten dollars in a restaurant. It was a good burger—damn good. And (Steven clenched his fist again as he thought about it) Michael was about to absentmindedly stuff it into his face while he watched anime.

WHAT REMAINS

IT DIDN'T HELP. Steven was pissed off—maybe even sort of furious. At mom and Ben, for existing; at Michael, for living wrong; even at this burger, for wasting so much time but not making him feel better. He'd overcooked it a little: a sign of failure when he bit into it. It was gone in just a few bites and all it left him with was a film of grease on his fingers and a faint pressure in his stomach... which would turn, maybe half an hour later, into the need to shit.

He'd made a lot of dishes while he was cooking. That made him angry too. It took almost twenty minutes to clean, which usually wasn't a big deal, but he didn't want to do it. Michael should help—Steven had cooked him food and Michael should fucking help him clean. But he knew, already, what would happen if he went to ask. Steven was here as a favor to him, it was practically a privilege to have him here; he wasn't a fucking house maid.

It had seemed, while he was doing them, that the dishes were the problem, and when they were done he'd be okay. But that wasn't it either. It had been building all day, but Steven only felt the full force of it now: the sense of an utter, complete *wrongness* around him, a wrongness that needed to be fixed. It was little, small things, but already piled so heavy Steven felt them like a weight on his shoulders.

Maybe it was that he needed to unpack; but afterwards all he thought about was how the house was still a mess and he would have to be the one to clean it. He spent an hour doing that, but it only made it worse. It would take days, maybe months before he could really relax. But that knowledge, too—it made him resentful.

Michael should help, Steven thought again. But he wouldn't. Michael couldn't shop or pay the bills, so Steven would have to do it, even if he didn't want to. Knowing that, it was strange. It made him angry, but it also made him feel good, like he wanted to do it so he could prove himself. Already, Steven wanted Michael to see how much he owed him; and he wanted to hear Michael say it, that Steven was a better person than him and he knew it. But first, Steven wanted Michael to apologize about that burger.

It was an unpleasant, crippling feeling, so much Steven could barely sit still—but he had to. There was nothing he could do; distantly, he knew that even if all of this happened he wouldn't feel better. He'd felt like this in Chicago too, just for different reasons: he couldn't just settle down and relax, because something was always wrong. His roommates—they were dirty, or loud. Steven felt both angry and resentful when they had people over, which was often: angry because of the noise (as he sat alone in his room, watching TV or, less often, doing homework), resentful because a part of him wanted to be the one with friends over, but he hardly ever was.

It had been an unpleasant realization. Steven had thought, when he left Niles, that things would be different—he would have lots of friends, and he would be cool, and he would finally have that thing, that special energy (or maybe it was a hollowness, an inability to see the shittiness and uselessness and fakeness of the world) that allowed everyone else to live their lives so easily. It hadn't happened.

It wasn't that he hadn't had the chance. Steven had been invited to parties, met girls, even made a few friends. But it never seemed right. Half of the time, for reasons he didn't properly understand, when someone invited him out he would just say no, go home, and watch TV. It hadn't felt right yet—these hadn't been the right people, the right party. But there was more time, he'd always told himself... until there wasn't. And now he was back

here where he'd started. He felt like a Hanson again, being home
—except this feeling, he didn't feel like himself.

He felt like dad.

It was a stunning realization, when it hit him—this sense of
wrongness, this obsession with little things that could never be
fixed, this sense of endless injustice. It must have been how dad
felt, except Steven had only been here a few days. Dad had lived
like this for twenty-five years: slowly, steadily, unchanging. This
was what it felt like to be inside the beginning of that cool, slow
anger—except Michael wasn't afraid of him, like they'd been
afraid of dad. Michael wouldn't do anything Steven said. And
even that knowledge didn't fix it: it just made it worse.

So he did the only thing he could think of.

He stopped cleaning, went out into dad's den, and started
watching TV.

That should fix it, it should make Steven feel better—but no.
All he did was sit there flipping through channels. Maybe because
it was still early and there wasn't anything on yet—Steven passed
through a bunch of talk shows, settled on a rerun of *The Simpsons*
—but it wasn't enough. The sense of wrongness, of just not being
right: it was still there, only it receded into the background a little.
Probably this was also how dad had felt all of those nights when
everyone was so afraid to talk around him, full of that monumen-
tal, barely contained anger.

Steven knew it, god damn it, but even that didn't make him
feel better. It just made him feel sad too. Which was worse.

Then it hit him, what he should do. Such a good idea he was
almost proud of himself. He stood up and shut off the TV and was
about to get ready—except, right then, the doorbell rang.

It was Halie, a little earlier today, standing outside with a half-
empty box of cigarettes in her hand, wearing a My Chemical
Romance sweater.

"Yo," she said.

"Hey again." Steven stepped back to let her in. She didn't take
her shoes off this time, which didn't bother him. (It usually would
have.) "So, you come over here every day apparently?"

"It's summer."

"Right."

Steven closed the door as she walked past—which, all of the

sudden, he didn't want her to do. But she was already on her way to Michael's room, and he needed to say something to stop her.

"Oh wait," he said—and it worked. She turned, hands in the back pockets of her jeans; and he decided that maybe My Chemical Romance weren't so bad after all.

"Yeah?"

Now that Steven was actually talking to her he felt very old and big and uncool, in his basically normal clothes (still wrinkly from his bag), with his stupid, embarrassing fixations and his degree in general studies. He wanted to seem cool, seem younger (even if he wasn't old, twenty-three wasn't old), but he wasn't the cool kind of older guy, though now he wanted to be.

"Sorry about earlier. With Ben."

At least he could buy them alcohol—yeah.

"It's cool," she said. "Michael talks about him all the time. He didn't seem so bad."

"He's not." Steven wanted to say something else, but he couldn't find the words; and Halie shrugged.

Her eyes, Steven thought, were huge in that dark makeup.

"No problem," she said.

THE SCENT OF BLOOD

AT FIRST WHEN she was gone Steven felt a little lost, almost empty, but then he remembered why he'd gotten up. It was barely five—there would be time. It was a bit late for a drive to Chicago, but it was what he needed: to get out of this house tonight. It was late, so he would sleep there tonight—maybe even a few days, since he'd paid the rent there through next month. He could stay a few days, maybe a week; say goodbye to a few of his friends (it felt good, even to himself, to pretend that was necessary); and then when he felt better he could drive back to Niles.

The idea was so sweet it was almost delicious. He was already about to follow Halie into Michael's room to tell him, until—part of him knew this was a bad idea, but he couldn't help himself—he thought of that stain of blood in the back yard. Michael said he'd tried—he'd tried, but given up. What the hell was that supposed to mean? One last thing. Maybe Steven would just clean the fucking thing himself and get it over with.

So he went outside, still feeling good about himself, and that was when he saw the cat.

It was dead, Michael had told him. Steven had known, distantly, that there must be a body, but hadn't thought much about what had happened. It seemed too much, too ridiculous, to think that Michael would just leave the thing sitting there in that pool of its own blood: the stiff, matted fur of its belly molded to

KYLE MUNTZ

the bloody grass, head down over those two outstretched paws, even its ears stuck down to the side of its head.

It seemed impossible that Michael would leave it there. It's just weird—it's nasty and wrong to let a dead animal sit in your backyard... leaving it there to bake all day in the sun, that little mangled mess of skin and thin bones. Leaving it so long that, throughout the day, not just the flies, but other animals would smell the scent of blood.

But Michael had.

It was even worse to see it in full daylight. Beneath the muck, a few spots of fur still showed through—surprisingly, a raccoon hadn't carried it away during the night. Just looking at it brought back that weakness in his stomach; and Michael had come out here twice today. What had he been doing? Smoking weed while he looked at the corpse?

There was one last thing Steven noticed, though he only caught a glimpse, and didn't want to think about it for long. The cat's mouth.

Along the side of the cat's mouth, going back nearly to the base of the head, the flesh had been torn, almost as if it had been pried open. It was a ridiculous, stupid image—Michael reaching into the cat's mouth, one hand on the upper and lower jaw, pulling until the skin split. It was a disgusting, pointless image, but that was the only thing Steven could think of: Michael prying open the thing's mouth to look inside.

The alternative, well, that was just stupid—the only other reason a mouth could open so wide was if it broke at the base of the jaw. Fucking stupid.

It could only open so wide to make room for something to come out.

74

THE FEELING

A SHAPE IN THE GRASS

IT WAS PROBABLY BETTER that Steven had left, Michael decided—did he really have to get so angry all of a sudden? Even a few days later, Michael still thought it was weird how Steven had thrown open the door of his room and started yelling about the cat. Then he'd said something about going to pick up his stuff. He'd be back tomorrow, or next week; Michael didn't care really.

Steven had always been uptight. Apparently college had only made him worse, which was a shame since he'd been mostly cool since he came back. It sort of annoyed Michael, except he had other things on his mind. He'd hardly slept the last few nights, thinking of what he'd seen—and all the stuff with Steven, well, Michael just didn't care very much about it. It was like dad. Just ignore him and eventually he would calm down and go away. Maybe.

He understood, though, how weird it was to leave the cat there. And so did Halie when he mentioned it to her, but not for the same reason.

"So it's just been sitting there?" she asked.

"I thought something would come eat it or carry it away, I don't know."

"But apparently not?"

Michael shook his head. "It's just sitting there."

"Hum." That's how Halie said it: not a sound, but the actual word, 'hum,' which was probably supposed to be a thinking sound. She leapt out of the bed—forgetting to step over Michael's controller, which jerked the PS2 forward and knocked it onto the floor."

"Fuck, Halie."

"Let's go look at it." No apology—whatever.

"Now?"

"Duh. Come on."

It was maybe four in the evening, still bright as they walked out the door—at first Michael wondered if it would be there, but no. The thing he'd seen, it only came out at night, and there was no sign of it. Only the dead cat. Which was almost familiar to him by now, but Halie hadn't seen it yet.

"Wow," smiling and laughing as she said it. "It's so nasty."

"It hasn't rained for a week." Michael felt the grass crunch beneath his sandals, dry and sort of crispy. "I thought it would wash away the blood for me."

"It's disgusting!" Still laughing. Michael wasn't surprised—she was the one who liked all the violent parts of everything they watched, so much she'd called out 'yeah!' and started laughing at the scene where the guy got his eyes gouged out in *Elfin Lied*. And she couldn't stop giggling like a crazy person while people's heads blew up that one (and only) night they watched six episodes of *Fist of the North Star*. That show was dumb as hell but they still made jokes about it now. And there was something else, one show he wasn't thinking of, right on the tip of his tongue.

"It's like something from *Gantz*!" Halie said. That show, which they'd watched early last year, about a bunch of people in black body suits with guns that made things explode in the most ridiculous way when they shot them. "Except worse."

"That's what I was thinking," Michael said. "I couldn't remember the name."

Except Halie flinched. "Sorry. I know you liked this cat."

"It's fine."

"No really, I'm sorry." She stepped away and patted him on the arm. "Maybe we should go inside."

"Do I look sad?"

"See, you're getting defensive. Let's go."

So they weren't out long—Halie hadn't had time to look close. If they had (it was harder to tell now that the rot had set in, and with all the flies) maybe she would have noticed those bloody lines around its mouth, though she couldn't have guessed what it meant. She was smart, Michael had always thought Halie was way smarter than him, but even her, there was no way she could guess what he'd seen that night. Or what he saw, later that evening, when he went outside without her.

It was almost routine at this point. He'd gotten so used to going outside with dad to see the cat. Even without dad, after it got sick, Michael would go outside and sit with the cat for hours. The cat got sicker and sicker. But even afterwards, after what happened, nothing changed. He still went out to see.

Only now, it wasn't a cat.

Michael went outside around eight today, holding a beer in one hand, a tin of cat food in the other. It was still light, the sun slanting yellow and heavy over the trees, but he didn't mind waiting. He sat down in the same spot on the edge of the deck, smoking a cigarette and drinking the beer—he would need to ask Steven for more whenever he got back—but he didn't have to wait so long after all.

Twenty minutes later, and he made out the rustling in the grass.

It was hard to say what it was—but that was normal at this point. He was used to it; or he thought he was. There it was, rising up at the edge of the trees. At first, it almost seemed like something crawling beneath the ground, some worm the size of his thigh churning up the earth. But no.

It was there, an outline, a shape on the grass. Up closer, it looked like a shadow, like maybe the light wasn't hitting it right, like it was standing in something else's shadow. But no. It wasn't a shadow itself—you could see, when you looked close enough, meat behind the shadow, cool and black or gray. Only sometimes it was there, and sometimes it wasn't.

When the creature stood near the base of the deck—beside the bloodstain—it even, from the right angle, looked almost like a cat. Were those protrusions on top of its head like ears? But it was a cat with no fur, heavy shoulders; leathery black skin, then not skin at all. A protrusion like a nose on the face, except it wasn't a nose. But there were eyes: huge, staring eyes. And beneath them, a mouth.

"There you are." And then, in a gesture he imagined the creature wouldn't understand, Michael chugged all of his beer as he stood up... or tried, except he coughed at the end and spilled the last little bit on the ground.

It stared at him. Silent, like a cat. But this wasn't any cat.

"You're bigger today." Michael put both hands out as if to measure it.

The creature—which, for the most part, did not remind him of the cat—seemed glad to come back and listen, but it didn't have much to say.

Michael said, "A lot bigger, actually."

Days ago, when this creature had come out of the cat's mouth —wrenching the jaw so it nearly fell off—it had still been small. Enough that, if he wanted, he could have held it in his hand. But now it was... not as big, yet. But at this rate in a few days it would be the same size as the cat.

And then, what, would it keep getting bigger?"

"I've got your food again." Michael reached for the tin of cat food. Damp and soft on his fingers; the faint residue left behind when he tossed the food onto the grass.

But no, nothing.

The creature didn't even look at the food as it fell. Its eyes were still fixed on him—but, though Michael knew this was technically scary, for some reason it was comforting.

"You must be hungry. But you're okay, right? I want you to be okay."

A motion—Michael had asked questions before without ever seeing something like it. And even a moment later he didn't believe. But he would have to try again, to test it.

"That's good," Michael said. "I'm glad to hear that."

He'd spoken again, but no movement this time.

He wiped his hand on his shirt, feeling the residue of the cat food stick to the cloth. Not all, but some of it.

"But you're okay?" Michael asked.

There it was: that movement again. Michael felt crazy, asking the question he was about to ask, but at this point who cared? If he was crazy he was crazy. But he was also curious as hell.

"Do you understand me?" Michael asked.

There it was again: the creature nodded. It was a gentle, faint

gesture, but undeniable. So now he asked another question, probably the most important one.

He asked:

"Are you going to hurt me?"

The creature shook its head—that thing shaped like a head.
There was no way to be sure, but he would have to trust it, and he
decided he did. Though the question he asked next was the
craziest of all.

That question was: "Do you want to come inside?"

A QUIET GUEST

MICHAEL KEPT his eyes on the creature as they went inside—held the door open for it (though he knew it didn't need him to), following behind it through the house. Eventually they had to wind up in his room; there wasn't anywhere else he would go. All that time, he kept thinking that soon, when the light was right, he would get a good look at it. But he never did. Like even when he was staring right at it, he was still looking from the corner of his eye.

It was quiet, so quiet it might not have been there at all. Michael sat down on his bed; the creature stared at him. It stared, and stared, and Michael looked at the rigid line of that shape that wasn't a neck. It stared at him but what did it see? He didn't know, had trouble imagining. He felt strange, and naked, and terrified... even though, the longer he looked at it, maybe it seemed like a cat again after all. It would be so much easier if the thing still had some fur.

Then it dashed forward—so quick Michael flinched. It was going to bite his legs, mangle his calves and bite them deep to the bone... so he lifted his legs up, which wouldn't work, but it felt like the right thing to do.

Only the creature passed right beneath him. Under the bed.

And it seemed content to stay there. Almost a minute later, and it hadn't moved, so Michael did the only thing he could think of, the only thing that made sense. His legs were so weak he could barely stand, but he found the strength for it somewhere.

He stood up, turned on his PS2, and started watching anime.

He was still rewatching *Evangelion*, only he was about done now. For the first twenty minutes he could hardly focus, so scared he could barely move—what would happen when it got tired of waiting? When it pounced? He was crazy to have invited it inside. Probably he'd just killed himself. When he reached the end of an episode, he realized he'd probably have to watch it over again, because he'd been so busy imagining different ways the thing beneath his bed might kill him. Or at least hurt him terribly.

He restarted the episode, and thought: what was done was done, and it was stupid to worry. So he did his best to enjoy it. Midway through the episode he realized he hadn't thought of the creature in five minutes. And when it was done, while the credits played, he wondered something else, something very strange.

The creature had been watching with him, so yeah—he wondered if it liked it.

It had been long enough, nearly an hour. He couldn't stand the suspense anymore. So he decided he would look under the bed.

"Hey," he said. "You there, little guy?"

Though that didn't sound right. He was still talking to it like a cat. And that wasn't any cat. He wasn't sure what it was, only that it was strange enough it could have come from an anime. And that wasn't good. Characters in anime got hurt all the time.

"I'm coming down there. Is that okay?"

Nothing. But it was now or never, so Michael got on one knee at the edge of the mattress, tilting his head down to see beneath the bed. There was a lot of junk down there—wrappers for food he hadn't eaten in months, a bunch of quarters, knots of lint. But way back, by the wall, was covered in shadow.

Only when he'd been down there almost a minute, still staring, he realized for sure.

The creature wasn't there.

But where was it? Michael stood up, feeling this intense pressure in his head—a pounding ringing in his ear. He felt awful and tense and worried; and, when he stood up again, he had to take a piss terribly. It took an effort of will just to hold it in, and there was a second he almost thought he'd piss himself.

A few minutes later, when he entered the room again, it was even worse. The creature could be anywhere, except it seemed like it was nowhere. That was worse: knowing it was there, but not having a point of reference. It had been okay, somehow, when it was under the bed. More manageable.

Now maybe it wasn't in his room at all. He didn't know where it would hide—beneath the bean bags? Even there he'd hear it. It was there, but it wasn't there, and that was maybe the worst thing he'd ever felt.

But he didn't want to look for it either, didn't want to risk making it angry. And he didn't see it again the rest of that night. Halie wouldn't come over again until tomorrow—that left him alone with it.

How the how hell could he get it to leave? And what would he do when Steven came back?

Michael didn't know, he didn't have any idea what he should do. But that didn't stop him from thinking about it all night. He already knew he couldn't sleep, so he just sat there for hours, watching anime. He paused it to think, and when he blinked it was morning and he was still alive. Which, that was good.

Except he wasn't alone.

It was standing there on top of one of his shelves, looking down at him. Probably it had been there for hours, staring at him as he slept. But it didn't react even when he screamed.

And afterwards, when it was still just there, staring at him, something changed. Michael felt the shift in himself, like somebody had flipped a switch. He wasn't scared anymore.

"Hey again," he said. "Been there long?"

He hadn't expected an answer—but it nodded, and he laughed.

"Don't kill me, alright?" He paused. "I guess you already said you wouldn't. Probably I should have remembered that."

The creature shifted slightly. That was about the time Michael noticed it wasn't really standing on top of the shelf—it was clinging to the side, sort of like a spider.

"What are you?" he asked. "What do you want?"

He should have known better than to expect a response. But sometimes there was no helping it.

"I should tell you," he said. "My friend Halie is coming over in a few hours. Don't eat her either, okay? Even if she looks like she'd taste good."

No nod this time. Hopefully it understood.

"Don't eat my brother Steven either, even if he's sort of a dick." Michael's stomach rumbled; he reached down to grab it. "Oh yeah, I'm hungry aren't I?"

They didn't blink. The creature's eyes didn't blink. It wasn't natural. But maybe they weren't eyes.

"I didn't eat yesterday," Michael said. "It's all your fault. But it's okay."

That said, he stood up, went into the kitchen, and ate a bowl of cereal. Frosted Flakes. Steven had given him shit about Frosted Flakes the other day—they were too sweet, they were for kids, they were bad for him. But Steven didn't like anything Michael ate: pop tarts, ramen noodles, probably even pizza rolls. He needed to relax.

Speaking of relaxation, Michael almost felt proud of himself now, how relaxed he was. Look at him. He'd invited a monster into the house and he was keeping his cool. That was something special, right? That was something to be proud of?

When that feeling came, it didn't go away. He felt it the rest of the morning, which he spent playing *Tekken* and doing pretty damn well. He felt good about himself, and he felt interesting, and that feeling only intensified until around noon, when Halie showed up.

"I let myself in," she said. "The door was open."

"Cool." Michael didn't talk again until he finished the match. Which he won.

"So I was thinking," Halie said. "Your brother was pretty pissed the other day, wasn't he?"

"He gets like that." Michael started another match. "I wouldn't worry about it."

"He's supposed to be living here now, yeah?"

"He can come back whenever he wants."

"Are you pissed at him too?"

"Umm." He squinted as his character got punched in the face. "Give me a second."

"Are you pissed at him?

"Nah." He tossed the controller aside, still getting beaten up onscreen. "It's just sort of annoying."

He turned around to look at her—and that's when he saw the creature. It wasn't standing on anything this time, just sort of lurking in the corner of the room. But it wasn't staring at him. It was staring at Halie.

She'd said something, he realized a second later, but he didn't know what. He only heard afterwards, when she kept saying his name.

"Michael," she said.

The fear came back, icy and powerful. But he had to act normal, so he said, "Yeah?"

"When's the last time you took a shower?"

It could pounce on her, Michael realized. An idiot. He was a fucking idiot.

"Umm," he said.

"When?"

"A few days ago."

"Gross," she said.

"I'm fine."

"I was—what are you starting at?"

"It—it's nothing."

"You're being weird, Michael."

She hadn't turned because there couldn't possibly be something there. And a second later there wasn't. It slipped back beneath the bed, stealthy and silent. And for the rest of the day, even after Halie was gone, Michael mostly forgot about it again. He played more games, took a shower, ate two peanut butter sandwiches for dinner. It only occurred to him around seven, when he sat down to watch more anime, how tired he was. And when he remembered being tired, he remembered why he'd stayed up all night.

That didn't stop him from falling asleep. There was fear—it had been there all day, even when he felt good about himself. (Probably what had felt good, more than anything, was how good it felt to be in denial.) But eventually he needed to sleep, and even the fear couldn't stop it.

The TV was still on when he woke up, but it was dark. Little red numbers on the clock said it was one in the morning. Probably the light from the television had woken him up. He started to get up to turn it off—except that's when he noticed the shadow. The shadow of the creature leaning down above him.

The light was faint, so he could barely see it. But enough to see it move: closer, like it was taking a step, a subtle drift.

Then it lowered its mouth.

THE ABSENCE

PAIN—MICHAEL expected pain. As a child, he'd been bitten once by a dog. Not a small bite. A serious one. He remembered the teeth sinking into his forearm: the sharp pain of it, but the stranger part was looking and seeing the holes. The blood leaking out. The knowledge of a solid thing (his body) except now it had a hole in it. The pain was all part of that. The breaking of the solid thing.

Only this wasn't his arm—it was leaning down over his face. It would maul his face off, and eat his eyes, or tear off his lips... and if he survived probably he would need that weird, fake-looking reconstructive surgery. He would rather die than be so ugly. When the creature was done, he would look in the mirror, and if it was too bad he would shoot himself.

What a stupid thing to think. He would never do something like that. But he thought it—maybe because he was too scared to look at that mouth, that mouth that wasn't a mouth, leaning over almost like it wanted to kiss him.

And yes, it wasn't a kiss, but maybe in some ways it was like one. Or at least, it wasn't like being bit. Because being bit hurt, and this didn't hurt.

The feeling was hard to describe. At first—but only for a very short moment—it felt strange, but even then it wasn't painful. It just felt... unfamiliar. It was a feeling like his dad must have experienced the first time he saw Michael wearing girls' pants: a sense that the world wasn't quite like he imagined it. And in that brief, barely conscious moment afterwards, came a resistance, a moment where his understanding of everything had to change; and that was a hard, rough moment.

But then it ended.

It ended—and what came after was the feeling.

It was a hard, maybe impossible feeling to describe. The problem had to do with words—the problem was we only have words for the familiar, for things outside us. Even feeling, the interior of it. Those things are so hard to describe.

This was something different, something new. But Michael did know something.

It felt good.

Maybe it even felt damn good.

There was a kind of discovery in it—it didn't make any sense to him that first time, but later he would find words for it. That first time it was as strange and impossible to understand as anything had ever been. He didn't find the words for it that first night—though he would fall asleep, soon after. Maybe he would never find the words.

But he knew that afterwards, he felt good and he felt sated. Maybe better than he'd ever felt before. And when he looked at the shadow above him he didn't feel fear—probably he would never feel afraid of it again. It was impossible to be afraid of something that made you feel like that.

He fell asleep, but even in the dream, the feeling was still there.

CONTRAST

STEVEN CAME BACK a few days after that, but Michael didn't pay much attention to him. He didn't pay attention to anything. He felt good, and he felt calm, and he felt alive: more alive than he'd ever felt before. Every time, it was always the same—it seemed impossible, but every time it was the same.

For the first time, over that next week, Michael walked out into the backyard and he understood why mom and dad had liked sitting there so much, sitting and watching the leaves and just waiting for animals. It had seemed boring to him before. But wow—the world was so beautiful, it had always been beautiful. He just hadn't cared to take a good look at it.

On the surface, not much had changed. It was summer—the beginning of a long, beautiful summer. And Michael was happy. He spent that whole first week watching anime with Halie, and even Steven coming back couldn't ruin it, no matter how hard he tried.

Michael had always understood this, but now he understood better: that it was important to relax. That life is good and beautiful and really there's nothing to worry about, everything will be great if you just sit back and enjoy it.

On the surface it was all the same, except Michael spent more time sitting outside. A few days after Steven came back, he walked out while Michael was sitting there, and just stared at him a while. Then he walked up and sniffed Michael's shirt.

"Damn," Steven said. "I was sure."

"About what?"

"That you were smoking weed out here."

"Nah."

"You've been so out of it this week."

"It's summer. Just relax."

Which, of course, Steven had never been good at doing. After those first few days, Steven and Michal didn't talk much; but two or three times a day, Steven always showed up with some complaint. Afterwards, Michael couldn't have said what they were, just that he didn't much care.

He didn't care about anything—except afterwards, when he did.

The feeling was as strange and unfamiliar as the first—only this time it was the opposite. Not pain exactly... more like, waking up. It was a simple feeling, and easier to describe: an almost immediate return to the way things had always been. There was no pain, no physical unpleasantness. Just an abrupt, unwanted awareness of things—like waking up from a dream, where you're just on the cusp of it and want to go back, but can't.

It was like that, only it could happen at any time. The first time, Michael had been sitting in his room at night, when all at once it seemed really truly dark again, and for a second he felt lost and confused and wondered (really truly wondered) if life was even worth living.

Then he just felt... normal. It wasn't so hard, coming back to normal; but even that first time, he felt different knowing there was something else, some other way to live. And he felt it in him now—vaguely the first time, and more clearly as the days passed. That reserve of... something. He'd never noticed it before—never known he should think about it. But now he felt it: almost a pressure, an awareness.

Of what, it was hard to say. It could be a lot of things. Sometimes it was as simple as annoyance—others, the knowledge that humanity was doomed, had always been doomed, simply by being born human. Michael had never been a very philosophical person, and it was a small punch in the jaw to realize he believed things like this.

He almost wasn't sure where they'd come from, only that they'd been there a very long time: like armor he wore in order to face the world. And like armor, all of these parts of him, they had a weight... something heavy, pulling him down when he walked. But they were even there when he laid down.

It was only the third time, when he went back to normal, that he really understood it. He'd been thinking about his dad, which he did a lot... not an important memory, and he wasn't sure what reminded him of it. But he was thinking about a store dad had taken him to when he was young—Lunker's, a fishing store.

This was back when he'd thought dad was a good fisherman. (Later he'd discovered that dad was really very casual about it, just like he wasn't a great golfer, in fact he was almost kind of bad.) But this store—it was closed now, either that or dad just hadn't gone in years—it was off half an hour away in another town, Goshen or Elkhart, it didn't matter.

Going there as a kid, it had been a strange, revelatory place: more like a museum than a store, with huge mounted fish along all the walls, fishtanks, nature-displays, even a bridge in one room with a fake riverbottom beneath it. Every time dad mentioned going Michael always wanted to go with him. They would eat at the restaurant there; Michael would start to want something he saw—a tent, a fishing pole—fervently wanting dad to buy it even though Michael didn't know what it was used for. And dad would say no and Michael would forget about it, and that was fine.

It wasn't an important memory, not really. But it's what Michael thought about the third night—and that's when he understood the difference, what had changed. Because before, it had felt good... like a kind of casual stroll through the past, one without any real purpose, just to see.

But then it had changed, then the weight had come back, and now he felt sad. Actually, he didn't just feel sad, he felt terrible; and even if he was just in his bed, staring at the ceiling, it didn't matter.

He started crying, maybe harder than he'd cried since dad died—but again, it wasn't anything new. He'd just gone back to the way things always were.

THE BLACK PELLET

THE CREATURE WASN'T JUST MAKING him feel better, Michael realized—though after a few days, it was hard to believe he'd ever been afraid of it. It was strange, yeah, and unfamiliar; it wasn't always shaped the same, really it didn't have a shape. But now when he saw it he just felt good; sometimes when it wasn't there he actually missed it.

Not that it had any answers for him. It would only answer his questions sometimes, not often. Which left Michael alone to sit and think... not that he minded. Nothing had ever been so pleasant as sitting alone and thinking this week.

The creature wasn't just making him feel better. It was eating something. Though that... that was the hard part. Putting words to it. Mostly Michael thought of the feeling. But it became easier when he figured out a way to generalize it.

Absence. That's what made it so beautiful. It wasn't that life was better than it had been before, or that he had more reason to enjoy it; it's just that the shadow, the underside of it, was gone. The creature had taken all of those things from him, had eaten them—but then, after long enough, they came back. That's why it felt like an absence, a reserve to be emptied and refilled.

There was so much he didn't understand. It didn't make it hard when he just went with the feeling. But there was one thing that confused him, that almost would have scared him if he still had room for fear in him... though another part of him, even while it happened, knew that he should be terrified.

It happened again, maybe on the fourth night, he didn't remember. He felt an itch on his left forearm, right where there had always been a vein—but it wasn't a normal itch, even though it felt good to scratch it, it felt so fucking unbelievably good. And it wasn't a welt he felt there, not a normal one.

It was big, the size of a quarter—maybe half an inch high, firmer than the rest of his skin. So eventually he turned on the light, because he should look at this stupid huge thing. But he was wrong, it hadn't been a welt.

He saw it there, buried in his skin, but at first he didn't believe it—a rounded, black shape, pushing out of the skin. It was only later, when the feeling went away, that he realized he should have been afraid; that really this was worse than anything he'd ever dreamed, as bad as that dream where he'd looked down at his arm, except inside the pores were so many eyes.

It was like that, except now he just felt curious. When he scratched the black shape, it moved, inching a little closer to the surface; if he grabbed it right, maybe he could even pull it out.

And he did. And when he was done he was holding a little black pellet, the size of a ping pong ball; and the skin of his wrist, well, he'd thought it might be bleeding, thought there might be an immense hole. But now it felt good too.

Not just an absence—he felt actual pleasure where the black pellet had come out. A sort of good, pure, rush in his skin; the sense of being purged, of being empty and pure and fresh. Probably that's what made it easier, the reason he wasn't terrified. And why, when he looked up, and saw the creature on the floor beneath his bed, he just felt curious, not scared.

He said, "Hey there, buddy."

Its head lowered, then rose, beckoning.

"You want it?" Michael held the black pellet up in the light. It was a little soft, like rubber—if he squeezed hard, it would give. Though it wasn't too soft either, not the kind of thing that would leave a mark on his fingers.

It nodded.

"It's not like I have any use for it," Michael said.

Michael tossed the black pellet onto the carpet at the creature's feet—it bounced once, rolled. Michael could feel when the creature was pleased, even if there was no visual change. It was only a few days later, again, that was when he started to think how strange this part was too.

He felt very close to the creature, like he'd given it a gift in exchange for all it had given him. And he was actually happy when he saw what happened next, it made him feel good—there one moment, gone the next, as the creature lowered its head.

Lowered its mouth around the black pellet, and ate it.

THE REMAINDER

MICHAEL SPENT the first few hours the next morning in a state of total, utter stupefaction. It wasn't like him just to lay around in bed for hours. One thing about Michael—he was still a Hanson, and Hansons are never still. They're always doing something, whether it's building, or playing video games, or getting angry. But this morning Michael didn't feel like a Hanson. He just felt confused.

What he should have felt, he thought, holding his arm up into the light, was fear. The arm seemed to be mostly alright, but not unmarked—the flesh was raw and puffy where the black pellet had emerged. At first it reminded Michael of popping a zit: how you found this weird, greasy, alien pus in your skin, except afterwards it was okay, the surface sealed... and sometimes for years, when he looked at people (especially politicians and pretty girls) he wondered how everyone had gotten used to this strange life, this insane, disgusting life where everyone had these weird deposits of slime building beneath their skin.

Weren't they disgusting, people? What was this life they were trying to live, just looking at the surface of things when beneath it there was this accumulating, greasy nastiness... like snot, or shit, or blood? But that's how it all was, all surfaces—and when you saw what was beneath the surface, your first thought was that, well. It should have stayed hidden. Surfaces should stay closed; that was a proper, good life.

And when Michael thought about it like that, he understood people—he understood his dad, always insisting on making things right, making things the way they should be, even though the world was imperfect. He understood those fussy, stupid schoolteachers with their rules and their words that couldn't be said. He even understood Christianity (but not, he told himself, enough to sympathize with his mom) because, when you just thought about things a certain way, when you pretended the world was as it seemed to be, it was so much easier, and you didn't have to think about those greasy insides.

Michael couldn't stop—all morning, he prodded at that raw, soft flesh on his arm, and it wasn't like popping a zit. It took him a while to find it, but right in the center, where the black pellet had come out, there was a hole. So small—just a pinprick. The hole was still fresh: it was small, but it could stretch.

And he realized, after picking at it for a long time, that if he wanted he could stick his finger all the way in—like as a child he'd buried it up to the knuckle in his nose to pick away the crust along the sides. The skin wasn't meant for it, it was a one-way hole, but with enough prodding he could make the skin part, and it didn't even hurt very much.

But no—there was nothing down there to touch, nothing in the greasy interior except maybe a bone. And if he kept at it maybe the skin would be all flappy and stretched... and yeah, actually, when he took his finger out of his arm it kind of was, except there was no blood... if he'd gone down far enough maybe he would have found some strange gland, which had produced the black pellet and built it up. Maybe everyone had one and just didn't know about it, or it needed the right stimulus to start, or—

It was morning, so Michael felt like he should be alone, but no. The creature was standing there at the foot of his bed. The longer it stayed with him, the more it looked like a cat... only, sometimes when it moved, its limbs weren't stable, they transformed.

Like now, when it stepped forward, its head raised—but it didn't just look up. The neck actually *elongated*, until it jutted a foot off the torso; it tilted, leaning to the side as the creature stepped forward, until it was close enough to touch.

"What did you do to me, little guy?" Michael held up his left arm, the raw skin facing up. "What is this?"

The creature took another step, so close it pressed against him through the covers.

"What the hell are you?" Michael asked again. But it was a gentle, relaxed question, and he didn't expect an answer. He just wanted to lay back down and relax—and all this time, he hadn't felt scared. He just felt confused.

They laid there together for a while, Michael and the creature, and he thought it really was a pretty nice morning. At one point, he reached out to pet the creature on the head. Its skin felt exactly like he'd imagined. Not warm and soft, like a cat, but cool and smooth, like leather.

He dozed off, and woke up to the creature's mouth on his arm, where the black pellet had emerged. And yeah, just like before.

It felt good.

THE PLAN

MICHAEL WASN'T CONFUSED VERY OFTEN. Life had always seemed pretty simple to him—if people left you alone, and you had something to do, it would be basically okay. Whenever he was confused, there was only one course of action: he had to talk someone about it. And, of course, there was only one person he could talk to.

That meant, somehow, he had to let Halie know about the creature. Which was harder than it seemed. Even Michael, who'd never been a stealthy guy, knew he needed to keep the thing a secret. What could he do? She'd think he was crazy if he tried to tell her about it, but she'd also just freak out if she saw it.

He spent a full day thinking about it, which didn't seem to help, but he knew it needed to happen. It still needed a little planning though. He told the creature his plan a few hours in advance, and hoped it understood, but it was impossible to know for sure.

Halie came over early that day, around two, and he didn't wait long before he brought it up.

"So you know the other day," he said, "when I showed you that cat?"

"That was last week," she said. "Is it still there?"

"Probably, but—"

"I wonder what it looks like now? Let's go check it out."

"Ok, but wait—"

No good. She was already headed towards the door, so Michael followed her out onto the deck.

"Whelp," she said. "Still dead."

The skin was starting to look almost baked and crispy—dry, from all that sunlight, like the grass. But the body was still whole. He didn't remember his biology classes so well, but he was pretty sure nothing would eat it now.

"Dead as fuck," Halie said.

"There's something I wanted to tell you," Michael said.

"Yeah?"

"Well, when the cat died, it died but also it didn't die. Something else came out—you see there, around the mouth?"

"Okay."

"A creature." Michael had never talked about it out loud, and it felt so strange—especially knowing that, if the creature listened, it would be underneath the deck right now. It would be listening to his words. "Only it's not a cat."

"Then what is it?"

"I feel like I should just show you." Louder, he called: "You can come out now."

A long silence followed, maybe thirty seconds of Halie just looking at him—and it occurred to Michael, surprisingly for the first time, that maybe he was just insane. Maybe he was a weird, crazy person who had invented all of this. It was worse because he was seeing things that weren't there—it only took half a minute but he was already coming up with an explanation, some way to tell her it had all been a joke. It would take an idiot to make a joke like that.

It appeared, swiftly and quietly, from beneath the deck. Only it didn't keep its distance and stay in the grass, like Michael had said it should. Which maybe, sort of, might make it less scary.

Halie didn't scream, like he'd expected she might. She just stared at it, stared for a very long time, until she said:

"It's bigger than the cat was. I thought you said it crawled out the mouth?"

"It grew.

"Okay then." Another of those long pauses. "So it's a Pokémon right?"

"I wish I knew."

Halie leaned down close to the creature.

"Hey there."

It flicked its tail in what might have been a reply.

"If it had spines," she said, "it would look like a chupacabra."

"Chupacabras aren't real," Michael said.

Then Halie looked at him, and he realized why it was funny—and both of them laughed. Michael laughed so hard his vision blurred, and he had to sit down. Halie doubled over, except instead of coming over to one of the chairs she just kneeled down in the center of the deck.

It went on so long, maybe five minutes. Both of them laughed, and laughed, and laughed, and by the end of it Michael's stomach hurt, and so did his throat, and there were tears in his eyes.

Even when it was over—mostly, kind of over—they still had trouble talking because whenever they tried one of them would start laughing again. They even laughed at the silence.

What made it worse, or maybe better, was how the whole time the creature just looked at them with those immense white eyes.

"It's kind of creepy, isn't it?" Halie said.

"Nah," Michael said. "You get used to it."

"But what does it do?"

"Well, that's what I wanted to talk about."

THE VIRTUES OF
HUMAN FRIENDSHIP

MICHAEL HAD DONE his best to explain—which probably wasn't very good. It had all come out in a rush, both true and shapeless. When it was done, Michael felt he'd explained a few things well, and most of them hardly at all. He hadn't expected Halie's reaction, but probably he should have. It must be that he was pretty dumb. How could you be friends with someone for so many years and not know the first thing they'd want to do?

"I need to try," she said. "Come on."

"It might not be safe," Michael said.

"That hasn't stopped you."

They'd gone back into Michael's room eventually, both sitting on the floor at the foot of his bed. Michael realized the importance of keeping their voices down. What if Steven heard? Well, maybe not. Steven would just think they were talking about an anime or something.

"Come here," she said.

The creature didn't move. It looked at her. At Michael.

"I think..." she trailed off, but then seemed to become sure. "It's asking for your permission."

"Umm."

"Don't be a dick."

"Okay," Michael said—and the creature walked towards her.

"Wow, it really does understand us."

"It just doesn't have much to say."

Michael wondered. Was it private, what was about to happen? Should he leave the room? Part of him wasn't sure what he was about to see—he'd tended to close his eyes when it happened.

Halie didn't seem to mind, so he stayed where he was, watching as the creature stepped forward. He expected it to go for her arm, but instead it pressed its head against her ankle.

"Here?" she asked. "Okay, yeah."

But her pants were too tight to roll up, so after a minute of trying she just took them off.

"Mysteries of the universe." She grinned up at Michael. "Yeah?"

The creature's head touched her ankle. Michael had always imagined it as a sort of licking, like a real cat would do—but from this angle its mouth looked like a suction cup, maybe even the mouth of a snake.

Michael thought a few things, in the next thirty seconds or so.

First he thought about Halie's legs. They were nice, and thin, and a bit pale, and high on her thighs he could see the faint, faint down (the same thin, colorless hair he saw on girl's backs when they bent over and the shirt rode up, which he spent so much time thinking about in real life but never noticed when he watched porn), but also not so different from his, because all legs were basically the same right?

But then its head pulled back. He'd thought it would take longer—sometimes, with him, he imagined five or ten minutes. Except with Halie it was over in less than a minute.

There was a point, near the end of it, where all the tension went out of her. Halie sighed, and all her muscles relaxed, a sound like someone setting down all the weight they'd ever carried; and her voice was tranquil and sluggish when she spoke, but what she said was simple, it was exactly what he'd expected.

"You're right," she said. "It really does feel good."

"Right?" he asked.

Both of them laid back, and it felt the same as after they smoked weed, except different. It seemed, for a while, that there wasn't anything to say. They just laid together in the crystalline sunlight, the bed frame creaking whenever one of them shifted.

They laid together, their hips touching just a little, until Halie turned, her face squashed down into the pillow. "Hey Michael."

"Yeah?"

"You wanna give me a kiss?" she said. "I feel like kissing somebody right now."

Michael turned his head to look at her—the hair falling down over her face, across her eyes, the thin body in bed next to his. Maybe this was it, he realized. Probably she could see it: the insistent, oppressed boner down there, struggling with the tight fabric of his jeans. He didn't just hear the sound of her breathing; he could feel it a little on his face, and it felt good.

He looked down, a quick flick, towards the crotch of her jeans: a kind of innocent, barren flatness where her legs came together. (That was what jeans were for—to hide the genitals underneath them.) But if he reached over right now, maybe even put his hand down her jeans, probably he could discover the soft, warm parts of her, maybe even the wet ones.

Maybe, he thought, in just a second he would reach over and feel the pressure of those breasts inside her shirt. Maybe a few minutes after they would have sex—the familiar, impermeable exterior of her would give way except it would be sweet inside, and he would fuck it: fucking until that reserve in him, that other, unsettling pressure, was empty; and instead of being in him, being his burden, it would be in her.

He sort of smiled, thinking of it, and reached over to run one hand along her arm—and felt, down in the hidden world of him, this electric, almost painful jerking against hard cloth: and it was such a hard, strong jerk that he almost came, almost finished right there so he would have to get up stealthily and clean his boxers.

But he didn't do any of those things. Instead, he pulled his arm back and said:

"Naw." When that didn't seem like enough, he added: "Maybe later."

Another rustle as she turned over on the bed, pressing her face down into the pillow.

"Okay then," she said.

And at some point soon (it didn't take long), both of them were asleep.

DINNER PLANS

THEY FELL ASLEEP, yeah, and they would have stayed that way most of the day—except, as he did with an insistent regularity, Steven barged into the room: not knocking, just throwing open the door so it swung and bounced against the wall.

"Am I interrupting something?"

Michael pried his eyes open and rubbed them (ineffectively) to make the blurriness go away. It took a while, but eventually he managed to say:

"Just sleeping."

Next to him, the pillow sighed when Halie nodded. "What he said."

"Okay." Steven always came here for a reason, to nag Michael about something—for a second he hesitated. But Steven never gave up.

"I came to tell you. I'm going to the store, then when I finish cooking we're going to eat."

"Why?" Michael asked.

"Because I said so." His eyes flicked noticeably to the side. "You can come too, Halie, if you're still here."

"Sure," she said.

"I don't see the point," Michael said.

"Because I'm not a fucking maid service." Steven said it with an authoritative awkwardness, as if he'd been trying to direct the

111

conversation towards it. Probably he'd been rehearsing it by himself all day. Maybe multiple days.

"I'll still be here," Halie said.

Michael reached over absentmindedly to scratch his arm. The feeling must be gone, because he was sort of annoyed. Maybe not a little—a lot.

"I don't see the point," he said again.

"Good," Steven said. "I'll see you two later."

The door shut again, and it occurred to Michael to look around for the creature. And yeah, it was right there: on the far, right side of the room, as if sleeping in the corner. Had Steven seen it? Probably not. That would have to be enough.

"He's being an asshole again," Michael said.

"Don't worry about it." Halie's voice was clearer—she must be waking up too. But of course she wasn't annoyed. She still had the feeling. Michael felt the absence of it acutely, an absence that felt like an itch in his left arm.

"He's a good cook, right? My dad never cooked decent food in his life."

"But he's such an asshole about it." Michael scratched vigorously at his arm, hard enough Halie noticed and looked down.

"What's that?"

"Nothing." Except he looked too, and it wasn't.

There it was again: another of the black pellets, embedded in his skin. It looked a little like a black, lidless eye: one that could only open, not close on its own. A black eye, just staring at them.

"It's like I told you," he said.

"Gross." But Halie put her face closer, didn't pull away. Probably it helped that she still had the feeling. It was much harder without it—this feeling like his left arm was barely his property anymore. It was scary: and fear, he decided, felt basically like needing to piss. Which happened a lot in the movies.

It would be the worst thing ever to piss his bed in front of Halie. She would tease him about it forever. He would never hear the end of it.

"Fuck," Michael said. He didn't want to itch it anymore, but he couldn't help it.

"And you said it comes out?"

"Fuck."

He couldn't stop itching, no matter how he tried—as he scratched, the black pellet made its way towards the surface. It reminded Michael of something he'd seen in porn but not understood: a woman pulling a string of beads out of her asshole. But slowly, so slowly, so the edges of it puckered as if a baby were being born; and he hadn't felt turned on, he'd felt confused, the kind of confusion that wouldn't let him look away.

But this wasn't his asshole, this was his arm... and now the black pellet, the emerging sphere, it was halfway out. Until finally he didn't scratch anymore—he just pushed with two fingers, so that it rolled down onto the bed.

"That's the most disgusting thing I've ever seen," Halie said.

The black pellet just sat there on his bed, innocuous and still. A part of Michael was relieved that there was no blood or slime on it. So he wouldn't have to clean up the blanket.

The creature crept closer.

"Can I touch it?" Halie asked. There was an expression on her face, one Michael recognized: a kind of intense, focused curiosity she only felt towards monstrously fucked up shit. He associated it with anime and horror movies, not with real life. Kind of weird, kind of cute.

Michael said, "Umm."

But of course, she didn't wait for permission, just picked up the black pellet and held it in the light. She squinted and turned it from side to side.

"What do you think it is?"

"It's feeling," Michael said. "Human feeling."

The creature was only a few feet away.

"Okay," she said.

Then, turning her hand palm up in the light, Halie did a very strange thing—maybe the strangest thing anyone had ever done.

She opened up her mouth, and put the black pellet inside.

CLEANING UP THE MESS

SHE SWALLOWED IT AND GRINNED, a satisfied look on her face as if she'd just made an especially funny joke; and there was a brief period, maybe ten seconds, before she started to vomit.

It didn't last long.

There was a powerful jerk as she curled forward, arms pressed in around her belly—but the look on her face was still casual, more confusion than anything, even as the first spray gurgled up between her teeth, out onto Michael's blankets.

The second was a long moan—Halie with both hands down on his bed, vomiting right onto the covers. Once, twice. Only the vomit wasn't green, or yellow, or that weird puce color that vomit usually was. It was an evil, cloudy black, pooling all across the bed, leaving inky trails around her mouth.

In the middle of it, Halie paused, her head hanging weakly on her neck, and let out a sound that reminded him of the dying cat. Michael felt like he should comfort her, but also he was sort of pissed. So he wanted to do a lot of things but didn't manage to do any of them.

"Halie, what the hell?"

"It seemed like a funny thing to do."

She laughed, only it became an awkward, lurching black belch. A softer spray this time—one that barely made it to the bed but mostly got on her shirt.

"The bathroom," Michael said. "We should get you to the bathroom."

The creature was just staring at them. Michael had never seen it look so pissed.

"I just thought it was funny," Halie said, and laughed again.

She wasn't in any hurry. Probably it was the feeling—even after that, she was sort of oblivious and relaxed. Michael felt almost jealous, having to deal with this like normal.

"I mean, the look on your face!" She pointed at him and laughed, keeling over—normal laughter this time. "Wasn't it funny?"

"I mean, yeah. It kind of was."

"Right?" She waved her hand down over the bed. "It's probably still here somewhere. It's not like I chewed it or anything."

"He looks kind of pissed at you."

"He'll get over it."

"But come on," Michael said. "That's your favorite shirt."

"It is, isn't it?"

Halie laughed, sitting and just staring at the cat. Then she burped again and more of the black shit came out. This time it was half a minute until she looked up, just kneeling down with her arms curled over her stomach.

"Michael," she said. "I don't feel so good."

And yeah, she really must feel bad—so bad she didn't laugh, or even freak out, when the creature put its head down and started to eat up the vomit. Michael noticed, enough it distracted him… and somewhere in the pool probably most of the black pellet was still intact.

"Come on," Halie said again. "Don't be a dick."

So they made their way to the bathroom across the hall (the only other thing on the second floor), and Michael stayed with Halie while she puked again. He didn't do much, just stood there while she kneeled over the toilet. Mostly he noticed how her torso contracted every time she wretched. But the strangest (and also most fortunate thing) was that it hardly had a smell. Which didn't make any sense, because vomit was stomach acid and stomach acid smelled, but the black pellet seemed to have neutralized it somehow.

It wasn't a quick process. They stayed in the bathroom for almost an hour and a half, not talking much. Halie threw up maybe every ten minutes—at least, there seemed to be less every time.

"I feel like shit," she said.

"You're right though," Michael said again. "It really was sort of funny."

After the third time, she started laughing while she vomited. That made it weird and awkward but Michael laughed too. And both of them kept laughing while she wiped her mouth with toilet paper.

"You're nasty," Michael said—except he didn't really think so. The longer they sat here, even without the feeling, he was almost glad it had happened, because it was so funny.

"It's a bonding experience, right?"

Halie got paler the longer she threw up, but she seemed basically okay.

"Sure," Michael said. "Like—oh hey there."

The door was cracked open, but Michael hadn't seen it move as the creature made its way inside. It seemed out of place against the sterile white tile everywhere in the bathroom. That made him laugh too.

"I'm sorry," Halie said. "Please forgive me?"

The creature's silence was a pissed silence. But it came over to Michael and put its head on his arm, and that was good.

Yeah, Michael thought, it was good—so good he barely even noticed the creature do the same to Halie afterwards, and for a while they just sat there. Just sat there in silence even while Halie threw up again.

When half an hour went by without Halie throwing up, they made their way back to Michael's room. The bed looked almost clean, but they still didn't trust it, so they just laid on the floor (after Halie had changed into one of Michael's shirts), using the beanbags for pillows. And Michael thought it was pretty fun even though neither of them should ever do that again.

But there was one thing Halie said, one thing he would remember for a long time. Later he didn't remember what had brought it up, he only remembered how serious Halie had seemed when she said it; how it had been followed by a silence that seemed so out of place amidst the feeling.

"Michael," she said.

"Yeah?"

"I think…. I think I miss your dad."

A WORK OF ART

STEVEN WAS ANGRY; maybe angrier than he'd ever been before. As a kid, he'd never had much time for his own anger—there had always been dad's to worry about. In Chicago, he'd felt frustration, but that was different, private, he knew he had to keep it under control, it was his problem and no one else's. But this, well.

Nothing in life had prepared Steven for living with his brother. What made it worse was the understanding—which ought to be simple and obvious to any human being—that living together like this, they had a responsibility to each other and the house. The difference was that Steven wasn't Michael's dad; they were brothers. Brothers both pitch in to take care of whatever needed doing.

It seemed so obvious to Steven—but not, apparently, to Michael.

Steven had felt okay in Chicago, cleaning out his apartment. He'd stayed there a few days, loaded everything into his car, and come back feeling that, yeah, he was ready for this life. (He hadn't seen any friends in Chicago. He'd thought about it but, well, he didn't know who.) He was okay, and he was calm, and he was ready for this year of living at home, rent free, on someone else's money.

Like a vacation—he could spend the whole summer watching movies, or he could do something productive. Start jogging or playing sports or something. Without any schoolwork, no job.

He'd be full of energy, right? What could be easier than this perfect, relaxing life, where he could cook good food every day and no one would ask him for anything, and he if ran out of money he could just ask mom for more?

It went okay the first two days. Steven spent most of his time unpacking—cleaning up his old room and making it one he wasn't embarrassed to sleep in now. He didn't have any energy because of all that unpacking, even if it only took a few hours, spread over two days. And when it was done, no reason not to just sit down and watch TV, right? There'd be lots of time later.

He wasn't even thinking of the dead cat in the backyard, drying out in the sunlight. (He just wouldn't go outside, and that was that.) Everything seemed okay, and at balance, and now Steven would be ready to enjoy himself. And maybe he would have been able to—if, that second day, Michael would have taken out the fucking trash.

Steven had done it the week before. It was only fair. And so, seeing it was full in the evening, he went upstairs and told Michael to do it. And Michael said, yeah, sure. Except he hadn't. Steven went up again—Michael said he would do it. Two days later: the trash was still there. Overflowing. Steven had seen Michael hesitate as things fell off the top, then shrug and walk away.

That was when it came back, that same sense of wrongness, an unmoving edifice of fury. Steven had taken out the trash himself —but he'd done it to spite his brother, to prove he was the better person. A few days later, he took it out again. After that he stopped sharing what he cooked. Michael didn't seem to notice, and that made Steven even angrier.

What he hated most, he realized, was the impotence of his anger. He could go up and yell at Michael, but even that, would it do anything? Afterwards he would look ridiculous. So instead he just went up to remind Michael of things with an increasing, embarrassing frequency that made him ashamed as it increased, but he couldn't help it... and Michael, who seemed weird and out of it that whole week, he just didn't notice anything at all.

Steven was careful, mostly, to go up when Halie wasn't there, because he was ashamed. A part of Steven knew it was weird and sort of stupid to get caught up in this, but he couldn't help it. He'd even decided a few times, whispered it under his breath: I don't care. I don't care. I don't care. But it hadn't done any good. It was a bodily feeling—a reminder that he was still a Hanson and he was going to fixate on stupid shit like taking out the trash for as long as he lived.

This time he didn't care. When they came down to dinner (both of them) he was going to sit Michael down and tell him what he expected of him. He had terms and Michael was going to follow through on them, or else—and the first would be sitting down to a proper dinner.

It was a work of art. Steven had bought fresh flank steak for tacos—corn tortillas, of course. In the center of the table, he'd covered an immense, wooden cutting board with toppings: finely sliced lettuce, tomatoes, onions, and cilantro (which Michael wouldn't like); a little pile of roasted corn; wedges of lime; two bowls of freshly made salsa and guac. Next to the cutting board, a big bowl of rice and black bean salad.

Steven had made it all, to be honest, because he knew Michael liked Taco Bell and he wanted to hear Michael say this was better. Which he might. But also he probably wouldn't. And knowing that made Steven a bit angry too.

They didn't come down on their own—Steven had to go get them—but eventually they sat down at the table, both Halie and Michael. Except something didn't seem quite right.

"Halie," Steven said, "you look pale."

"She's sick," Michael said.

Halie nodded solemnly, and added, "I'm sick."

"What the hell happened? She seemed fine earlier."

"You just couldn't tell," Michael said. "She's been sick all day."

"That's why we were asleep," Halie said.

Michael nodded. "Because she was sick."

"Can you eat?" Steven asked.

Halie turned her eyes towards the table, and Steven's stomach fell a little when she said, "Probably not."

Steven said that was okay, but it felt sort of weird to eat, just him and Michael, with a sick girl watching them. They must have smoked earlier, since they both seemed so calm, a little out of it. Surprisingly, being around them was actually relaxing—Steven felt better and almost relaxed by the time he finished his second taco, and for a while he didn't want to do anything.

But no. He had to. He was a Hanson and when he set his mind to something he did it. He started with, "Michael, there's something we need to talk about."

"Yeah?"

"It's—" It felt even weirder to try to say any of this out loud. It made so much sense in his interior world. It felt kind of clumsy and awkward even thinking of saying it. But Steven found the will, and he said: "You need to help out around here."

"Sure," Michael said. "I will."

"I mean it," Steven said. "If you don't start helping, I'm going to leave." Michael didn't respond, just took a bite of his taco, so Steven said it again, with more emphasis this time. "I'll leave. And that means mom will move in."

That, well, that got Michael to look up.

"Ah."

It was a shitty thing for Steven to say, petty and shitty—worse because he didn't want to do it and might not follow through on his own threat—but he'd said it anyway. And now that he'd said it he couldn't unsay it.

"I mean it," he said, a third time.

Steven wasn't sure what kind of reaction he'd expected. Probably something more than he got. Which was Michael taking another bite of his taco.

"I'll do my best," he said.

"Okay then." Steven felt uncomfortable as he started making his next taco, like there was something more to be said, to be done, but he didn't know what it was. He felt like there was nothing more to say, so he was surprised by what Michael asked next.

"You okay, Steven?"

"What do you mean?"

"You don't seem so good. Don't you think so, Halie? He seems stressed out."

She nodded, but didn't say anything. Steven had never seen her so quiet. Probably because she was sick.

"It's summer," Michael said. "It's just us in this house all summer. There's nothing to worry about. Shouldn't we just relax?"

There it was. Steven felt it: the rigidness coming back at the base of his spine.

"It's not that simple," he said.

"Maybe it is."

"Then maybe you'll be fucking living with mom next week."

A crash: rattling plates and the cutting board. Steven had hardly noticed his fist come down on the table. But the others had.

"It's okay," Halie said. "Nothing to worry about."

Coming from her it just made him feel ashamed. And feeling ashamed also made him angrier.

The shame wouldn't be enough. A minute or two more of this and he'd be yelling at Michael, and it would be ridiculous but it would be righteous and it would feel so, so good.

He could feel the anger making its way out of him, more of the iceberg rising to the surface.

"I'll be right back," Michael said.

"The hell you will."

"I need to take a piss."

Except Michael went upstairs and stayed there for way longer than he would need to take a piss. That left Steven sitting alone with Halie. She could have left, too, but she didn't. Sitting alone with her was embarrassing, and Steven felt ashamed and even his taco didn't feel taste good, and he was glad to sit it down when she said something.

"Sorry I can't eat," she said. "It looks good."

"It's okay," Steven said. "Another time, hopefully."

"That'd be good." Halie shrugged. "My dad cooks sometimes but I don't like to eat it."

"That's why I learned. Our parents—dad was okay. But mom couldn't cook at all."

"Another time."

"That'd be good."

Another silence, but Steven decided he would break this one, that he was tired of silences. Not that he picked his question very well.

"Why do you hang out with Michael so much?" he asked.

She shrugged. "Why not?"

"Do you like him?"

"He's my best friend."

"I mean, like—"

"He's my best friend," she said again. "We've been friends forever."

"I remember," Steven said. "I used to see you here when you had normal hair."

"I was a hideous little girl."

"You looked fine."

"Hum," she said.

"I'm still pissed at Michael."

"He's avoiding you, I'm pretty sure. He thinks you're annoying."

"I know."

"He says you're like your dad was."

"I know," Steven said again. "I can't help it."

"Well, you seem okay."

"How do you mean?"

"Like, you seem fine."

"I'm under a lot of stress.

Halie didn't reply to that, only looked at the cutting board. "Maybe I'll have a taco."

"They're good," Steven said.

"Tacos are always good. It's a—Michael, there you are."

Walking slowly down the stairs. He shrugged and sat down.

"I thought you needed to relax," Michael said.

"I mean what I said," Steven told him.

"These are good tacos," Halie said.

"Glad you like them," Steven told her.

"I thought you needed to relax," Michael said again.

"Really though," Halie again. "These tacos are fucking good."

Steven was torn between wanting to thank her again, and wanting to yell at Michael. But then he felt something, a sort of gentle rush again his ankle. He reached down to brush it away but didn't feel anything.

Until, all at once, he felt very, very good.

THE WINDOW

STEVEN KNEW INTELLECTUALLY that something strange had happened. They'd explained it all, explained everything—even then he'd known it was strange. But he hadn't minded so much, even when he looked down and saw the strange monster that had put its mouth on his ankle.

He hadn't been afraid, and probably that's what was strange about this, about the feeling. Steven had always been afraid of something. He was so used to fear it had become invisible to him: this accumulated, immovable growth.

But the bigger absence, yeah, was the sense of *wrongness*. Even after what they told him, Steven still remembered how he'd sat all that night on the couch watching TV. It was a basic, normal thing to do, and he felt normal too—no strange feelings in his body, blurring in his vision like he was doing drugs.

Except he sat there and everything felt *right*, maybe for the first time in his life.

Sometimes Steven had wondered, wondered what made life so easy for everybody else—he felt they must have something he didn't, something that let them just sit there and be themselves. He'd always wanted that thing, wanted it for himself. It was something he'd never had, just like their dad. Something shimmering and shapeless that maybe didn't exist—but had to. And now he had it.

That first night, he just sat there and watched TV. He fell

asleep early and woke up late, and still felt good. So he woke up, made coffee, and, while he drank it, sat down at the dining room table, watching the light come in through the broad windows in the front room. It was so bright—a beautiful morning, full of eternity, heaving with potential.

He remembered how, when he was young, he would wake up some mornings to come out here, right in this very spot, and look at the lines of light on the floor, and think of how pure and beautiful the morning was. The light would be strong and warm when he touched it, so bright it hurt his eyes to look out at the sun. And every one of those mornings, there would be a feeling of potential. A feeling he could do anything.

Steven had thought of that feeling for years, but mostly felt he imagined it. When he woke up now, usually he felt sore, and tired, and in those last few moments before he was really awake, he felt a cloud somewhere in his head—the shadow of something ominous and bad. It seemed distant, formless, right when he woke up, but it took shape as he went about his day, and he would remember that the world was wrong and not fair and really he wasn't the person he wanted to be, maybe he didn't like himself much at all, and that was brutal and inescapable, because it was him, it was *him* that was wrong, and that could never be fixed, there was no medicine for that, there was nothing.

Steven had wanted, for years, to regain that sense of potential in the morning, but it had never occurred to him. The only way would be some strange alien creature—well, not an alien, but it kind of looked like one. Whatever it was. He knew he ought to be afraid of it, but right now he wasn't afraid of anything.

He drank his first coffee slow, with a generous amount of half and half—the way he really liked his coffee, even if he knew it would make him fat. By the second cup, the sort of tingling, shimmering feeling in his arms, his legs, the knowledge of feeling good and alive, it felt even better with two cups of coffee in him.

He was going to cook again today, so he went to the market. Afterwards, just for the hell of it, he stopped at a liquor store and came out with two six packs of beer—Bell's Oberon, because it was summer and he was in Michigan, and an Amber just because he liked it. A thing of Vodka too, in case Michael wanted it. Then he stopped at the Chinese restaurant near Martin's supermarket, the one that had been there ever since he was a kid, bought General Tso's chicken with rice, took it to the park and ate in the sunlight, and all of it just felt so good.

It was nearly two when he got home, late enough that Michael would be up. Michael was on his bed, playing video games—which was normal except Halie was still on the bed, asleep. Steven could see a little of her hair, but otherwise she was curled up, not quite but almost in a ball, on the far corner of the bed, and seemed to have no trouble sleeping through Michael's game.

Maybe the strangest thing was seeing the creature, just sitting there on the carpet. Its eyes followed Steven as he stepped inside, and stayed on him as he said:

"That was a hell of a night."

Michael nearly didn't pause, but he did. "It's nice, isn't it?"

"What about Halie?"

"She woke up earlier," Michael said. "But she fell back asleep."

"Is she okay?"

"I don't know, I guess."

Steven stared at the pause screen for a while, like he'd forgotten what he came here for. He watched Halie sleep for a few seconds before he remembered.

"So you call it the feeling?" he asked.

"It just seems like the right name."

"I get it." Steven said it again, he didn't care that he was repeating himself: "It's nice."

"It makes it easier. This way I don't think about dad so much."

"I guess it does."

Michael looked back at the TV, at the controller in his hands. There wasn't anything to talk about, not really, but still Steven didn't want to leave. It was a strange feeling—unfamiliar and shapeless. An odd feeling, but a good, comfortable one. A feeling like he'd imagined when he first saw the old house, one it had taken him a long time to find.

"What are you playing?" he asked.

"*Tekken*." And as if to explain: "I play *Tekken* a lot."

"Yeah?"

"You get to be a badass."

"Sounds like it."

Michael unpaused the game; played one match. Steven

watched, and it was kind of nice. When the next one started, Michael looked at Steven and asked: "Do you want to play?"

"Maybe I do," Steven said.

It was hours later that the feeling went away—Steven noticed the glaring, stark absence of it. He'd gone downstairs because he was hungry, and all at once he felt strange, not right anymore. Wrong. It was a terrible feeling even if it was how he'd always felt. It felt bad, bad enough he almost felt sick. He went into the front room to sit down.

He sat there for ten minutes, feeling strange and tired and kind of empty, until Halie walked down the stairs. He heard her, but didn't look up. Though he hadn't expected her to stop above him, or to hit him with a pillow.

"Hey guy," she said, and hit him again. "How you doing?"

"Not so well."

"It wore off, yeah?"

Steven sat up, but slowly and only halfway. "I don't know."

"If you feel like shit, then it wore off, obviously."

"It's not that." And her just standing there. "You want to sit down?"

"I guess, why not?"

He made room for her and she sat down, just a few feet away, clasping her knees up against her chest. She had very thin legs. Basically she was just a small person. Steven had always felt too big, sort of clumsy, like his body took up too much space. It wasn't a physical thing, it was something inside him.

He wondered how she felt when she moved through the world, if she didn't feel huge and doughy and clumsy. How would anyone feel, living like that?

"I wanted to think..." He shook his head, but went on. "I wanted to think it came from inside me, you know?"

"Maybe it does," she said. "I mean, it's not like a drug. It's not adding things to us. It's just taking them away."

"Yeah, but... shit, I don't know what I'm saying."

"I get it."

"Do you?"

She nodded. "I remember thinking, that first time: I'm okay

now. I'm okay now, I'm fixed, I'll never hate anyone again. I even felt that way when I was sick."

"Yeah?"

"That's what it does though. It doesn't change us, it just gets rid of the parts of us that are bad for us."

"Maybe," Steven said. "For some reason it's sort of depressing."

"That's a dumb way to feel."

"What, why?"

"Because you can just do it again. It's still here."

"But that's dependency, right? It's like doing a drug."

"Which is fine too," she said. "The problem with drugs is they aren't free, right?"

"Ah," Steven said. "Maybe you're right."

"Of course I am."

Steven decided to drop it, but still he didn't want her to go. "Do you have it now?"

"The feeling? Nah."

"But are you okay?"

"It's only so hard coming down the first time. After that it gets easier."

"Maybe that's why. It's still the first time."

"It depends who you are I guess."

Halie glanced towards the stairs, but didn't get up yet. Steven needed to say something else, needed to say it now, or she would go soon. Of course she would go. She didn't come here to see him. She was Michael's friend, not his. But he didn't want her to go.

And that's when a feeling he'd noticed in small amounts crept up and become stronger. A familiar feeling, not one he liked. The best word for it was probably jealousy. But even that word, even jealousy, was tied into that feeling of wrongness. That he would get left down here while Halie would go up to Michael. Even though, if Steven wanted, he could go back up there too, they'd been hanging out all day.

But it felt weird now, without the feeling.

"Michael said you had to go talk to your dad the other day?"

"We had a fight."

"Yeah?"

"He said—this is how he put it. 'You're never setting foot outside my house again.'"

"That sounds like my dad. He was always getting mad about the smallest things."

"It's not the first time."

"That sucks."

"I wanted to bring more with me, but I only had my bike."

"Ah, yeah, right." Dad must have complained when he saw how Halie left her bike on its side in the front yard all the time. It was kind of a funny thing to think about, the things dad had gotten angry about—until Steven remembered himself, and felt ashamed.

"You live, umm… over—"

"Up by the river, on Copp."

"So wait, is your dad super rich?"

It was strange to think about Halie's home life. Steven thought about her a lot, but always as this strange person who came from nowhere. Probably that was because of how she behaved, a certain sense that she was anyone or could do anything. For some reason he'd always assumed she lived in the trailer park. Maybe because of her clothes, he didn't know why exactly.

Or maybe it was because he couldn't imagine who would want to come here—especially a girl. This was the old house, the Hanson sanctuary. A place that kept the world out. Steven's whole life, growing up—or just really, life as a Hanson—was a life without girls, except mom. But then Halie was just here.

"He likes to think he is," Halie said.

"So you don't like your dad very much?"

"Not really."

"I suppose that's pretty normal." He looked at her skin, how pale it was, and remembered. "Oh wait."

"Yeah?"

"How do you feel?"

"Still sick," she said. "But better."

"That's good."

"I'd say so."

Halie glanced at the stairs and said, "I think I'll go."

"Yeah, sure. Thanks for talking. It was nice."

"Yeah." She smiled, and Steven was actually surprised to see it. "You coming back up?"

"I'm not sure, maybe."

"See you soon then, maybe."

She got up slowly, creakily, and made her way to the stairs. But stopped at the bottom, and turned around.

"I need to pee," she said. "I almost forgot what I came down here for, to pee."

But after that she was really gone, and Steven just sat on the couch, looking up after her. He was hungry but he didn't want to cook. He felt strange and unsatisfied and disappointed, in himself or in everything, he didn't know—and, like always seemed to happen whenever he was disappointed in himself, now he wanted to masturbate. It was a stupid, silly thing, but it seemed right: like no matter what went wrong, or what he couldn't do, or what he wasn't, he could still masturbate, so at least he had that.

"What's wrong with me?" he said. "What the hell is wrong with me?"

He just sat there for a while, still on the couch—except now he didn't feel full of possibilities, he felt empty and sad and still hadn't masturbated yet. He wasn't sure how long. Maybe ten minutes, maybe an hour.

Until he looked up, and saw he wasn't alone. He saw the creature, a sleek shadow, leaning down on the couch above him—its neck not just elongated but curved down towards him in the dark.

"There you are," Steven said. It occurred to him that he should be afraid, but even now, he wasn't. "I've been thinking about you all day."

The creature was still, which Steven had expected.

"Listen to me," Steven said. "This is very important. No one can ever see you, you understand? Only me, Michael, and Halie. No else can see you, ever."

It nodded this time, which made Steven feel better. They were right, it understood them, which meant maybe this would work after all.

"Nobody," Steven repeated as its mouth came close.

Not ever.

SOMETHING NEW

IT ALL STARTED when Halie stubbed her toe on the stairs a few days later. It had been an uneventful week—Michael's perfect summer. One that seemed like it would last forever, and one that surprisingly involved hanging out with Steven a few hours most days.

Michael didn't think much about it when Halie stumbled into the room, complaining about how she'd hurt her toe. But he paid attention afterwards, when the creature lowered its mouth down around her foot—and she sighed. Not how she sighed when the creature gave her the feeling. Different, deeper, so powerfully her shoulders shook, and she reached out and grabbed his bed, and even when the creature finished she just sat there for a few minutes, shivering and breathing deeply.

She looked at Michael and said, "That felt good."

They experimented with it for a few hours. Experimented in small, sort of silly ways—even tried saying mean things to try to hurt each other's feelings, which hadn't worked. The problem, yeah, was that they had to hurt themselves. It was different to talk about it, as opposed to really doing it; but there they were, sitting on Michael's floor, talking about hurting each other.

"Bite me," Halie said.

"What?"

"Right here." She held out her hand. "Hard."

"That's super weird," Michael said.

"But it'll hurt."

She pressed her hand close, against his lips so he felt them fold back across his face.

"Don't be a bitch," she said.

"I'm just—this is dumb, Halie."

"Shit, Michael. Here, give me your hand."

"For what?"

Except he knew—and there were her teeth, small and sharp. Michael hadn't been bitten by a person in years, not since he was very young, a toddler, and he had gotten in a fight with another little kid for a reason he didn't remember. It was a strange pain, not like other pains. But it was definitely pain; and a second later he was trying to get his hand out of Halie's mouth.

"Halie, come on, damn it."

"There." She wiped her mouth and let him go, then held the hand up to inspect the fresh red marks. "That should be enough."

"Fuck, Halie. It hurts."

"That the goal, stupid." She turned towards the creature and waved her hand. "Come on little guy."

"Halie—"

But no, nothing happened. She waved her hand again, and the creature didn't come. And again. And she got sort of frustrated.

"What the hell?" she said.

"It's—I think it's waiting for me."

"Then stop making it wait."

"Right, yeah." He waved to the creature too. "Come on, it's okay."

A few seconds later, Michael felt its mouth—

And then his hand came.

That wasn't how to describe it, maybe. Halie had said it felt good, yeah; but it wasn't like an orgasm either. What it made him think about was something he'd realized years ago, when he burned his hand on the stove while dad was cooking: that pain is more intense than pleasure; that for some reason, the human body is built to hurt more than it feels good.

Maybe it was survival, maybe it was evolution, he didn't know. Really he didn't care. Just, he'd always had this subconscious awareness that life can get much worse than it can better.

That pleasure is quick and fleeting, like a plateau you get used to. But pain is endless; it can always get more intense, always get worse. Even from something mild, like a bite on his hand.

Only this feeling now, it felt like feeling all that in reverse. Like the pain itself was being drawn out of him—and he could feel it, feel how pure and good it felt, as the deep, spreading well of it drained up out of his skin. It felt good, and it felt real; and it felt natural too, like this had always been meant to happen, like he was discovering some carnal, deeply embedded sensation in his lizard brain, even if really he'd never felt anything so good in his life. Even coming.

He could feel the roots of it all up his arms, feeling like they glowed some bright, translucent color: a stream of fire in his veins, glowing brightest, glowing so beautifully strong, on the back of his hand where Halie had bitten. He closed his eyes and still, fuck, he could almost see it; only he saw just the light of it, the glowing pure stream.

It glowed brightest for maybe thirty seconds. Until the thinner tendrils, higher up in his arm, started to deplete; and the thing as a whole became softer and softer, until it was just a faint pressure in his hand. Then nothing.

"You were shaking," Halie said.

"Yeah?"

"And you made a funny face." She laughed, soft then loud. Michael would have laughed too if he'd had the energy, but right now he just felt satisfied and tired.

"Wait, I need a second."

"You even started moaning, it was hilarious."

"Did I?"

Michael shook his head, looked at his hand—and he was surprised. Actually it was sort of weird. Because after all that, he thought his hand would be healed. He could still see the indents of Halie's teeth. Later that night they would bruise. But there wouldn't be any pain.

"I see why you liked it," he said.

"It feels good doesn't it?"

"Maybe better than anything."

A little while later he said: "I have an idea." Though she had thought of it too, yeah; and after what had happened, it was hardly even scary.

That's how, a few hours later, they wound up in the bathroom, sitting first on the floor—after talking about it a little more, in the bathtub. Both of them had decided, with a strange kind of surety, that they were going to be very adult and responsible about this, so over the sink they'd gathered everything they could find: paper towels (Halie had a big bunch of them in her hand, too); some kind of disinfectant spray; a lighter. There were no big bandages in the house—there was no reason a family would have something like that—so Halie had actually ridden to Walmart to buy something she thought looked right.

And also, in Michael's right hand, they had the knife.

Neither of them knew much about what you were supposed to do when you cut yourself. In movies, people always used straight razors, but straight razors were weird and neither of them knew where to get one. So instead they'd gone downstairs and looked in the kitchen, the big drawer with a lot of knives in it. Because it looked cool, they'd settled on this big huge knife, almost a foot long, which Michael had never seen anyone use to cook.

The creature was curled up on the floor outside the bathtub.

"Okay," Michael said. "Let's do this."

But for a while they just held the knife up, looking at it. Michael had it first. He passed it to Halie. She passed it back.

"Wait," she said. "We should take off our clothes."

"What, why?"

"Because they'll get blood on them, duh."

"Not if we're careful."

But then they set the knife down on the sink, and threw their clothes in an awkward pile on the far side of the room. Michael sat down in his boxers—which were too big for him, enough it was a struggle to stuff them into his pants when he wore them—suddenly anxious he might get a boner.

Halie stepped across from him, not naked but close enough. Her stomach creased as she sat, the shoulders drooping forward.

"Fuck," she said.

"Come on, what?"

"Wait, I'll be back."

She stood up again—out the door, dashing into his room. She

came back holding an mp3 player, the old one he hardly used anymore.

"We should have music," she said. "What do you have on here?"

He said he didn't know, so she searched for a while. The song she settled on, which was a bit of a surprise to both of them, was *Kids,* by MGMT.

"There we go," she said. "Perfect."

She climbed back into the tub, handing him one ear-bud to put in as the soft, familiar synths of it hit. Michael had loved this CD a few years ago—both of them had.

"You're right," he said. "Good choice."

Halie wasn't listening yet. She'd put the bud in one ear, except it kept falling out, and she ended up just holding it there with one hand.

"Sorry," he said. "They're old. The shitty plastic kind."

"Whatever, it's fine."

"So who should go first?"

"Not me."

"Me neither."

"You afraid?"

"I'm not afraid of anything."

"I knew it," she said. "You're afraid."

"Fuck you, I'll do it."

"No, no I'll do it. Come on."

"You sure?"

"Yeah I'm sure, here."

Halie stuck out her free arm, the one not holding the earbud, and it was white and pale in his hand, and he hoped she didn't look down since if she did she would definitely see his penis sticking up, not quite hidden by his boxers.

Her voice, soft as she sang along, almost speaking:

"Control yourself. Take only what you neeeed from it."

"Don't sing," Michael said. "It's weird."

"Are you going to do it or not?"

Her hand, it occurred to him now, was almost close enough to touch it.

"Okay," he said. "I'm doing it. Really."

"Really?"

"Yeah, really?"

"Little bitch," she said. "I knew you weren't—ah, fuck."

Her blood, even with such a shallow cut, welled up like burning floodwater.

RESIDUAL PAIN

LATER THEY DECIDED they should have thought it through better—what had they been thinking, making the cut on their arms where everyone would see it? But even then, Michael didn't care. It had been so intense when his turn came around, he barely remembered what happened; but he remembered how Halie's eyes had closed, and the long, low, deep moan; and how her whole body shook so bad he put the knife on the floor outside the bathtub, in case she cut herself again.

What had she said next? It was so hard to keep track of things. She'd smiled, the biggest smile Michael had ever seen on a human face, and she'd said something like:

"Somebody had a good idea."

"Yeah?"

Halie's eyes were bright, excited, but her hand shook a little as she reached out for the knife.

"Wait." Michael grabbed her wrist and felt the tremble beneath the skin. "Are you okay?"

"Of course. It's just, a lot to take in."

"Are you going to kill me by accident?"

Halie fell forward into the bathtub and laughed. Only Michael didn't laugh this time. Her blood was all over on his hands; a red print still showed his grip on her arm. Something she seemed mostly oblivious to.

"No way," she said. "You think I'd do something like that?"

"Just give it a second."

"Don't be a baby."

"It's not that, I'm just—"

Before he could finish, Halie grinned and swatted his penis with the back of her hand. It was a quick, decisive blow; but it hurt, even if it also made Michael laugh, feeling it sort of thwack against one leg then stand up again.

"Halie, fuck—"

"No excuses," she said. "It's your turn."

"I'm not scared, it's just—look at the blood."

He put up his hands, both hands, in front of his face. But she didn't look because she'd turned, both reaching and crawling over him in order to reach the knife.

"Look at your arm," Michael said.

She did—holding it up into the light with the blade of the knife turned away. She was acting like a crazy person, Michael thought. But pretty soon he would understand. His head had felt cloudy before, except that was nothing. A cut this size drained you.

"It's still bleeding," he said.

And yeah: like heavy tears from a crying mouth, dripping down her forearm and back towards her elbow. Soon, his arm would match hers, and they would spend nearly half an hour clumsily wiping up the bathtub—forgetting they could just turn on the shower. It was a kind of mistake they would become used to making.

"It's getting on your bra," Michael said. "Down by your armpit."

"I'll survive." She turned the knife towards him. "Where should I do it?"

"The arm. We should match."

"You sure you aren't going to freak out?"

"No way. I'm looking forward to it."

He really was, he told himself. Though he bit his lip and gritted his teeth when he felt the knife touch his skin.

"This is crazy, isn't it?" Halie said.

"But it's worth it," Michael said—because he knew what to

expect. And when Halie finally made the cut, it was everything he'd wanted.

But also more.

AFTERGLOW

The tiredness hit a while later. It was good they'd almost managed to clean up—only the knife was still laying underneath Michael's bed, and the next morning he would realize they'd completely forgotten to use those bandages Halie had bought yesterday. But it was okay. Everything was okay. Everything would always be okay.

The tiredness hit Halie first, and she said that wow, she was fucking exhausted—but Michael was getting there too, so when they finished cleaning they both stumbled back into Michael's bed and collapsed. Even now, he'd never felt so drained; but it felt good, to be empty and used up, it felt satisfying and good; and it was even better to know Halie felt the same way.

They used each other as pillows to fall asleep, and Michael felt himself grinning just faintly into her cheek. In those last few seconds, he felt her breath against his neck and thought it was weird how wet breath feels.

Being human, he thought, is fucking weird.

Then he was asleep, and it was a good, comfortable, dreamless sleep—a rest he somehow felt he'd earned, as if he'd accomplished something; and maybe they had, and maybe they hadn't, but it was enough just to feel that way. And, as he fell asleep, the first thing on his mind—formless, nebulous, the way things are when you come out of dreams—was that maybe he sort of loved the creature. How could you not love anything that made you feel so good?

That feeling, it was better than anything people worked for. Food. Driving a new car. Even drugs or (he presumed) sex. It was better than anything. Even Halie—he'd been her best friend for years, but being with her was just a normal good thing. This was special, better than anything else.

Even the thought of it made him grin, which is why he still felt that same happiness stretched across his face. Only there was a glow behind it: a light. Not a glow in his mind; someone had turned on the lights in his room. His left arm itched like hell.

"That's disgusting," Steven said.

Michael opened his eyes, but he didn't recognize what he was seeing—the creature didn't have a shape as it leaned over him. As the days passed, it had looked less and less like a cat. Now it seemed like some strange, long legged bird with tentacles for wings, dipping down with its beak in his left arm.

Where the beak touched, it prodded at another of the black pellets.

"It's okay," Michael said.

"I mean, yeah. But goddamn."

It felt good like this—better than getting it out himself. Thirty seconds later the creature had dislodged the pellet with some kind of gentle suction. Michael sighed, still feeling good, and laid back as the creature went to the corner of the room.

"Goddamn," Steven said again.

"Nah," Michael said. "It's fine once you get used to it."

"That's…" Steven rubbed his forehead and laughed. "You know that's the same thing you said to me the other day?"

"When what?"

"When I was trying to get you to eat potato chips."

"Man, don't be weird."

Michael stretched, yawning—but felt bad when he set his arm down roughly on Halie, and she sort of jolted.

"Shit," he said. "Sorry."

"What happened?" she said.

"Don't worry about it, it's my fault. You can go back to sleep."

Steven said, "It's eight in the evening, guys. What the hell have you been doing all day?"

"Sleeping," Michael said. "Obviously."

"What happened?" Halie turned onto her back and stretched —and, maybe by accident, maybe on purpose, punched Michael in the face.

Not hard, but she did it.

"Good job." Steven had started laughing. "Now get him with the left hook."

"It was an accident." Michael nursed his jaw with one hand. "I think."

Halie rubbed both her eyes and sat up, and asked for the third time, "What happened?"

"Nothing much," Steven said. "I was just seeing what was up."

"Us, apparently," Michael said.

"Did you make any food?" Halie asked.

"You were asleep."

"Useless," Halie said.

"I'll leave you two alone. You can come down later if you want."

"We'll see what happens," Michael said. "We may be too tired to stand."

Steven turned to leave, putting one hand on the doorknob, but stopped before he'd taken his second step.

"That reminds me," he said. "Mom and Ben are coming around tomorrow. Prepare yourself."

"Around when?"

"Like noon or something."

"I can't believe he's coming back," Michael said.

"That's why I'm warning you."

"Cool, thanks," Michael said.

Steven left for real. Michael laid back down, still feeling tired. He watched as she reached down to scratch her ankle.

She noticed him looking, and shrugged. "It's itchy."

Michael glanced down towards the faint film of the black pellet beneath her skin. He put his hand on her wrist.

"Wait," he said. "I'll get it for you."

"Sure, whatever."

So he reached and scratched above her ankle, thinking how strange it felt to do this for someone else.

"That actually feels pretty good," she said.

"I'm getting better, check this out."

Just a minute later and it was out, clasped between two of his fingers.

"Don't eat it this time, crazy girl."

"I'm not hungry."

"I think I know who is."

Michael tossed the black pellet towards the creature—only the throw was short, way short, and it would have landed and rolled on the carpet if the creature hadn't stretched its neck to catch it. How long, he wasn't sure. Two, maybe three feet in an instant.

"Good catch," Michael said.

Halie hadn't seen, so she just said, "What?"

"Don't worry about it."

Michael sat for a while, looking at the creature, and something hit him—something he couldn't quite explain. Somewhere between a feeling and an intuition, but it wasn't a guess, it felt solid. Like something was happening, some form of communication. But even now, it was hard to believe, so he asked:

"Do you feel that?"

"Feel what?"

"Look at the creature." Michael pointed. "Can you tell what it wants?"

"Umm." A rustle in the bed as Halie sat up, then shrugged.

"So you don't feel anything?"

"Hungry, a bit."

"No, I mean from the creature."

"No."

"So it's just me then," Michael said.

The knowledge was in him, so sure and clear that he didn't even feel odd asking—and it made him feel privileged, it made him feel privileged and good to know, since a part of him was glad to think of the creature as his (he shared it with Halie, and sort of with Steven, but in the end it was his), and this new thing, well, it was proof. Proof that it was special, that he was closest to it; maybe even that it loved him back.

"I can feel it," Michael said. "You want to go outside, don't you?"

The creature nodded.

OUT FOR A JOG

STEVEN WOKE up around eleven the next morning—late, for him. He'd woken up without the feeling, which meant he felt like shit... but not as bad as before. It was hard to keep track of the days, but he'd been feeling pretty good this last week or so. Actually he'd even been having fun.

He felt sort of tired and groggy as he made coffee, and just as tired as he sat around drinking it. But he was actually a bit glad as Michael and Halie came down the stairs with the creature behind them.

"So wait," Steven said. "Did you sleep all that time?"

"Most of it," Michael said.

"Though we woke up around three," Halie added, "and we watched an episode of, umm—"

"*Ghost in the Shell*," Michael said.

"Right."

"Do you want some coffee?" Steven said.

"I thought you remembered," Michael said, "I don't drink coffee."

"But I do," Halie said. "Bring it on."

They sat down at the table. Michael went and got a Mountain Dew, so he had something to drink with caffeine in it. Halie was one of those people who drank her coffee weirdly sweet—lots of cream and like three sweeteners. Steven watched her add them meticulously, one by one. She looked in time to see him cringe.

"Shut up, dick. I like what I like."

"I didn't say anything." Steven shrugged, but he felt the grin on his face.

Michael added, "You know she puts ketchup on her eggs? I've never seen somebody put ketchup on their eggs."

"Fuck you, Michael." Halie took the last sweetener packet, still half full, and threw it at him. It spun in the air—but only made it half there, whipping and flinging white powder all over the table.

"Ah," she said. "Sorry."

"Whatever," Steven said.

"She has terrible aim, too," Michael said.

"Be careful," Halie said. "I'll cut you."

That started them laughing. At first Steven laughed with them, but they kept at it for almost two minutes, and it was weird.

"I don't get it," Steven said.

"Don't worry about it," Halie said.

"So are you going somewhere?"

"For a walk," Michael said.

"I didn't know you went for walks," Steven said.

"We do now," Michael said.

"Yeah," Halie said. "The creature wanted to go outside."

At first Steven didn't register what she'd said—but then it hit him, hard, and he said, "You realize, right, how dumb that is? What if someone sees?"

"No one will see," Michael said. "You know how it is. Sometimes it's just not there, even when it's with us."

But not now. The creature was standing over by the couch. Today it looked huge—the size of a big dog, practically up to one of their waists, with heavy shoulders and a face lost somewhere in the lumbering mass of it.

Steven said, "You're a fucking idiot, Michael. Do you, Christ—do you have any idea what would happen if somebody found out?"

"No one will see." Michael's face was hard and determined as he took a drink of his Mountain Dew, and Steven thought again—stupid. So stupid.

"I didn't realize it was a big deal," Halie said.

"It's not," Michael said.

"But it is," Steven said.

Michael took another drink of his Mountain Dew and gave Halie a look. One that said, *Look at Steven being ridiculous.* He and Michael had given each other looks like that when dad got angry, and it pissed Steven off to see Michael do one about him.

"An idiot," Steven said. "You're a fucking idiot."

Michael still had that same, stupid, determined look on his face. Halie didn't seem to care. But she also wouldn't be any help.

"I don't know," she said. "Whatever, right?"

"It's the perfect time," Michael said. "When do Ben and mom get here?"

"Twenty minutes," Steven said.

"See? It's the perfect time."

Steven's fist clenched beneath the table, and he was still angry. He wanted to hit the table again, as pointless as that was.

"There's no such thing as a perfect time," he said. "It needs to stay inside."

"But it wants to go outside," Michael said.

"That doesn't make any sense. How would you know what it wants?"

"I just know."

He looked sure—a completely sure, confident idiot. And that was exactly the moment (the first, but definitely not the last) when Steven realized how stupid the feeling made them. It didn't get rid of inhibition, not completely… actually it was hard, maybe impossible to describe. Everything was still the same intellectually; even now, Michael must know the risks. He knew them and understood them, like he understood everything.

He understood, but he wasn't afraid. Because it's feeling, really, that makes people do what they do—not understanding, but feeling. When you had the feeling, sometimes you would feel like a normal person, you would act like you were scared or intimidated, but it was almost like playacting. You cared, yeah, but not the way you're supposed to care about yourself; it was more distant, like something happening to someone else.

Michael wasn't afraid, so it didn't occur to him to worry about what they had, or what they might lose.

"You can't go," Steven said. "No way."

"You're not dad," Michael said. "You can't tell me what to do."

That was approximately the moment, they all decided later,

that the front door opened, and Ben stepped inside. He was wearing shorts and a blue windbreaker, with an obnoxious red sweatband over his ears.

"Sorry to bother," he said. "I saw the door was open."

A jog, he didn't have time to say, but it was obvious. Mom had told Steven that Ben would come over first, but he didn't realize what she'd meant—that Ben would jog. Maybe he'd gotten here early in order to talk to Steven alone. Or at least, when they thought he'd be alone."

"I hope I'm not interrupted something," Ben said. "Your—"

Your mother, they guessed later, was the word he'd meant to say—they weren't sure when Ben actually saw it. Maybe he'd glanced down and only then started to register it. Maybe it had just assumed.

But they knew for sure: that exact moment the creature's tail (what they had sometimes called a tail, but might also be more like a tentacle) took him through the forehead.

There was another instant as Ben's body went slack. His limbs limp, the smile falling away from his face. Barely a second as the creature opened its mouth—only the mouth didn't just open.

It was huge, Steven thought, like a gate into some vast, endless darkness, spreading nearly six feet, enough to catch Ben's whole body as it fell.

Wide enough to eat him.

DEALING WITH THE SITUATION

LAST YEAR, Steven had seen a video on the internet of a snake eating a man in his sleep. It had been terrifying, but also sort of ridiculous—this bloated, lumpy, almost cartoonish snake, laying there with a person inside it, enough you could see the line of the man's shoulders inside it, enough you almost thought he might be alive, though he was dead, dead and boiling in acid.

For a few seconds you could see what was left of Ben, a lumpy outline within the dark, bloated bulk of the creature. Followed by an aggressive, gargantuan contraction: the thing's body shrunk like a trash compressor. And after that, nothing.

The creature didn't look at them as it walked back towards the couch to lie down. Its movements were a bit sleepy, heavier than Steven had ever seen them—and it was disappointing, almost, not to see something else. Steven expected more. He wasn't sure what. But it seemed like there ought to be more.

They were still, all of them, as still as the creature taking its rest. Steven wanted to ask the question, wanted to ask *What the hell just happened?* It was a stupid question, because he already knew. That was the main thing Steven thought about. That he didn't want to look stupid.

It was Michael who spoke, his voice so dull and matter-of-fact it seemed as out of place as the sleeping creature.

"I didn't know it could do that," he said.

"Me neither," Halie added.

It was so sudden, Steven still felt Ben had stepped out of the room—like he was in the kitchen except Ben wouldn't like anything he found in there. That was so much easier to believe, because even movies hadn't prepared him for this. When someone died, there was supposed to be something left of them.

But this: nothing. It was just nothing. It seemed impossible, and probably it should have been.

"Fuck," Steven said.

"It'll be alright, guys." Halie, her voice not sounding nearly as calm as it sounded. Maybe she said it to make them feel better. There was no way she could actually believe it.

"But Ben…" Steven trailed off, restless and full of the most uncomfortable lightning. He stood up, walked halfway around the table, and stopped. "I can't take this right now."

"I think I need to go," Halie said. But didn't stand. Just saying it dully, and sitting in her chair.

Only Michael still seemed calm. Instead of just sipping at his can, he threw back his head and drank the Mountain Dew all at once.

"What the hell are we going to do?" Steven asked. "Ben—"

"He got what he deserved," Michael said.

Steven's head whipped towards Michael, and he could tell he didn't have the feeling, because he was furious. Enough that he wanted to jump over the table and hit Michael. That same idiot face. Again and again and again. Though none of it would be enough.

"The hell he did," Steven said. "Somebody just died."

"It was only Ben," Michael said.

"You fucking—fuck, what's wrong with you?"

Steven wanted to so bad. All he had to do was walk around the table and punch Michael in the face. Maybe that would make him understand—though even then, probably not.

"I think I need to go," Halie said.

"We go can now," Michael said. "Like we planned."

"Hell no you aren't," Steven said. "Everyone is staying right here."

Only then, it occurred to Steven that he didn't like standing with the creature at his back. But he turned and it was still just napping.

"What?" Halie asked.

"It's…" Steven sighed, covered his face. "What are we going to tell mom?"

"Nothing," Michael said. "We're not going to tell her anything."

"But, that would mean—"

It made sense, Steven realized—there was no body, nothing to say Ben had ever been here. There was no way out of this. No way good. Even if they told someone what happened, no would believe them. It was an impossible thing, what had just happened. At least there wasn't any blood.

Only it didn't make Steven feel good, not at all. Already he felt this terrible sinking feeling in his stomach—guilt, so heavy he almost felt the nauseous film of it across his skin. The same guilt he always got when he thought of mom, of Ben, only now it was different and so much worse.

"This is going to ruin mom's life," Steven said.

"She'll get over it," Michael said.

"Jesus Christ, Michael. What's wrong with you?"

All the anger went out of him at once, as he asked it. Instead he just felt tired and bad, and so many things he'd thought were good, well, they were bad too. It was a hard feeling; the knowledge they might lose everything, all of them. It was a weight, a heavy thing he would have to carry: and it would just get heavier the longer he carried it.

He turned to look at the creature, he had to, because he didn't want anyone to know he had tears in his eyes.

"What's wrong with you?" he asked. "Why the hell would you do something like that?"

Then he remembered, remembered the words he'd said to it in this room only a few days ago. He hadn't meant them this way—hadn't thought much about it, since it seemed like the creature only listened to Michael. But maybe it had listened. Maybe it taken what he said seriously.

No one can see you, he'd said. *Not anyone.*

He'd meant to hide, of course. To stay out of sight, inside the house, and make sure no one saw it. But how would the creature know that? It wasn't human, even if it could understand their language. Maybe it was really a monster, the most terrible monster—only they'd invited it into their house. It was living with them.

And even if he wanted to, Steven couldn't make it leave.

"Don't do that again," he said. "When someone's around, don't do that again. Just hide, you hear me?"

It didn't respond, didn't nod or anything, so he called over to Michael: "Tell it. Tell it not to hurt anyone else."

"Sure," Michael said. "He's right, don't eat anyone else."

This time the creature nodded. But it still didn't move, just laid there, and Steven felt tired and evil and bad.

"What are we going to do?" he asked again. But he knew no one had an answer, not Halie and especially not Michael.

"I think I need to go," Halie said.

"Sure," Steven said. "But Michael, you're staying here."

"Whatever, fuck it."

Michael stood up and threw his can down onto the table—it bounced and made a scraping sound, making its way towards Steven, but didn't go far enough. He'd always been like this; relaxed most of the time. But stubborn, when he got something in his head.

Steven couldn't tell right now whether Michael had the feeling. Though he was surprised, as Michael made his way to the stairs, that the creature didn't go with him. Maybe it really was tired.

Halie still sat in her chair, sipping coffee. She took another drink, so loud it was almost a slurp, and said: "It's getting cold."

"Sorry," Steven said. "I'm a mess. I'm a fucking mess."

"It's okay. I get it."

Steven only noticed now that he'd been pacing this whole time, frantically like he was going somewhere. He needed to calm down, needed to relax. Only he couldn't, of course. This was all stupid and terrible and wrong, and it was just like Michael, to go upstairs and leave him here alone.

"I'm glad you're still here," Steven said.

"What, me?"

"Actually no." Steven pointed towards the creature. "I need to relax before my mom gets here."

A STORY FOR MOM

STEVEN WOULD NEVER HAVE BEEN able to deal with mom without the feeling. He hadn't known what to expect, but the feeling was just the same as always, leaving him clear and bright and knowing what needed to be done. Mom got there right as Halie was leaving. They talked in the front yard for almost five minutes—enough that Michael would have been annoyed if he saw it.

"There's my boy," Mom said when she came inside, and Steven gave her a long hug. "It's good to see you."

"Glad to see you too, mom."

"Where's Ben? I thought he'd be here by now."

"Haven't seen him."

"That's not like him. He was supposed to be here by now." She shrugged. "But at least I get to see my boys. Where's Michael?"

"He's sick. I think he's sleeping."

"That's a shame. Sick in the summer."

"It really is, mom. Have you eaten?"

She hadn't, it turned out, so Steven made her lunch while she waited. It felt very natural, casual—and, probably because of the feeling, there were points he forgot what had happened. He even enjoyed himself at times: maybe enjoyed himself a lot. What a strange thing. That only now he could really enjoy just sitting and talking with his mother.

"It's so strange," she said again when they were done. "It's not like him to be late."

"Maybe he forgot?"

"Maybe." Her face looked kind of pinched and uncomfortable as she said it. "But I should go. I have some things to do."

"You got it, mom. Thanks for dropping by."

She'd given him the money earlier in the conversation—and when she was gone, it seemed, that was the end of it. Steven felt good, and he felt okay, so he sat down in dad's den and watched more TV, and he didn't think of it again until later that day, when the phone rang, and he picked up and heard mom's voice.

"Steven," she said. "Have you seen Ben yet?"

"Not yet, mom."

"Okay." She didn't sound so good—actually she sounded pretty bad. "He's still not home yet."

"Weird."

It felt very casual and normal to lie to his mom. In some ways it was a familiar feeling—the first person any child lies to is one of their parents. This was different but in some ways it didn't feel different at all.

"I wouldn't worry about it, mom."

"It's very strange," she said. "This isn't like him."

"I wouldn't worry, he'll be home soon."

"Okay then." And then: "I love you, Steven."

"I love you too, mom."

And that was it. Steven hung up, went back to watching TV—and didn't hear from mom again until two days later, when she called back and told him (of course) that Ben still wasn't home, and she wasn't sure where he'd went, and was he okay, and what might have happened to him? She was so worried, and sad too (which was how Steven remembered her, it had been almost strange to see her happy these last few years, though he would have time to get used to a sad mom, to a crushed mom who felt overwhelmed and alone and couldn't do anything), so worried, and she'd been staying in that house alone for two days and could he even come stay with her a while?

Which he did—Steven didn't quite move in with her, but he spent quite a few nights that summer staying with mom. Sometimes her friends stayed, but mostly it was Steven. They talked a lot on those nights, more than they'd talked in years, and Steven would think a lot that it was weird and awkward and just unpleasant to watch your own mother cry. Most of the time she just kept saying those same things—that it wasn't like Ben to disappear like that, that she wondered what had happened to him, that she missed him.

And really it was a terrible thing, what had happened, terrible and cruel—and Steven told her so, quite a few times. He'd say, *Mom, it really is the worst.* And: *Mom, I wish I knew what to tell you.* But especially, *Mom, I'm sorry.* And again: *I'm sorry, I'm sorry, I'm sorry.* Eventually he would say it to almost everything she said, over and over again, that he was sorry. He was sorry—and yeah, he really was. Maybe that's why he said it so many times, but it only made it worse when she would say no, it wasn't Steven's fault, Ben was just gone and nobody knew what would happen, nobody could explain. And Steven would wish, maybe more than anything, that his mom was right—but no, it was like before, mom was never right. Not about this, especially.

But Steven wasn't thinking about any of that after the first phone call. He just sat in the dark, watching reruns of *South Park*. There was some kind of marathon, which was good news. Probably he would watch it all night—though maybe he wouldn't make it long since he was getting kind of tired, and probably he would have fallen asleep soon if Halie hadn't knocked on the door, so he had to get up and let her in.

"I'm surprised to see you back," he said.

"Yeah, well. Better here than at my dad's."

"I wasn't complaining. Come on in."

Halie stretched as she came inside, but instead of going up to Michael's room she leaned back on the couch as Steven shut the door.

"That was crazy earlier," she said.

"For sure."

"You okay? You didn't seem okay."

"I guess I'm as good as I could be."

"So, like, somewhere between shitty and still surviving."

"Something like that."

Steven walked near the edge of the table, bracing with one

hand on a chair. But it was dark, so dark he could barely see her, so he reached up to turn on a light.

"So what is up with you and your dad?" he asked.

"He's crazy," she said. "An insane person."

"He doesn't, like, yell at you all the time or something, does he?"

"Nah, not that kind of crazy."

"No breaking stuff?"

"Naw."

Steven laughed, which seemed to surprise Halie a bit. Maybe she thought he was serious and it was strange for him to laugh. Maybe she was right, who knows.

He said, "Our dad, he used to break stuff."

"I remember."

"You do?"

"Not when I was here. But Michael told me a bit."

"Like right here." Steven walked to the screen door to the laundry room, right next to the table. "He got angry once, and just punched right through this."

"Angry about what?"

"Don't remember. Dad got angry about a lot of things."

"But he didn't, right—"

"Nothing like that."

"Okay."

"Just, like, once. I remember—dad had us working on something outside, I couldn't tell you what it was. But I'd been out there for hours alone, and I decided I wouldn't do it anymore. So I went inside. Dad was… umm—"

"It's okay, he was somewhere else."

"Yeah. And when he got home and found me inside, man, he was pissed."

"Yeah?"

"Pissed as hell. I was inside, watching TV, and he found me and smacked me in the face. Hard—I remember it was sort of shocking. And I thought... it's hard to put into words. I thought: okay, it's official. My dad is my enemy now. My dad is my enemy and someday I'll get him back."

"Did you?"

"Nah. It was just a thought—and after that he never made me

do it again." Steven shrugged. "Dad was a bit boring but he was okay. Did you ever talk to him much?"

"Not really."

"Right, it's mom that always talks to you. Dad was always fine leaving people alone. I used to think it was weird—even when he was with his friends, these old men, he was always careful to say he was too old for things. He was saying it even when I was young—that he was too old, that the world was changing and he didn't understand it. But I think mostly he liked saying it. That something about it was almost comforting."

"Weird." Halie shrugged, looking absently over Steven's shoulder, and said, "My dad, he's super religious, yeah?"

"So a crazy person, right? Like my mom."

"Not quite." Halie made a sound like a laugh, but not. "Did Michael ever tell you? We tried going over to my house once."

"No," Steven said. "Michael and I don't talk about things like that."

"I never take people to my dad's house."

"That's how we've always been," Steven said. "We always thought it was weird to bring people here."

"Maybe," Halie said. "So we went into my room, and started watching TV. My dad—the door was still open, right, but—"

"He wouldn't leave you alone, yeah?"

"Sort of," Halie said. "Once we'd been there twenty minutes, my dad came over with a screwdriver—or tools, whatever—and he started taking the door off its hinges."

"What?"

"Just like, staring at us the whole time. But he didn't say anything until the end, and he said one of those weird things. The kinds of things my dad always says."

"What did he say?"

"*God is watching you*," Halie said. "That's what he said. *God is always watching you.*"

"Fuck," Steven said.

"There's still no door in my room."

"Yeah, well—you want to go upstairs right?"

Steven had asked because actually he wanted her to say no— or because he didn't know what to say. There was no chance, really—of course there wasn't. But he wanted her to say no, maybe she would stay down here and get drunk with him and watch *South Park*—and he could feel like... how would he feel? Like he wasn't alone? Like there was someone who understood him in this universe?

It felt symbolic, enough he must be imagining it and making it up, projecting things onto her and imagining she meant things that really she didn't. But that's what he'd always done, how life always worked. Everyone lives alone, really, with versions of other people who live, isolated, in their own imagined realities; and sometimes, not often, maybe they manage to understand each other, to not feel alone. But not often.

"Yeah," she said. "I should go."

Then she was gone, and Steven didn't feel so good, in fact he felt abstractly bad, even with the feeling. It was a strange, contemplative sadness, one he would get very used to that summer: the feeling of knowing that he hated everything, that this whole world was wrong and had no place for him; but it was okay, he just had to live with it, and maybe if he pushed through he would be okay eventually. But not now. For now he could just masturbate; but tonight he didn't even have the energy to do that.

More than anything he was grateful for that *South Park* marathon, and even more grateful when he remembered the beer he'd bought the other day. So he went out to the fridge and cracked open an Oberon and drank it right there, out by dad's old work bench.

He cracked open two more, and took them inside.

THE RIVER AT NIGHT

MICHAEL HAD STASHED his bike beside the house earlier that day, but he was glad he'd waited to go out—long enough for Halie to come with him. It didn't just feel good, riding at night with the wind against his face, Halie behind him and both of them laughing every few minutes while they peddled as hard as they could—it felt perfect and liberating and fine, and maybe for the first time, he regretted spending so much time sitting in his room watching anime, when life could really be so much more, full of so much energy, and all he had to do was go out at night to feel it, to ride so hard his lungs gave out and his legs were sore and he felt the perfect cool of sweat on his forehead.

But it was especially nice, more than anything, to know the creature was with him—that he was special. This wasn't just sneaking out at night: this was like a hero's journey, a rite of passage… a symbol that he was… well, a 'chosen one' sounded like too much, but also it was exactly right. He'd been chosen and the creature would go with him forever—he was the same, his body and his life, but now he was sort of a Pokémon master, with a servant that listened only to him. Halie—it was nice to have her around, it was okay. But even her, she was just a sidekick, someone there to remind him how special he was, how good all this felt, how amazing life could really be.

It wasn't a long ride—twenty minutes, maybe twenty-five. But it felt like forever. It didn't matter how long, he didn't care. He felt so free, like all his life, everything he'd ever done, had been building to this. It was a hard thing to explain, and not in a rational way, but he felt it all the same—the same way he'd felt it earlier, when the creature killed Ben.

All that time, there was hardly any sign of the creature behind them as they rode. Michael looked back a few times but only saw Halie pedaling and laughing—maybe a rustle in the bushes as the creature followed, but also maybe not. It hardly mattered; he didn't need to see. He could feel it there, feel it in some subtle ephemeral way, and that was enough.

They stopped at the riverpark at the north end of Bond Street, letting their bikes fall on their sides in the grass. Halie stopped too, and they recovered for a minute, kneeling over and breathing hard. And even in the dark, Michael became sort of fixated on the sweat stains beneath her armpits, the heavy sound of her breath matching his, the sign they'd really done this, that they were really doing something.

"Let's just go," he said. "Come on."

There was a path here, stretching for miles, where during the day middle aged women went in groups to 'power walk'. (That's what mom always called it.) Or sometimes there would be men by themselves fishing, or old ladies feeding the birds. He'd been here some when he was young, always with his parents. Not much for years. Michael hadn't gone outside a lot since he started watching anime, and he didn't especially care to change that.

"You can still sort of see the factories." Halie pointed out across the water—and you could, these heaving, dark behemoths on the far side of the river, with jutting smokestacks blocking out a thin beam of stars. The other side of the river seemed monstrous, like something out to get them—but that, too. It made Michael feel powerful, like he'd come here to fight it.

The first stretch of the park was well lit, so he could see the shadowed yellow grass all around him—but it cut off sharp at the edge of the rocks. And the same up ahead, the first awning like a gaping mouth in the dark.

"Hey," Michael said, "there's somebody there."

Of course, the paths weren't empty. There was a group of kids their age under the awning in a small group, their voices startlingly loud in the dark—falling to a sudden quiet as Halie and

Michael approached. Michael heard whispers—they were worried about police, or just adults in general. But when they saw two kids instead, they asked if Michael and Halie wanted to hit the joint they were passing.

"What do you think?" Michael asked.

"Why not?" Halie said.

So they hit it, twice—but it was already pretty low, a roach, by the time they got there, and pretty soon the group wanted to leave. They were going somewhere else, but, no, Michael and Halie just wanted to walk in the park. So they kept going, Michael feeling swirling and weightless now—sometimes forgetting, for long stretches of time, what exactly they were talking about.

"It makes the air feel so tingly on your skin," Halie said. "Like this."

She brushed the tips of her fingers against his arm. It felt good —distant but strong, like everything did when he smoked weed. It made him think, distantly and lazily, about how everyone said sex feels so good on weed, or even a blow job—and he thought again, what would it feel like to fuck Halie in this tunnel, or in the grass beside the path? She would do it, probably. Maybe he wouldn't even have to use a condom.

He wanted to, yeah—but there was still something that wouldn't let him do it. It wasn't that they were friends, though they were. It was something different, a feeling he had trouble putting into words, something even he knew he shouldn't talk to her about. It wasn't that she wasn't pretty, because she was; and it wasn't that he didn't like her, because he did.

It was the knowledge, spoken or unspoken, that if they ever had sex, they would be attached to each other in a different way. In Michael's head, somehow, Halie had always been a stand-in for other girls, like practice, only she was cool and liked the things he did—maybe even the popular girls, the ones he stared at all the time in gym class and sometimes talked to but didn't have anything in common with. Michael liked Halie; sometimes, not often, he even thought about her while he masturbated.

But he didn't want to be stuck with her. It would be fine if, after they did it, everything was just the same—they could be friends who fucked, and that would be nice, because anything is better if you add fucking to it. But Michael didn't want to feel tethered down, even if he wasn't going anywhere; even if no one else was interested in him. He felt like the chance would come, eventually, and he didn't want to have Halie there, clinging to him.

He was special, he'd always felt—he was, in the end, the main character of a story. But it was only today, sitting in his room, that he'd really felt the difference, that he'd really understood something about himself, why he didn't leave his room. Because there, watching anime, he could pretend to be someone else, someone who was special. Even Shinji in *Evangelion*—he was pathetic but he was special and everyone around him knew it.

Michael had felt something click today, some strange difference, when he realized it—that now, he didn't have to be someone else. He could be himself, and be happy about it, because he was special: he'd been chosen by the creature. It would do whatever he told it; he was powerful. He'd always felt, somehow, that he deserved it: that he had that certain something, the thing that made him different from everybody else.

That's why it felt like a celebration, like a becoming—that's why he walked so quickly ahead, feeling almost good when Halie said, damn it Michael, slow down, she was getting tired. He kept visualizing the same two things: pushing Halie down in the bushes to fuck her; and Ben, his eyes slackening just a little at the last second, as the creature killed him.

They'd been talking for a long time too, saying things, but Michael wasn't sure what. He'd tuned out, half because of what he was thinking, but probably mostly because of the weed. As he walked, he kept one hand in his pocket to keep ahold of his boner —every once in a while he gave it a squeeze, and it felt good, the rough cloth of his jeans through his boxers.

"What?" he asked.

"Where are we going?" Halie repeated. "All the way downtown?"

Michael paused. They'd been walking, how long—half an hour? Forty-five minutes? He sort of wanted something to eat— Taco Bell, probably. McDonalds would also be good. But they were far as hell, so neither of those would work. Instead they'd have to go home. He'd seen a bag of Cool Ranch Doritos there earlier—the only thing Steven had bought after Michael asked for them. As soon as he got home (Michael felt the saliva gather just thinking of them) he would grab a handful, a huge, rough handful, and throw them all into his mouth and bite through like ten of them at once, so much they would be hard to chew, so much the corners of the Doritos might cut the roof of his mouth, but he wouldn't care, because they would taste salty, and sort of tangy, and maybe a little spicy, in that way that only Cool Ranch Doritos did—and he would chew them, he would maul the fuckers, and already he could feel no amount would be enough. After the first mouthful—hell, before it was gone—he would grab a second, and start chewing those too, and he remembered the feeling from that last time he was high: of eating chips, but too many to swallow, so they sort of got caught in his throat and a little falling from the front of his mouth, and it was ridiculous but it felt right and primal and good, and goddamn he was hungry.

"Yeah," he said. "Probably a good time to turn around."

"Wait." Halie raised her hand to point ahead. "There it is."

"What?"

"The creature. It's in front of us, now."

"Yeah?" Michael had to squint—he'd been staring at something, but he wasn't sure what.

"It's going on ahead."

"I guess we have to follow it then."

Michael wasn't happy about it—he was still thinking of those Doritos. But he'd never seen the creature move like that, as if it had somewhere to go. (He'd never seen the creature outside of the house since its initial appearance in the yard, so that was no surprise.) Loping ahead like some heavy, hulking monstrosity of a dog.

"Jesus," Halie said. "Where's it going?"

They had to jog to keep up, then sprint. They were close to the riverpark now—ahead was an area with an open pavilion where they held a fair in summer, and every weekend there were concerts where a lot of old people gathered to be old, and a little beyond that was a park where Michael had played some as a kid. They were close to the pavilions now—lights on those too.

"Shit," Halie said. "There are some kids ahead."

And maybe the kids saw too—Michael wasn't sure. The creature was so quick, passing beneath one of the street lights—but he saw the movement first, from the corner of his eye.

Something across the river. He didn't know why, it just stood out. But Halie saw it too, what happened next.

It was swift, so swift—a leathery shadow.

Something fell out of the sky.

THE MAW

BACK TO CHURCH

THE NEXT MORNING, Steven woke up and felt pissed off—and he would feel that way a lot throughout that summer, probably the longest season of his life, pissed off and frustrated and alone, even as the eternity of June faded to July, the beginning of August. So many of those nights, Steven would sleep on the couch in dad's den, usually with the TV still on. Even with the feeling, he still had trouble sleeping like he had as a kid; in July he got into the stranger habit of sleeping on Ben's couch. Except Ben wasn't there, only mom.

That morning, he woke up, looked around the house, thought about cleaning it, but decided—fuck it, nobody cared, not even him. There was nothing he could do. Nothing that mattered. He had felt okay the night before, sitting and drinking beer and watching *South Park*, enough he woke up with a hangover. He felt bloated and massive and useless this morning, but at least coffee and a big, greasy breakfast might do something about that.

Michael and Halie didn't walk downstairs—they came in through the front door. Only they didn't look so good. Michael's shirt was ripped in the back, and dirty, and he had dirt on his face too, and he was limping, though he tried to hide it. Halie looked better mostly, but there was a big scratch along her arm, a red mark on her right cheek. Both of them were covered in sweat, like they'd been walking for hours.

"The hell did you two do last night?" Steven said. He was still proud, weeks later, of how he'd handled it—because his first incli-nation was to yell at them. Not just Michael; Halie too. They'd gone out exactly like he said they shouldn't, and they'd stayed out all night, and they'd done it all right after Ben was killed. He wanted to yell at them and throw his coffee cup at them, and he didn't care who it hit, either one of them—but, he didn't want to think, not just because it had been dumb. That wasn't the only reason.

"We went out," Michael said.

"Obviously," Steven said.

Michael flinched—he must know. He must be able to feel how angry Steven was. How much Steven wanted to throw that fucking coffee. And that was why, later, Steven was proud—why he felt like he'd matured, or grown, or whatever, when really all he did was say:

"You might want to get a new shirt."

Michael blinked. "Yeah."

Steven walked around the table, set down his coffee cup, and said: "There's not enough for everyone this morning."

"That's okay," Halie said. "We'll manage."

And they didn't talk about it anymore.

They didn't talk about it even the next day, when Steven was flipping through channels and stumbled on the news—which he didn't watch, only when he was bored. If he did, he would have gotten the story yesterday when it happened. But there'd been a huge... something, downtown. Gas explosion, that's what they were calling it. No one knew what had caused it. Only that a quarter mile of the park downtown by the river had been leveled, and there was nothing left of it, only skeletal, ashy trees and burned grass.

Steven remembered that area very well. It's where the Wonderland Theater, the only good place to see movies in Niles, had moved a few years ago when it stopped calling itself the Ready Theater. It was the cheapest place to see movies pretty much anywhere, and once every month or two, he remembered going to watch a movie there, then afterwards half of the time he'd gone and walked in the park by the river.

The park that had been leveled in the explosion—and there were missing people too, a group of kids. No one knew what had caused it. They only showed the pictures: the playground, with slides torn in half and monkey bars sitting on the ground… then, a long ways away, the amphitheater leveled, damage all over the place. In some ways, the footage looked haunted and strange—in others, boring and normal in full light, with local reporters talking over it.

And Steven knew—he didn't know what, or how, but it must be. They'd caused that, whatever it was, by going out last night, Michael and Halie—they'd caused it and they hadn't told him about it. Why? Well, it wasn't hard to guess—because he'd get angry. Because he wasn't one of them. And it pissed him off. Not that he'd ever been one of them. Even when they were relaxed, Steven always knew he was the intruder, that they did their thing and he stopped in sometimes. But it pissed him off.

That wasn't all. It made him feel left out—of what? He didn't know. Michael and Halie seemed very mysterious to him, in some ways. Maybe because he was around so often, but not with them. They could be doing anything in Michael's room. They could be fucking all day. They could be shooting heroin. Whatever it was, they did it without him; and here he was, where he'd always been, sitting alone and watching TV.

It made him feel excluded, but it also made him feel proud— proud of how, that night at dinner, he hadn't mentioned a thing. Even when Michael seemed sort of awkward and nervous, Halie too. The creature hadn't come down even though it usually did when they ate, maybe because Michael didn't want Steven to think about the creature. Steven was proud of himself, and maybe he was still being like dad but that was okay, he felt like he'd figured it out, that he needed to just relax, really.

He did relax, too, which is why July passed so much easier than June—he was used to this life, he was even really enjoying it. But he wouldn't have been able to do it normally. Whenever the feeling went away, he felt pissed off and anxious… but every time, it felt a little further away. Of course it would. It had been a while since it happened—and even with the mystery of the riverpark, it was better than thinking about Ben. What had happened. How the creature had killed him.

The feeling made all of that intellectual though—something he could think about, without feeling. And what he settled into, in

the end, was a kind of resignation... a resignation that was almost
pleasant. Every morning he woke up early, made coffee, and felt
he was doing the right thing. He was still alone, or more alone
than he'd wanted to be; but that was okay. He was a Hanson and
he just wasn't built to be around people—and there was no better
place to be a Hanson than here in the old house.

All he needed to feel okay, all he'd ever needed, was the creature. It made it bearable, that sense of wrongness, even if it was
still there—even if, by the end of summer, part of him hated the
world more than he had ever hated it, even if he'd never felt so
alone. But he understood, he really did. The problem with every
person, ever, was that they were born themselves. He'd been born
who he was, which meant he could never change; which meant he
had to get used to this, and the sooner he did, the better.

And that was why the summer passed so easily. Because every
time he didn't feel right, he could just go back to the feeling. So,
even though he was angry at Michael, eventually he forgot about
it; but he was angry at Halie too, and he got used to that.

He had a purpose at least, something worth doing, and it had
nothing to do with that—going to see mom. It was weird being in
Ben's house—an expensive suburban place, so much bigger and
nicer than dad's. It was weird sitting and talking with her for
hours as if this was something they'd ever done before. It wasn't,
and a part of him still didn't want to, but it made the one thing
better. It got rid of the guilt—or pushed it down. It was okay, even
if Ben was dead, and dad too—even if he had never spent enough
time with dad—even if dad was rotted and full of maggots and
hidden in the earth, even then.

There was always someone with her. That's what Steven
learned from all this—that it was improper to grieve alone. Most
often it was grandma Granger, who sat for hours, sometimes
wheezing a reply, while mom talked about various things. Others
it was her friends—Tiffany, or some other middle aged woman,
usually on their way out as Steven arrived. Less often (almost
never) it was one her sisters, Steven's aunts.

It was night when he came over most often. He would cook
dinner for her, and they would sit and eat—and mom, for the first
time Steven had ever seen, would drink sometimes, usually too
much. She had the silliest taste in alcohol—she didn't like beer

(too bitter), or wine (too bitter), or especially liquor (just terrible), but she liked those bottled malt beverages like Smirnoff Ice or Mike's Hard Lemonade, and she drank them with a kind of worldly, put-on air, like an actress performing sadness. She wasn't pretending, or Steven assumed she wasn't; but she always seemed like it, like someone who felt so bad they didn't know what to do, so they tried to grieve like someone else, like someone from a movie.

"I just don't understand," she said many, many times. "Where would he go?"

"I don't know, mom."

"I loved him, Steven. I loved him so much."

"I know, mom."

"He was so nice to me. So good."

Steven said he knew—and that's what he said, when he wasn't saying sorry. He would listen to mom talk about Ben taking vacations with her, or cooking, or taking time off work to spend with her; or his little mannerisms around the house, even (once) little details about how he smelled, which Steven really didn't want to know. She had two moods on nights like that: ones where the memories, everything she had to say, would just spill out. Others where she seemed awkward and nervous and could barely respond to anything Steven said.

There was one thing for sure though, most of these nights as they sat at Ben's table in his nice house—it would happen at some point, and every time, Steven didn't know what to say."

"I just don't..." She would trail off, and her voice would start to break, and she would reach over to grab Steven's hand or up to wipe her eye—and then she would say, "I don't..." but she wouldn't finish, because then she would cry. She would cry: sometimes loud, others hushed and simpering, and Steven would watch and not know what to say, and he would feel embarrassed (all the time), then awful, and he would hate himself, he would say, *Steven, you deserve to die,* and then he would wonder—even this, all this, why did even her grief seem wrong to him? Like she wasn't doing it right, like she'd never done anything right—and it was a tough question, one he didn't know the answer to, but like every question, that didn't stop him from asking it. He wondered, and wondered, and felt like shit, but he never excused himself, because it seemed like a point of pride, maybe a punishment: a sign of something he'd done wrong. He hadn't known, he really hadn't—but he knew the answer, he knew that. But he couldn't tell her. He even tried, once, opened his mouth like he had something to say—but no. What would she say? That he was crazy? It would be even worse if she believed him. Because there was nothing that could be done. They'd come this far and they couldn't go back, and telling her wouldn't make a difference, it might not even make him feel better. Nothing would make him feel better. He didn't deserve to feel better. He didn't deserve anything: to feel happy, to feel important. Maybe he didn't deserve to eat. He didn't deserve to live in a nice house or take her money. He didn't deserve to enjoy himself when he watched TV. He almost, he thought once, felt he like deserved to go to hell— that strange, imaginary place where he would suffer, just suffer, and he would do it forever, because it would be what he deserved, suffering. For ruining this. For ruining. But not that—it went *back* further. Because he was wrong. He'd always been wrong. His whole life was a mistake and what he was doing now was just an extension of it... the real, the true confirmation, of how awful he was. He had led to this, somehow, by letting Michael do what he did—by being himself, but not stopping it, by saying what he'd said. And now he was paying the price: only it wasn't just him. It was a price mom had to pay—and he felt uncertain and lost and bad, but maybe, more than anything, he felt alone.

He started doing things for mom—shopping for her, even cleaning, and that was fine. All of that, and he still couldn't believe where it led. It happened early in August, when the summer was starting to die. Sometimes he went out with mom now—even, on the Fourth of July, to one of her family parties, which he and Michael had hated for as long as they could remember. But after all that, he'd never considered she'd talk him into going to church.

She didn't even have to try hard. It was the guilt that made it happen in the end—a quick suggestion one day, and he felt bad and said yes. It wasn't a surprise. Everything about him was guilt. And he felt bad about it. He felt bad about everything. But he still went.

Steven drove, because mom had always been a terrible driver, but first they went to pick up grandma Granger, who mom took to church every Sunday. They were almost twenty minutes late already because mom had been doing... something. But when they got to mom's church (the same sort of factory building in the middle of nowhere it had been years ago, but transformed and newer looking, somehow more real and vaguely effervescent) they found a seat in the back without trouble.

And that was all it took. They sat down and Steven listened and he was feeling bored but okay—he looked out at the faces around him, all these pale, doughy faces, eyes narrow and focused, like soldiers. They'd come here for a purpose, because they felt they had to. It was responsibility—responsibility to other people. Not everyone had it, but he did, and that was what made him better. That was why he could sit here for an hour and a half and listen to an old man talk about god. Because he understood responsibility, and that made him a good person.

Only, it turned out, he couldn't. It was hard to tell when it would go, which was part of what made life so difficult—but the feeling went away in the middle of the service. It went away and Steven could barely sit still. He tried, he legitimately wanted to, but he started sweating and sort of wanted to hit somebody, sitting there because *their eternal souls depended on it,* so eventually he turned to mom and said,

"I need to go to the bathroom. I'll be right back."

Only he didn't go to the bathroom. Instead he went outside the church and sat down on the grass, facing out into the big field behind the church. There was something growing in it, corn probably—he didn't know who it belonged to, only that it had been there years before, as a kid when he and Michael would sneak out of church. Beyond it was a line of trees, a line going back, way back, maybe forever, into the terrible immensity of the horizon, and Steven looked up at the sky and felt damned and lost, pained and confused. While he was sitting there he thought about a lot of things. He thought about mom crying, more than anything. He thought about Michael and Halie not thinking about him. He thought how even watching porn didn't make him feel better. Nothing would make him feel better—he went through the motions of life, yeah, he went through them, but that's all they were, just motions, and when he felt comfortable, well, it wasn't real comfort. It was an illusion, a seeming: a bastard feeling. His whole being, everything he was, had ever been: he was just this stupid, useless, swinging cock—the kind of picture people draw on the walls of bathrooms, a symbol of stupidity and uselessness and nastiness. That's what he was, that's what he'd always been inside, and no matter what, no matter what he did to forget it, it only became more true. He was as useless as an old man's cock and balls, he was as unsightly and nasty—except his whole life, his whole stupid fucking life, he'd done his best to hide it, he'd tried to seem like a person who deserved his sliver of space on this miserable fucking earth. He'd tried, but even then he'd known—known he'd failed, known that really, truly, everyone was laughing at him, everyone knew he didn't belong, that he was a failure and stupid, he was a Hanson. And in the end he'd be like them, a stupid picture someone draws on a bathroom stall—scribbled over and forgotten.

Steven's ass hurt, and there was dirt on his pants now, and his eyes ached, but he kept sitting, kept sitting because there was nowhere else to go, and he only went inside when he knew the service was over. There would be a crowd, enough that mom wouldn't know where he'd been (unless she saw the dirt on his ass but she wouldn't, she was mom), and it didn't take long to find her talking to some of her friends.

"Steven!" she said. "There you are! I wanted to introduce you, this is—"

"I don't feel good, mom. I need to go sit in the car."

She tried once more to introduce him, but no—he walked away and sat down in the car. It was hard to be still, there was nothing decent on the radio... and, just because it felt good, he banged his head three times against the seat. It didn't hurt—all that happened was he bounced back. But it felt like punishment, a punishment he'd imposed on himself—like coming here. Like existing. It felt so good, like what he deserved, that instead he decided to bash his face into the steering wheel.

Only that didn't feel good at all—it fucking hurt, and he'd honked for just a second, and his face felt crushed in and swollen at the same time, and when he reached up there was blood coming out of his nose. Was it broken? Shit, he couldn't tell. He fussed around with it; looked for a tissue in the glove box. There wasn't one, so instead he held up a spare shirt of mom's to his nose, getting it all covered in blood. And that's how he sat for almost half an hour, waiting for her to come to the car, except it took so fucking long.

"Steven," she said. "What happened?"

"I told you, I'm sick."

"Your nose—"

"It's fine, let's just go."

Though she drove this time and yes, no, he wouldn't be able to go again. Even though it made him feel bad. He was so impatient to get away, to get home, that he could barely wait for the drive to be over, and his shoulders ached and he wanted to blow his nose but he knew if he did all that would come out was a spuming glot of blood. But even when he got home, the feeling didn't go away. He just filled the sink with red—noting, fortunately, that it stopped a few hours later—and sat on the couch, not watching TV, not doing anything, just sitting there hating everything—everything, but himself in particular.

He was surprised, almost a little annoyed that it took so long. Almost half an hour until he saw the creature standing above him, a lithe shadow perched on the edge of the couch. Not judging him, just looking down.

"There you are," he said.

No movement, of course, no sign it had heard him or understood him. It only gave those to Michael. Michael was the only one who understood it, the only one it really communicated with. And that, too—it wasn't fair. It was another reminder that Steven wasn't important, that he was always an outsider, even with the creature, even with the thing that ought to make it better, ought to let him bear all of this. It didn't love him. It didn't love anyone, except maybe Michael. It was only here because it was hungry. Because it needed to eat.

There it was again—jealousy. Michael was upstairs right now, probably with Halie, maybe fucking her. And here Steven was, alone with his dumb fucking bleeding nose. And all he got was this, just a little bit of pity—but even the creature, even it would be gone soon. But that didn't matter. He knew, knew that what he wanted didn't make any sense, even if he didn't know what he wanted. And it hurt. It hurt like his nose. It hurt like that throbbing, pulsating nothingness, the churning fuckpit deep in the center of him—and the secret of that darkness, that emptiness, was that there was nothing inside it, but that nothingness had a form: it was pain, and fear, and emptiness, and he wished more than anything that the creature could take that too, that it could empty the boundless darkness inside him, but even it couldn't, even the creature had limits—and a part of him resented it for that, he realized only now, though the other part was glad just to see it.

"There you are," Steven said. "I needed you."

But what—why? It was leaning close, so close that for a second Steven was worried it would eat him—eat him like it had eaten Ben, if maybe that was only way to swallow that boundless darkness inside him, a universe of unbearable pain. Even then, the fear was distant—he had trouble explaining it himself, the more rational part of him, but it seemed absurd to be afraid of the creature, something so familiar, even knowing what it could do. So he wasn't afraid as it put its face close, close enough to block out all light, all sound of the dying, brutalized world—but it wasn't trying to eat him, of course.

No, he told himself later. It was more like it had given him a kiss.

FLASHES OF LIGHT

THERE WAS a reason why Michael never told Steven what happened—reasons, plural. More than one, so many they started to run together. But the first was that Michael didn't understand what had happened until much later—assuming he even understood it now. And maybe, after thinking about it so much, he'd made up memories: made up a clearer, more linear version of what, at the time, had just been chaos, just noise, just sound, just light.

He remembered glancing over, and seeing movement along the other riverbank. And now he might actually have invented something: seeing the long, sleek body on the other shore, amidst the gathered shadows—maybe even the churn as it leapt across the river.

As the second creature leapt, and came down on theirs.

They met with a shockwave: not an explosion, since you couldn't see it, it wasn't visible—but like a wall, spreading back. The wall hit Michael in the chest, knocked him down, pushed him away. Halie too, but she was further back, so it didn't hit her as hard.

He remembered that first punch, the breath going out of him, and falling back. Halie told him later how he flew backwards—eight, maybe ten feet. But he didn't just fall, he started to skid, which was why the skin on his face was so torn to shit. And why he missed some of it—just a few seconds. But a lot can happen in the right few seconds.

He didn't remember how he'd broken his ankle. Though maybe it hadn't been the shockwave at all. Maybe he'd just stepped on it wrong when he saw the second creature land ahead. Maybe he just hadn't noticed the pain. It was confusing being knocked off your feet, like having your whole body yanked up at the end of a string.

The two creatures fought for a brief, brief moment on impact— only they were so quick, churning and lashing and writhing at each other, their bodies wrenching and collapsing forward, their motions burning the grass. That part, it only lasted a few seconds, so quick it was impossible to follow—until one of them, Michael didn't know which, got knocked out of the light.

Over towards the pavilions, Halie guessed later, when she heard the crashing. Michael heard it too: a series of sudden, rapid roars, like thunder but not thunder. The sound of things breaking; the creatures' bodies meeting. But it was off in the dark, nothing to see.

That was the funny thing, how there was nothing to see. Michael heard the rumble off to one side—louder, deeper, like a bomb going off. Then it was over by the playground. It stayed there longer, ten seconds, maybe twenty, then: something gray. Like an explosion, only it wasn't made of fire. A gray sphere, visible but not giving off its own light.

It flashed into being almost instantaneously; then gone. Then again, rippling and crackling, half a dozen times in half that many seconds—but each time it was in a different spot, as if the creatures were knocking each other around as they fought. It was some *Dragonball Z* shit, they started calling it later—or at least it seemed like it. The thing was, in *Dragonball Z*, everything happened slow enough you could watch.

Here, even when the creatures went into the light, it all happened so quick that any lamps nearby broke. But he saw a few times—the quick, colorless death of the light, the grass peeling and rippling away from the earth, a tree lurching as its bark was ripped away.

It took maybe a minute, all together. Funny, considering he and Halie spent whole nights talking about it, trying to reconstruct what happened—until eventually they ran out of things to say. That night, though, for the first time, they hardly joked when it was done.

They didn't say anything during the fight, and nothing afterwards either, when the silence fell. A long, pregnant silence, full of danger. Michael tried to stand, and realized his ankle was broken. That would make him the first of their burdens, the reason it took them until morning to get back—he could hardly walk, so he had to hop on one foot all down the river. That took all night, but they kept at it—even, at one point, when they sat down beneath a bridge and fell asleep for a while. Eventually Halie poked him on the shoulder and they got up and started walking again, and it hurt like hell.

But it was good, in the end, that they had to go slow. Because it wasn't just them. For a while, after the fight, they started to wonder if they were alone—if the two had just killed each other. And even thinking of it, Michael almost started to cry... this feeling like everything that mattered to him, he'd had it and he'd lost it, and if it was gone what would he do? He wouldn't have anything. And it was a long, dumb wait, saying dumb things, until it crawled towards them. Crawled into the light, bleeding and shapeless and wounded.

It could still walk, yeah, but probably it didn't mind going so slow, didn't mind walking all the way down the river until Michael had his first try riding a bike with one leg. But it was okay, in the end. It was a long, shitty night, but that morning, when they walked into the house, Michael had a word for how he felt, and it was how he wanted.

He felt, he told himself again, like a badass.

So that was the first thing Michael thought about a lot that summer. The second, for the next few weeks, was how he would hide his ankle from Steven—he could go to the hospital, in theory, but then Steven would find out. And Steven already knew, but a part of Michael didn't want to give Steven the satisfaction, the acknowledgement that going out that night had hurt him.

Either way, it would have been great, the most perfect accident —and Halie was sort of jealous. Because he just kept walking on it all the time, kept walking on it every day even though it was broken. And not just once, but two or three times a day, the creature would kiss it, and turn everything that hurt into something that didn't. At first usually the pain might be distant when he stood up, like something subtle he could bear, until it became hard and sharp again; and it hurt, but even after weeks of it, he still looked forward to it, so much he almost wanted to break something else when it stopped hurting.

So those next few weeks, until the ankle got better, were a sort of bliss—except he hadn't thought so much about the medical side of it, until a few weeks later when Halie pointed out he walked with a bit of a limp now. Not terrible, but there—and even into August it hadn't gone away yet. Maybe it would never go away. At first Michael didn't notice it, but then he did—the way he sort of lurched at the end of every step, so he walked like an old person, or a cripple. And it bothered him, a little at first, then a lot—but also he didn't care enough to get it fixed. He just, he told himself, he would get used to it, maybe it would be kind of his trademark.

Even he knew he shouldn't go out much, not on a broken ankle, so until late July he did what he always did—stayed in his room all day, playing video games early in the day, watching anime late at night, pausing intermittently to masturbate. It was, he would have told himself last summer, his perfect life. No one around asking anything from him (even Steven), no demands or responsibilities, only the shadow somewhere in the distance, the knowledge that it would end eventually when school started, and he would have to go back there again even though he hated school, hated everything.

Dad had given him trouble, starting a few years ago, when his grades really started to drop. But just, damn it—Michael didn't care. He just wanted to be left alone. He just wanted to do what he wanted. And everything else, everything he was supposed to do, was just a weight other people wanted him to carry. He didn't want to carry weight for other people—he wanted freedom to be himself, freedom to just *be*, to find that terminal illusive point in space, in time, where he could just be by himself and the world would leave him alone, time would leave him alone, everything would leave him alone, and he could just stay like that, stay perfect and alone and at balance, in equilibrium with himself, forever. He'd never been able to achieve it, not really—that balance, that feeling of being completely at ease—but sometimes he'd come close, and that was good, that would be good enough.

And what it had meant, until just a little while ago, was being left alone in his room—sometimes by himself, sometimes with Halie. He would play video games and feel like a badass; he would watch anime and some deep, repressed part of him, a buried flower (he actually thought of it like that, like something shining and delicate and pure), would reach up towards the light, towards the sun, reach up and say to itself *I've gotten what I need, I'm alive,* and it was a good feeling even if it was only temporary, even if it didn't last forever, and it would go as soon as he left his space, his window towards himself hidden in the stupid, clumsy mass of an imperfect world.

The foundation of that, of all of it, was a very basic idea: the world, his life and his living it, was imperfect and shitty and not very interesting, so he had to go somewhere else, go somewhere more interesting. It had always been so obvious to him: how petty, thin and ridiculous real people are, how they obsess over their bodies and try to control them but really they're just animals, and the raw materials were never quite good enough, never quite right, never taking the shape they were supposed to. Real life, in some ways, had always seemed less real to him than anime—because in anime, you knew everything was *meant* to be how it was, people were the real actualized ideals of themselves, beautiful and innocent and good, or evil, their bodies didn't sweat or smell, they didn't take shits, their faces weren't masks covering disgusting pockets of grease, their bodies weren't thin flesh packets over churning sacks of gore. Organ machines—seeping, smelling husks of snot and piss.

The real world, it had always seemed to Michael, was a ridiculous, futile place: a place where the most important part of being human was to deny the futility, the insides of things. To imagine a version of the world where families are happy, and people love each other, though love is nothing but a selfish illusion—to imagine the body as something holy or pure, when really it was disgusting. These meat puppets, they liked to lie to themselves: they liked to pretend they were happy, or that the world was okay, or that certain things worked in certain ways, but they didn't. Because they were flawed—they were flawed and they'd been built that way by whatever created them, and their place in this earth, this world, was to fight it: to hate it, on some deeper, hidden level, because no matter how hard they tried, no matter what they told themselves they wanted, they could always see the flaws, or they created them: an awareness, initially small, negligible then gaping, of whatever was wrong, whatever didn't work, whatever it was that made this life so easy to hate, that made people not good enough, that made things not good enough, that made the world such a shitty place, that little gap, that little absence—the uncrossable boundary, in the end, between our idea of the world (a place where things work, everything has its place, a place meant for it) and the real thing.

Only Michael had crossed that boundary, because of the creature—and he'd realized it too, over the summer. He had it now, the thing he'd told himself so long ago he would never get. The creature, really, it was meant for him; but not just him. It was a natural thing, a means of achieving equilibrium. And that's why Michael knew it: that whatever the creature was—it had been created for him, by the earth, to fix the mistake it made in making him, for making all of them. Because human life, the human body, in the end, it was all a machine for pain: a means of generating pain. But the end result of pain is nothingness, futility; it doesn't lead towards anything, only pain—but now it did, for the creature it became food, and somewhere in that, somewhere in the balance it struck, Michael realized: it had fixed him, fixed him in a way he never imagined he could be fixed, and now, maybe, he thought it was okay to be alive in the real world, maybe he could even get used to this place.

That's why, for the first time, Michael felt bored all summer. He would play video games for hours but get bored, then look through his collection and never find what he wanted to play; and he would watch anime but it didn't seem right, didn't seem interesting enough, because whatever he wanted from it, he'd needed it before but he didn't need it now. And he would sit and talk with Halie but even her, she was boring. And as they talked, instead of paying attention, he would just look at things about her —he would tilt his head or lay back while they were talking so he could look up her nose, and see the little hairs there, or he would follow, day by day, the growth of the stubble beneath her armpits until she shaved again. And he would think that, for the first time, whatever he wanted, it wasn't in this room—and that was another problem, it made it harder, because if it wasn't here, where was it?

It hadn't taken long, in the end, to get used to the creature. Sometimes they sat around and just didn't notice it. It changed, over time, changed and stayed the same. Michael felt it, he could always feel it; but at the same time, he hardly noticed it. Halie, though—it always surprised her again, like that day early in August where she looked over and said,

"I just realized—it's bigger again."

"Yeah," Michael said. He was playing video games, and only sort of listening—but he wasn't really focused on the game either, he wasn't focused on anything. His head was just... it was somewhere else. Maybe it was even on the creature. But whatever it was, he didn't care to talk to her about it. Halie wouldn't understand, even if she spent so much time with it; no one would. Maybe no one could understand how he felt. No one was like him, really, because he was special—and maybe that's what it was, the thing he couldn't get off his mind. He was special and he kind of resented having to stay here—even with the feeling, always there, never going away.

He noticed it first in late July, but it was that strange kind of realization—the kind where something has been in the back of your mind for a while, it's been there but you sort of don't want to look at it. It wasn't just her—it was all this. Though maybe her first, because for so long, she'd been his partner in crime. Sometimes literal, actual crimes, after they started shoplifting... but mostly just, well, being themselves.

It had been a long time, really, since Michael asked himself what Halie meant to him. Sometimes she seemed like his sister, sometimes like his other half. But most of the time she was just there—like this summer. It had only occurred to him now, just recently, that he never asked Halie to come over anymore. She just did it, basically because she didn't have anywhere else to be. Neither did he, of course. It was just what they did—what they'd done for five, maybe six years now.

"I just hate everyone," she had said years ago, when they first met—and that, it was what had made them friends, the reason they could do what they did. Because they hated everyone else, all of these people (parents, teachers, but especially other students), for being normal, all the same. Neither of them had anything to say to that kind of person. That's why they only talked to each other.

"I meant to tell you," Halie said. "I've been working on a cosplay."

"Yeah?"

She said something else, but Michael was hardly paying attention. He felt restless and confined in his room, subtly at first, then more around the middle of July. That's why he started to ride his bike so often—sometimes during the day, but more often in the middle of the night. He would get on his bike and just ride, feeling the wind in his face, seeing light all around him, swirling immensities of light: and he would ride as hard and fast as he could, standing and peddling until his lungs gave up, then he would coast for a while and pedal some more.

And it was great, yeah—it felt good. But it wasn't enough. Because every time, every time he got off, he would have to go back to his room, and there was nothing there. Only his PS2 (he didn't even care so much now about wanting a PS3) and Halie. Every day he would go out further, but he always went back, and he didn't like it—and that wasn't all. Because in a few weeks he would have to go back to school, have to be like everyone else again, and he didn't want that—he felt beyond it, beyond anything.

"...and it's sort of expensive," Halie said, "but I thought it was worth it."

"Cool," Michael said.

"Like Mamimi from *FLCL*, you know?"

"Yeah."

"I was thinking, like—wait, Michael, are you listening?"

"What?"

"Are you listening?"

"Of course."

"Then what was I talking about?"

"Look at it." He pointed at the creature. "It really is growing, like you mentioned."

"I was talking about something, Michael."

"I was just, I was thinking about what you said earlier."

"Like ten minutes ago, dick."

"Well it was a good point."

"Yeah, but I made, like—"

"Like how big will it get? Probably if it wanted it could swallow a car. Maybe it could swallow a building."

"That's dumb. Who would want to do that?"

"Well, it might be sort of cool."

"But I was asking about—"

Halie never got to finish, because right then Steven opened the door—and he did it like he usually did, throwing the door open so it swung on its hinges and crashed against the wall. Something about Steven, Christ—he could never just relax. Everything was stupid, blunt force with him. Everything was simple and stupid. Even the way, shit. Even the way he opened a door.

"Hey guys." Steven's voice was gentler at first (the part also meant for Halie). Then it got lower and more rigid, like it always did when he said what he'd actually come to say. "Michael, I have something to tell you."

"Yeah?"

"It's about mom."

"Okay."

"Tomorrow I was thinking…" Steven trailed off, which meant —Michael had been dealing with this shit all summer—it would be something big, something he didn't want to hear. And even that, it sort of pissed Michael off. If Steven was going to say it, then he should just do it and get it over with.

"Tomorrow," Steven said. "I'm going to have her over for dinner."

"Have fun then."

"That's not it. I want you to be there."

Michael sat up. He looked at Steven and Steven looked like an alien. Like an insane, stupid alien.

"Why would I do that?"

"Because she wants to see you."

"Mom wants a lot of things."

Steven frowned. "I've been spending a lot of time with mom. She's not doing so well."

"Yeah, but she's mom."

"I think, like, she wants to make up with you."

"Sometimes people shouldn't get what they want."

"Aww," Halie said. "Come on, Michael."

"Fuck, Halie," Michael said. "You too?"

"It's no biggie, isn't it?"

Steven said, "It's you who always tells me just to relax."

"But it's mom," Michael said. And even saying it, *it's mom*, he felt in him—this huge, built up mass of… something. It was hard to know where it had begun… maybe even from just listening and agreeing with dad, but she just, shit. There was something there: he could feel it. This sedimented buildup of… rage, wasn't quite the word. Maybe resentment. It was inexhaustible, infinite—and he felt the truth of that just hearing the words, just saying them to himself. *She was mom.*

"That's the point," Steven said.

"She's just so fucking annoying."

"So was dad. Dad was annoying as hell and you got along with him fine."

"And you want me, what? To eat dinner with her?"

"Maybe even to be nice to her," Steven said. "Halie, you get it right?"

"Whatever," Halie said.

But it sounded to Michael like a full, complete yes. Like Halie, damn it, she wasn't on his side anymore either. Nobody was. Nobody got it. No one but the creature.

"Halie," Michael said. "What the hell?"

She said, "It's just—"

"Tomorrow," Steven said—and Michael saw it, a quick glance between Steven and her. The kind of glance two people give each other when they're on the same team, and a member of the other team (that was Michael, yeah? that was him, wasn't it?) wasn't being reasonable, maybe even being stupid or ridiculous or a huge dickwad. Steven was trying to bring the focus back to him, and that pissed Michael off too.

"I've already invited her," Steven said. "I'll be here tomorrow."

"You fucking—what?"

"She'll be here at five. I'll come get you when it's time to eat."

"Why should I?" Michael asked.

Steven's response to that was no response: a cool, accusatory leveling of his gaze. His eyes, it was like he wanted them to be weapons.

"I can't believe you would ask something like that," he said.

"Why the hell not?"

"Because we killed Ben, fuckhead."

And it was true, technically—Michael knew it—and he also knew, technically, that they were still living on mom's money. But something about it seemed wrong, underhanded, like Steven was being shitty and unnecessary and uncouth by bringing it up, by mentioning it. It just... it didn't seem right. It was uncool. And Steven, it was so like him to be like this, to be like he was right now—acting like he was right, like he was always right. That was Steven's problem, that he was a fucktard and he always thought he was right, when he wasn't, when most of the time he was just a monstrous douche.

This is when he would do it, Michael knew. This is when Steven would bring up the money, or he would say something dumb, something from a movie like, *She's our mom and we should love her.* People in stories cared about things like that, but Michael, he didn't care. He was different, and he hated everything.

This is when Steven would say it, Michael thought again—and Steven did say something, but smaller, something so simple it was like saying nothing at all, something like:

"We killed Ben. We have to give her something back, at least."

"Fuck you, bro," Michael said—but Steven was already closing the door, and he heard what Michael said but he didn't reply. What a, damn it—what a shitty thing to do. To leave before he could finish talking. That was so shitty.

"Fuck him," Michael said again. "Asshole."

"Well then," Halie said.

"That asshole."

"I mean—"

Michael stood up, and interrupted Halie by saying, "Fuck him."

He looked over at Halie, sitting on the bed, her eyes wide, like deer-eyes—except now even that, it pissed him off too, it didn't seem right and it pissed him off, because he wanted her to be angry too. If she was his partner, his best friend, shouldn't she be pissed off too? Shouldn't she be angry at Steven for being such an asshole?

But she didn't look angry, she just looked confused. She looked soft and pliant and confused, and somehow too—what was the word? Too feminine? That wasn't right, that wasn't quite right, but there was something missing, something no person had, something no person had ever had, but he wanted it, now it pissed him off not to have it.

"What are you looking at?" he asked.

"Me?"

"Yes you."

"I'm wondering—fuck, Michael. What's wrong with you?"

"Nothing. I'm just pissed."

"Are you, like—Jesus, are you okay?"

"I'm fine, fuck. Don't—"

"Don't what?"

She'd heard it, Michael realized, the words he was about to say. *Don't be a bitch.* But even now, even in his head, they sounded too much, callous, almost brutal, unnecessary, and he realized that if he said them she wouldn't just not understand, she might be pissed at him, and he didn't feel, damn it he didn't feel like dealing with another stupid person that was angry with him right now, he didn't want to deal with anymore dumb stupid fucking people.

"Don't worry so much," he said.

"How am I worrying?"

Her eyes—narrow now. She was staring him, with, like, this frown; staring like someone who wasn't happy with what they saw. And that, maybe, pissed him off most of all... because he felt, well, he felt okay, he was better than he'd ever been, and it annoyed him, it pissed him off, to have someone not get that— especially not her, that really he was more right now than he'd ever been.

"There's something wrong," she said. "There's something wrong with you."

"I'm fine."

"No, you just—"

"You just don't get it. I'm fine."

"Michael, I think—"

"Halie, shut up, I'm okay."

She did this time, she shut up, just shut up and looked at him —but that too, it made him angry. And maybe it wasn't her, it was this room, this box he'd shut himself up in. It was too much. It was all too fucking much, and he needed, something—he needed to feel good right now, he needed to feel better, and he knew how.

"The knife," he said. "Where is it?"

"What?"

Now her eyes—they were wide, almost scared. She was looking at him like some kind of alien, but she didn't, nobody saw what he really was, nobody understood him.

"The knife. What did we do with it?"

"It's, umm—"

"Downstairs, I remember now."

"But—"

"I'm going out."

"You're—what?"

"I'll see you later," Michael said.

Only he didn't step towards the door, because that way he would have to pass by Steven and he didn't want anything to do with Steven, not now. So instead he walked towards the window and looked down; two stories, not a bad drop.

The last time he'd done it had been months ago, when they went out that first time; only then his ankle had been fine. But he didn't care. He would figure out in a second, wouldn't he—and he felt proud of himself, proud and independent, as he lowered himself through the window.

And yeah, it was fine—he hit the ground hard, and fell on his shoulder, but it was nothing, just a little green mark on his shirt from the grass.

He got up, dusted his shirt off, and turned back towards the window. Halie was looking out the window, down at him.

"Michael, are you okay?"

He didn't answer, just shrugged. He walked a few feet towards the fence. This fence, it had always been here at the edge of their yard, separating it from the field on the other side, or what used to be a field. The fence was metal, a long, smooth lattice mesh going forty feet along the edge of the yard—and it wasn't the usual, it wasn't the knife, but it would have to do.

The fence, that wire mesh—he punched it, he punched it with his right hand, over and over. The mesh shivered each time, a wave spreading out; and it felt good to know he was affecting something, to see how it moved. And it didn't quite, but almost, felt good to feel the pain of the metal first scratching, then cutting into his knuckles.

He didn't count, but when he finished, it wasn't just a scratch, he was bleeding—and he could see the marks, the red, still lingering on the chain link fence.

It was good handiwork—funny, a funny word, considering it was his hand. But when he was done, he held it up to the light, saw the blood flow—not a lot, but enough of it, dripping down his fingers across the back of his hand, towards his arm—he saw the blood and he felt proud of it.

But most of all, he felt the pain.

"Michael," Halie called down from above. "What the fuck?"

Only then, there it was, leaping through the window after him —the creature. And it knew. Unlike her, it knew what he wanted, what was best for them, for everyone. Even with its bulk, Halie didn't have to move, it just slid past her, and then it was outside; and there it was, standing next to him.

"Here we go," Michael said.

And it was what he needed, exactly what he needed. He put his hand in the creature's mouth, and felt the beautiful, pure light of it, of all the pain going out of him—of everything he hated, everything impure, it was all going into its mouth, where it was supposed to be. And he felt it then—he felt real, and true, and happy. He felt complete. His pain, his everything, it all had an end, a purpose. It all made sense.

He wasn't sure how long it took, he never was, but in the end, when he took his hand out of the creature's mouth, when he looked up at Halie, he felt real, true happiness, the kind that was so rare, so impossible in this world, the kind he felt as he said:

"See? It's all better."

THE LONG DELAY

Steven felt good about himself, he felt proud—it had been tough, yeah, but he'd set it up. He was going to make this work, he really was... and in the end, when it turned out okay, or at least mostly okay, he would be able to tell himself, he could say, *Steven, it was a tough situation, but you did your best,* even if, well, even if it didn't turn out so well. At least it would be different from before. At least he could say he'd done his best. At least he'd tried.

Only mom was late. They were supposed to eat at five but, Jesus Christ, five came and went and nothing. Steven called her house—nothing. He called her tracphone next except she never answered the fucking thing. She was supposed to get here an hour before they ate... but then it was six, and Halie came downstairs and said she was hungry and Steven said he didn't know where mom was at and sent Halie back upstairs with a bowl of cereal (cereal!), and still mom wasn't there.

Until six thirty. More than two hours late—fuck, if that wasn't like her, to fuck things up, to be herself *right when it mattered most,* right when Steven, he really had, he'd been trying to do his best, and it wasn't for himself—it wasn't, really—it was for her.

Two hours late, fuck.

And the worst part, it was always the same—the worst part was how she sat in the car for like five minutes before she came in, combing her hair, or (even worse) if she was talking to someone on the phone he'd tried to call her on. It was like, Jesus it was like she had no idea of the importance of anything; and Steven had felt good earlier, he really had, and he still, well this was still for her, but he was so pissed that he hardly managed to stay in the house—when half of him, maybe more than half, half of him just wanted to go and pound on her window and say *What the fuck is wrong with you?* And he would do it, if he did it, with the profound, overwhelming, comforting conviction that nothing she said, no answer, would be good enough.

But he waited, sat down and waited, until she came and rang the doorbell, and when he opened the door she was holding two huge bags, one on either arm, so big they looked ridiculous and stupid and reminded him of everything that had ever annoyed him about mom, everything that annoyed him in the world.

"Steven!" she said. "It's good—

"What the fuck, mom?"

"Language, Steven."

"Do you—do you have any idea what time it is?"

He realized that he was blocking the door, that she needed to come in, but right now he practically just wanted to shut the door in her face. And her tone of voice, so oblivious and happy, that just made it worse.

"Aww, hon. I'm sorry. I know I'm a bit late."

"Almost three fucking hours."

"I just—I don't know. I got caught up in things."

"You always get caught up in things. You were, what —shopping?"

"For a while," she said. "I brought doughnuts!"

"Why would you bring doughnuts? I told you—shit, mom."

"They just seemed nice."

"Mom, god, you're so—" Stupid, he was about to say, such a fucking idiot—but he stopped, mid-sentence, stopped and just held it inside, and took a deep breath (a deep, deep breath), and let it out, and looked at mom with those two big bags full of shit he didn't care about, looked at her still even kind of smiling though he was yelling at her, and he said,

"Nevermind, let's cook."

"Aww, that's good bud. I really am sorry."

"It's—whatever. Let's go, alright?"

"Just give me a minute, I need to—"

"No. Let's go, okay?"

The plan, to begin with, had been for mom and Steven to cook together. Because she liked doing it, mostly—it had been a bit of a joke, but then sort of serious, the idea that he was spending the summer teaching her to cook. He did it for her a lot at her house, and he'd even been a bit proud sometimes when she cooked something decent for herself on her own, instead of eating out of a package.

He knew now—mom could cut vegetables, but anything else, that was sort of dangerous. The worse day (though it was kind of a funny story), the day he'd really learned, was a day he'd come over to make breakfast tacos. So he'd come over in the morning, and they'd gone to the store and bought a lot of stuff, and two pounds of bacon, and Steven did everything himself, just left mom to cook the bacon—only she burned it, not doing anything else, she burned the whole first pan of it. And Steven couldn't believe it, he thought she'd figured it out by now, but he left her at it and she burned the second pan too, she burned two pans of bacon in a row and it was her only job.

But Steven still liked having her there. Maybe because, something about cooking—it felt good to have an audience. And he knew she liked it. Today, especially with so much time to sit around beforehand, there wasn't much for her to do. He wasn't as hungry as he should have been because he'd given in and eaten a bowl of cereal at one point—and he blamed her for that too.

"We're making steaks," he said. "They're in the fridge—could you get them out?"

"That's great, hon. Where are they?"

"Just, like—in the fridge. And there's some potatoes in there too, in a container. I already cut them up earlier."

Steven got everything ready while mom hunted through the fridge. He sent her back eventually for milk and butter… except he'd forgotten that if he cut the potatoes early they would turn sort of brown, not much, but enough to annoy him.

"They look fine, hon," mom said. Which was what she always said—and Steven said he knew but just, shit, they were still a bit ugly.

He was hungry, enough to trust mom a little bit. Earlier that day, he'd gone to get the steaks from Shelton's—good, inch thick New York Strip, a big one for each of them, which had been expensive but worth it. So he was going to have her help him again even if there was a bit of a risk.

"Six dollars a pound," he told her.

"Isn't that a bit expensive?"

"It'll be worth it."

Steven always cooked steak the same: high heat, a crust of salt and pepper, oil on the steak (but not in the pan); sear the sides (especially the rind of fat on the New York Strip—you wanted it rendered down and almost crispy), and butter right at the end, which gave it a different kind of richness. Sometimes he'd add garlic or thyme, but with five of them to cook for, he didn't want extra ingredients in the pan. No matter what, he'd probably end up overcooking at least one. But that was okay. If he messed up, he'd just give it to Michael. Michael liked his steak stupidly overcooked anyway.

"Your dad used to love steak," mom said.

"I know, mom," Steven said—though actually, that's why he'd picked what he had. He didn't want to say it out loud because it sounded stupid, corny, but he was making the kind of food dad would have liked... the kind of food, technically, that might have killed him, since he died of a heart attack after all.

"I wish he was here for it," she said.

"Do you?"

"Of course. What do you boys think—that I wanted him to die?"

"No, I mean. Just, you know how he was. He would get angry."

Today especially. Whenever mom was late for things, dad would get furious, and he'd stay that way for hours, all night. If dad was alive, this whole meal, no matter what happened, they wouldn't have been able to enjoy it. They would have sat there eating in silence, afraid to say anything, afraid he'd explode. It was exactly like Steven had told Michael, stupid and annoying. But at the same time (Steven could hardly believe he was saying this) he almost missed it.

"I'll be honest," mom said. "I never understood."

"Understood what?"

"You boys—mostly Michael, but you too, Steven."

"Say it, mom."

"You always took your dad's side. Never mine."

"Only sometimes, mom."

"Always, Steven. Sometimes I felt, I don't know—"

"Like what?"

"Like I was barely family, Steven."

"It's not—wait, mom."

Steven checked the third steak with his thumb, and wasn't sure if it was ready for the butter but, fuck it, he wasn't going to cut it open and check. And mom's question, it was distracting him, he could feel it like a nail pounding into the side of his head, at first shallow then deep, so he just tossed the butter in, gave it twenty seconds on each side, and plated it.

"There," he said. Only instead of talking more, he reached for the fourth steak and put it in the pan—and it felt good, it felt right, when he heard it sizzle, and saw the steam, only he knew mom still wanted an answer, knew she would even push for it, and it didn't surprise him when he heard her say:

"You didn't answer my question, Steven."

"I know, mom, it's just—I don't know. You're family, you know, but..."

"You boys are always just getting angry at me, like your dad did."

"I don't know, mom. It's just, you get on our nerves. Like today. You just... you keep doing the same things."

"It's not just that. You won't go to church with me. You won't see my family."

"Church, mom? I tried."

"My family, then. You never liked them."

"I don't know, mom. It's just, I guess—it's just how it is."

And really, probably, he couldn't give a better answer. Something about them, something about their family—they'd always sided with dad, and Steven knew it. Not because dad was right... really, dad had caused a lot of the problems that made living in the old house so weird, so unpleasant, because dad was always getting mad at mom for being herself. And so, because it was normal sometimes, they blamed mom—but also, of course, it was dad's fault, for not being able to relax. Steven knew it didn't make sense, but it was just, well:

"It's just how it is," Steven said again.

"I don't understand, honey. I try my best."

"I don't know, mom. Sometimes our best isn't good enough."

"But you and Michael—"

"Wait, mom. Have you been checking the potatoes?"

"I—"

"Jesus mom, I give you one thing. It's been—the strainer, it's over there. They should still be okay, but—now, you need to take them out now."

So mom took the potatoes off the stove, drained them, and put them back in the pot. Steven turned off the burner while she stood at the sink. And, while doing his best to keep his eyes on the steak, he added everything he'd need to the potatoes quick, without measuring: butter, milk, seasoning, and (this is what would really make the difference) fresh parmesan, quite a bit of it. He told mom to start mashing, and he still managed to make it back to the steak in time to flip it.

"That should be good," Steven said. "Just go until they're smooth."

She did, and he was glad, yeah, that she didn't bring up what they'd been talking about, maybe there wouldn't be time. It didn't seem like a good enough answer, saying just *you get on our nerves*. The thing is, that made it sound like their fault, and he didn't like that so much, he disliked it enough he'd rather not talk about it, rather just, well, talk about anything else, enough that he was glad when he turned and saw Halie standing in the door, looking down at the steak with big wide eyes.

"That's a lot of smoke," she said.

Steven asked, "Are you okay with helping a bit?"

"I guess, sure."

"There are some salads in the fridge. Could you put them on the table?"

Only mom had stopped mashing the potatoes, and she turned towards Halie and said, "Aren't you cute today."

"Aww, thanks," Halie said.

"I always tell Michael. I tell him—you're so lucky, spending time with such a cute girl. Isn't she cute, Steven?"

"Sure," Steven said.

"I tell my friends sometimes. I say, my son has such a cute friend. And they say, not girlfriend?"

"Just friend," Halie said.

"For now," mom said, and Steven could tell from the tone of her voice that she was smiling, maybe she'd even winked, and he mostly wanted to be out of the room. "You know, my boys, I think they're great but they'll never tell me anything about girls."

Steven said, "It's your fault, mom."

"I wish they would. You know, I like things like that."

Halie said, "I'll go put the salad on the table."

"Thanks," Steven said, and flipped the steak, and while it was cooking he checked the mashed potatoes (success), and after this steak the only thing left was the asparagus, which he would have to cook in the pan once the steak was done. If they started setting the table now it would be only a few minutes until they could eat —and the knowledge of that, it felt good. It actually felt kind of great. That after all that work, well. It was going to work out. They were going to eat dinner together, and it was all because of him.

"Halie," he said. "Could you go upstairs and get Michael? It's about time to eat."

"Sure," she said, and then she was gone—and it took a few minutes, but by the time Steven finished the asparagus and plated everything (that was another of the biggest differences between an old family dinner and a new one—he liked to make the plates himself) there they were, everyone sitting down to the table to eat.

"There you are," Steven said to Michael.

Michael said, "I could smell somebody cooking steak down here."

Mom said, "Steven did such a good job. It was amazing!"

"Thanks mom," Steven said, "but I'm starving.

A FAMILY DINNER

MOM HAD BROUGHT WINE-COOLERS—THE same brand dad always used to buy. They were a bit warm (she hadn't thought to put them in the fridge), but Steven was actually a bit excited to drink them. They were barely alcohol, but they reminded him, would always remind him, of family cookouts forever ago, when dad and mom would let the kids share theirs, sometimes even drink a whole one.

It was mom's gesture that they were adults now—a silly, sort of childish way to do it, but Steven knew what it meant, and he actually appreciated it. Maybe Michael did too—and Halie wouldn't understand but that didn't stop her from saying,

"Hey, this is pretty good."

Mom said, "Like pop, right?"

Michael must have been thinking about the same thing—because when he picked up his first wine cooler he stared at it very hard, then threw back his head and drank nearly the whole thing.

"Whoa," mom said. "Don't hurt yourself, hon."

"I was just thirsty."

Steven said, "Here's the dressing. I made it a few hours ago—simple, just a balsamic vinaigrette. But be careful—it's strong."

"Thanks, hon," mom said. Only instead of using one or two spoonfuls, she used five.

"Mom!" Steven said. "That's too much—I just told you."

"Is there any cheese?" Michael asked. "I like cheese on my salads."

"This won't need it," Steven said. It was a good, crisp salad (romaine, endive, tomato, cucumber), except mom frowned a little when she took a bite, and a part of him wanted to tell her again, *I told you, you used too much*. But she wanted to pretend she liked it, so she said,

"It's nice, honey."

"Time for steak," Michael said, setting his salad down after a few bites.

"I tried to give you the most cooked one," Steven said, gesturing to Michael's plate.

Only mom had been biding her time—hardly eating, just staring out over all of them with a big smile on her face, and Steven already knew. It had been a while, but it was there in his muscle memory. It was time for her to say something sappy, only mostly it would just make them uncomfortable.

"Well then," she said. "I'm glad all our whole family could be here. Especially you, Michael. It's been too long. I've missed you."

"Sure," Michael said.

"Ben and I—we ate together a lot, and his family was so nice. But I miss eating here with you. Though Ben was always so nice. Such a nice man."

"Right," Steven said.

Steven glanced and saw Halie had gotten the rare steak—the red juice of it pooling on her plate. Which had always seemed... well, seeing meat bleed was a bit much, even for him. He worried for a second she might not eat it, but instead she speared a piece on the end of her fork and went back to dip it in the blood.

"I miss my boys," mom said. "Both of them."

"Mom," Steven said. "Give it—"

"No, I mean it. I do."

"We're here, mom. We're eating dinner."

Steven didn't like it. He'd gotten Michael here, yeah—but so far Michael had barely looked at mom. He kept cutting into his steak and then (weirdly) dipping the pieces into mashed potato, but even when he talked he didn't look up from his plate.

Only mom was set on talking to him now, so now she said, "Michael, how have you been?"

"Fine."

The answer took a while, but at least it came. Not that Steven liked the tone. Michael sounded so withdrawn, almost hostile, and he still wouldn't look up from his plate.

"That's great, hon. How have you been enjoying your summer?"

"It's okay."

"What have you been doing?"

"The usual."

"Aww, that's fantastic. Like what?"

"Nothing much."

"That's nice," mom said.

Halie said, "And thanks for letting me stay. It's nice of you."

"Of course, hon. You know I've always liked you."

"Steven cooks for us sometimes," Halie said.

"I'd hoped he would. He's amazing, isn't he, Michael?" And when Michael didn't answer she said it again, calling his name, only he didn't look up, just dipped another piece of steak in his mashed potatoes.

Steven said, "Michael likes it too."

"Ben told me he wanted to cook with you," mom said. "He was going to practice cooking meat—just for me, you know?"

"That was nice of him," Halie said.

"It really was. He was so sweet, such a nice man."

Steven said, "I've been thinking of eating vegetarian a few days a week. Because it's healthy."

"That's nice," mom said. "Isn't it, Michael?"

At last, Michael—who had been eating very quickly—took his last bite of steak. Now he looked up at mom, still chewing, but instead of replying to her question he stood up and said,

"I'm going now."

"Michael," Steven said. "Come on."

"Your mother is here," mom said—which only made it worse. It had always annoyed both of them when she talked about herself in the third person. "Can't you talk to me for a while?"

"I have things to do," Michael said.

"Jesus Christ, Michael," Steven said.

Even Halie chimed in when she said, "Can't you—"

"What?" Michael said. "Can't I what?"

"I pay for you to live here." Mom's voice took on that thin, almost fake firmness that Steven recognized so well. "The least you could do is talk for a few minutes."

"I don't have anything to say to you," Michael said.

There it was. The words—measured and cold—just hung all across the table, and they cast something, their own cold shadow. Steven knew that shadow, knew that no matter what he did the rest of his steak wouldn't taste good; but worse, that this, all this, the thing he'd set up, Michael was about to mess it up. And that pissed him off, Michael and his fucking stubbornness.

"Sit down, idiot."

Now Michael turned to Steven, that same look in his eyes, and said, "I'm so tired of you, Steven."

"What?"

"You think you can tell me what to do. You're not dad. I don't listen to you."

"I take care of the—"

"Bullshit, Steven."

Mom said, "Michael, please."

"No," he said. "I'm tired of this. I'm tired of all of you."

"Don't be an idiot," Steven said. "You're being—"

"I told you," Michael said. "I told you I didn't want to see her, but you wouldn't listen. No one ever listens to me."

"Michael," mom said, "can't we just—"

"No," Michael said. "It's no surprise Ben ran out on you. You're so fucking annoying."

The response was audible, or it wasn't. The response was silence. Even Michael—Steven had heard him yell at mom before, but this was too much. It felt wrong, like some line had been crossed, one he'd never imagined anyone crossing. And how could he—at Steven's dinner? It pissed him off, having this happen now. But to say the least, mom didn't like it either.

She said, "Michael, I'm your mother."

"I don't care who you are," Michael said. "And you were a shitty mom, anyway."

"How could—"

"I told you after the divorce," he said. "I don't want to live with you. I don't want to see you. I don't see why—"

"Michael," Steven said. "You're being an asshole."

"Me?" Michael said. "You're always an asshole. You're full of shit. I thought you might relax but, fuck, you just—"

"Michael," Halie said. "What's wrong with you?"

Another silence, at that—Michael just standing, looking over at her, his mouth open. And that gave Steven time to glance over at mom. She'd seemed strong, almost angry at first, but now her lip was actually quivering, Jesus she was about to cry, all this work he'd done and mom was about to cry.

"Michael," Steven said. "Apologize to her."

"For what? For telling her the truth?"

Mom was so close to crying now, but she could still talk, even if her voice quivered as she said, "I think I should go."

Steven said, "Mom, no."

"I should," she said. "I can't eat anymore."

"I'll stay," Michael said, "if she goes."

"Fuck," Steven said. "Fuck it."

Then Steven did something he never imagined he'd do, especially not to his own food. He picked up his plate, his own plate—half full, with steak and mashed potatoes on it—and threw it.

At Michael, was his first inclination, but no—he just threw it against the wall, a few feet away, and he heard the crash as the china shattered, and a dull thwack as the steak (his steak!) buckled and fell to the ground with pieces of plate on it, somewhere amidst the brutalized smear of mashed potato.

"Fuck," Steven said again.

But Michael hardly seemed surprised. He just looked at the remains of Steven's plate, tumbled awkwardly to the ground, and said,

"I'm taking the last wine-cooler."

He reached over the table, towards mom, and grabbed the last one out of the pack—orange. And he only said one more thing on his way to the door, turning towards Halie to ask:

"Are you coming?"

It must have been a lot of pressure, being put stupidly on the spot, but eventually Halie said,

"I'm going to finish eating first."

"Okay then," Michael said—and a few steps later he was gone.

The silence afterwards might have gone on forever—only it wasn't silence, because of mom crying. A part of Steven was used to silences at the dinner table. Only it was different now, because as a kid, no matter what happened, afterwards they could pretend to eat as if nothing had happened... except Steven had thrown away his food, he didn't have anything to eat.

But he was still the host, he had a responsibility, so he sat down and said:

"I'm sorry about that."

He wasn't sure who he'd been talking to. To Halie, for letting her see what she'd seen? To himself, for ruining his own plans? To mom, for ruining her life? Maybe he'd been speaking to the silence, and he didn't know who would reply, though probably he hadn't thought it would be mom who spoke first.

"I don't understand," she said. "I don't understand why he hates me so much."

"He doesn't hate you," Steven said. "He's just being Michael."

"I thought... years ago, when I had you two—I always thought I'd be able to stand before the gates of God and say I've been a good mother, but now I realize—"

"Mom, don't make this about religion. It isn't about religion."

"Now I realize—Steven, what did I do?"

"Nothing, mom. He just—"

Halie said, "Michael's going through a tough time."

"So am I," mom said. "But it's hard. Ben—he's..."

"I'll talk to him," Steven said. "I'll have him call and apologize later."

"I thought... Steven, I thought this would be a good idea, you living here."

"I did my best, mom."

"Why... why does nothing work, Steven? I keep asking God but I still don't—I don't know."

"Stop it, mom. I told you, don't make this about God."

"He won't tell me," she said again. "I keep asking Him, I ask—why doesn't my family—why don't they—"

"I don't want to—"

"Steven," Halie said. "Let her talk."

Only mom didn't have anything else to say, she just looked at the food, and now she stood up too, and said: "You did a good job on the dinner, hon. I'm sorry I was late."

Steven said, "You don't need to go, mom. You can stay the night."

"No, I need to be alone. I need to pray."

"Mom, don't—"

"God will know, Steven, even if He doesn't tell me."

"Fuck, mom, don't—"

Only then something went out of him, some rigid line in his back—the pressure, Steven had sometimes thought, that made him himself, that made him do so many of the things he did. It just went away, and he realized there was nothing he could do, nothing really worth saying tonight. So all that was left to say was: "Drive safe, mom. I'll call you tomorrow morning, yeah?"

"I love you, Steven. And have a nice evening, Halie."

"I love you too, mom."

And that was it—she spent almost a minute looking through those big bags she brought with her, but apparently didn't find anything. On her way out she told Steven she loved him again. Then she was gone, which left Steven alone with Halie, both of them just sitting in the most terrible stillness, amidst the wreckage of half-eaten food, but Halie, she really was the best, she finally broke the silence by saying:

"I meant what I said about this steak. The potatoes too."

"Thanks," Steven said. "That means a lot."

Except then he felt sad—so sad he almost felt like he was going to cry. And it was strange, because he didn't feel like he'd lost something, exactly... only this sense like, how to put it, like something was wrong. Something was wrong and he would never fix it and he would have to get used to it, which was the worst feeling, one he hardly wanted to admit to himself.

"I just realized," he said. "I'm still kind of hungry. Would it be weird if I ate what's left of my mom's food?"

"I don't care," Halie said. "Whatever."

So Steven walked around the table real quick, and grabbed mom's plate, and he said:

"I can't believe what he said about Ben. Did you—fuck, did you hear him?

"Yeah, I heard him."

"He said it like he doesn't know. Christ."

Steven felt, for some reason, like Halie probably nodded right then, not that he saw, he was looking down at his steak. But it was happening again—even now, when he needed it most, the food wouldn't make him feel better.

"Shit," he said. "I'm not hungry anymore."

"I can finish it," Halie said.

"At least somebody appreciates it." Steven looked up at her, taking the last few bites of her steak, and he felt—how did he feel? He'd been working for something tonight, but he wasn't sure anymore what it had been.

"It's just us now," Steven said. "You going up soon?"

Halie said, "Probably not."

"Maybe I should get us something to drink. You like red wine?"

"No."

"Good." Steven stood up and patted her on the shoulder. "Me neither."

A SCHOOLGIRL

STEVEN CAME BACK CARRYING a thing of boxed red wine—the cheap stuff. He didn't know much about wine, and never had, but he knew this wasn't good. He'd bought it a few weeks ago for... some reason? It was hard to remember. Maybe he'd just been being cheap. Because it was true—boxed wine had always been one of the cheapest ways to get drunk.

And they were out of beer. How had he let that happen? Steven felt vaguely dumb and guilty, letting them run out of beer—especially on a night like this. Not that he could have known. Except maybe he should have.

Steven set the box on the table between them, bigger than either of their heads, and Halie said, "That looks disgusting."

"It's perfect," Steven said. "Right?"

There were wine glasses in the cupboard somewhere, but Steven didn't care, so he'd brought along two red plastic cups left from the funeral—only for some reason opening the tab on the boxed wine was harder than it looked, and at first the wine came out too fast and he spilled a little of it on the floor.

"Maybe I'm not so good at that," he said.

Halie laughed and said that maybe he was right. She interrupted the laugh by throwing back her head to drink the whole cup in one gulp, enough she almost choked, and a few red tears fell down from the corner of her mouth.

"That's disgusting." She held out the glass to him. "Give me another."

"Why the hurry?"

"I've never liked wasting time."

She did the same with the second glass; on the third she coughed, spitting with her mouth half full of wine. It got it all over the table, even a little on her clothes. Afterwards she wiped her mouth with the back of her hand, which was a terrible way to clean up wine. So Steven got her a paper towel and she dabbed her mouth with it, then balled it up and dropped it on the table.

"Well," she said. "At least there's more where that came from."

She started in on her next glass, with Steven still only a few sips into his first, but she drank normally this time. And Steven felt strange but still actually, mostly okay. Though a part of him, somewhere beneath that, felt like it was dying.

"I don't feel so good," she said.

"Don't worry," Steven lied. "It's just the wine."

So they drank for a minute, until Halie asked, "What happened to your nose?"

"It broke." And then, to clarify: "I broke it."

"How?"

"It's kind of embarrassing."

"That sucks."

"Is it crooked? I've been worrying it might be crooked."

"Maybe a little."

"Fuck."

"Don't worry about it. You know Michael broke his ankle a few weeks ago? That's why—he walks with a limp now."

"Good for him," Steven said.

"He was trying to keep it a secret from you."

"That's what everybody does, isn't it? Keeps secrets from me."

This time Steven threw back his head and drank a glass of the wine (which was hard because the taste was sweet, but also bitter in the worst way), then refilled it, all without standing up.

Halie said, "Michael told me the other day. He wants to leave. It's all he talks about now—getting out of here."

"How do you feel about it?"

"I don't give a fuck where he goes."

"I thought you were, like—"

"Nope," Halie said.

Halie set her cup on the table and sort of slumped forward behind it. It must be the wine was starting to hit.

"You okay there?" Steven asked.

She sat back and asked, "Are you?"

"No, maybe not."

"What did you mean to do tonight? By having your mom over to dinner."

"I wanted to fix things. It seemed like the right thing to do."

"Well maybe neither of us are okay then."

"That's what we have the wine for." He took a drink, looked deep into the bottom of the cup, and said, "But where would he go? Michael, I mean."

"I don't know. I doubt he's thought that far ahead."

"That sounds like him."

"It's just—it's the creature. I think it wants to leave. And it's funny, because he always used to say he would spend his whole life here, which was dumb because can you imagine staying in this town forever? Sometimes we talked about college but Michael always said he would just get a job at Walmart."

"He's aiming high, obviously."

"Yeah," Halie said. Only now, as she finished her cup, Steven noticed her leaning back in her chair—leaning so far it fell over, and she flailed out and hit the ground and said, "Fuck!"

Steven stood up, bending over to put out his hand. "You alright?"

"Shit, oww."

"Is that a no?"

"It's a maybe." Halie reached to touch the back of her head—she was light, even lighter than Steven had expected, when she finally grabbed it. "I've never done that before."

She kneeled down, cautiously, to put the chair back on its feet.

Steven said, "I always worry, since I like to lean back in chairs. I've done it since I was a kid—leaning back all the time. And sometimes I feel like I'm taking it too far. Like, there's that point where you think you're in control, but then it turns out you're really not, and you hit that sort of endpoint, yeah? And that's where you lose control and start to fall, except you feel like you weren't there yet, only really you already were."

"I think I drank a lot of wine," Halie said.

"Maybe you should slow down?"

"Never," Halie said. "I don't take orders from nobody."

It had hit Steven too—he was feeling sort of tired and out of it, and instead of talking he just stared at Halie, looking down into her cup like she saw something there. But what would it be? What would be there, really?

"You know," Halie said. "If you'd asked me a few years ago, I would have said I hated everyone."

"I do," Steven said. "That's my secret. That inside I'm nothing but hatred."

"For what?"

"I hate people, for being themselves."

"That's dumb," Halie said. "I think it's how I feel too."

"Yeah?"

Halie was staring at him—but weird, not a good stare, and he felt sort of confused until she said,

"Your nose. It's bleeding."

"Shit." He reached up—and yeah, it was, enough the fingers came away red. It didn't hurt, but his first inclination, even now, was to find the creature and see if it could fix it. But that didn't make sense. The creature couldn't fix anything. That had always been the problem.

"Some napkins." Halie tossed a little bundle his way. "Here."

"Thanks." Steven balled one up beneath his nose and just held it there—he was afraid to look again because he knew what he'd see. The napkin brushed against his upper lip as he said, "I really regret breaking my nose."

"Why did you do it?"

"Because I hate myself. Because I hate everything."

"Your family is kind of dumb."

"I guess so," Steven said. "Would you miss Michael if he goes?"

It took Halie a while to answer, and actually she never did, because all she said after a bunch of thinking was, "I don't know."

"Why do you hang out with him so much, then?"

"It's like I said. He's my best friend."

"Okay."

"Only I'm not sure how much I like him. It's just that I hate everyone else—both of us did."

"Sounds pretty emo to me," Steven said.

Halie scowled. "Shut up, dick."

"Just stating a fact." And he laughed a little as Halie bit at her bottom lip. He couldn't tell whether she was mad or not. He never could with her. She really was just pretty weird.

"Sorry," he said. "Keep going."

"Now I don't want to."

"I won't interrupt, I swear."

Halie's scowl turned to a kind of contemplative look before she said, "We're friends, yeah? Except I was always worried, for years, that he would try to have sex with me. Because it wasn't like that, really—except a little while ago I thought he would try and he didn't. And it sort of bothered me."

"I've always wondered," Steven said. "Why do you come around here so much?"

"It's not Michael," Halie said. "Not really."

"It's just, what—your dad?"

"I don't want to talk about it."

"Come on."

"I don't like to talk about my dad."

"But..." Only Steven kept going even when he saw Halie frown, and he said: "We're friends, right?"

Halie shrugged like, *maybe,* but she said, "When I was young, sometimes my dad would make me kneel against the wall."

"He what?"

"He said—this is how he sounded—he said, *Halie, this is what you deserve.*"

"For what?"

"Just like, things. I don't know. I would have to stay there at least ten minutes, but sometimes almost an hour. And he never said it exactly, but I think I was supposed to be praying."

"Bullshit," Steven said.

She shook her head. "But I think about it a lot. Sometimes I want to do things, you know?"

"Like what."

"It doesn't matter. But sometimes—not all the times—I want to do things just because I shouldn't. I want to punish him."

"Your dad," Steven said. "He sounds pretty weird."

It was sort of disappointing. Maybe it was just the mood, or what had happened, but Steven had felt like they were opening up to each other, alone in the stillness of this awful, fucked night; like Halie was about to look inside him, look inside him into a place nobody ever really saw, no one except himself. The secret, of course, was that there was nothing there, nothing good or useful or valuable inside—and even Steven, he didn't like what he saw (he didn't like feeling and knowing that thing, somewhere in the core in him, whatever it was) because the secret was it was just pain, just emptiness. But it seemed like, maybe this wasn't true, but it seemed like if someone looked, if the right person saw, maybe that would make it okay. Maybe that would make him realize he felt empty but really he was full.

Was that how Halie felt when she thought about herself? Was that how everyone felt? Steven supposed he didn't know, didn't care. All that mattered was right now he felt okay, maybe he even felt peaceful, heavy as his body settled into place (probably that was the alcohol), contented, like the worst was behind him and now they could just relax and be themselves. Finally.

"We're fucked," Halie said. "You know that right?"

"We'll be okay," Steven said."

"You don't understand." Halie raised her hand as if to show him something, but that didn't do any good, he still didn't know what she meant. "After it happened, that's when I realized it. It wants to fight."

"What the hell are you talking about?"

"It's—he wants to go fight to become the strongest." And after a sort of sullen silence, she added, "Gotta catch 'em all."

"What?"

"Like *Pokémon*."

"Okay."

"It's such a shitty thing," she said. "And it's weird, because I don't even want to go. But it pisses me off when he talks about going off by himself and doesn't offer for me to come."

"That sucks," Steven said.

"You suck." But she grinned—a mischievous look, her face flushed as she leaned back in the chair again.

"Hey, be careful."

"Don't worry, I'm a big girl."

"Yeah, but one who just fell over a few minutes ago."

Then, yeah, both of them laughed, and Steven thought again how good he felt. But it wasn't just him—Halie was enjoying herself too. He could see it in her face. There was color in it and she was actually looking at him. Usually when she was around she just stared off, thinking about something else, even during a conversation. That must be how she was—always kind of off in her own world. Or almost always, because tonight, at least for now, she was in his. And it was a good feeling, it really was, enough he was barely surprised when she leaned forward, set her drink down, and asked,

"Do you like me, Steven?"

"Sure I do."

"I want to show you something."

She stood up—a jerky, erratic motion, knocking her chair back so it almost fell. Steven stood up, walking a little more carefully, but they didn't have far to go. She'd left it by the door—the same bag she used all the time, when she would bring things over.

"Here," she said. "Look at this."

Only he wasn't sure what she was doing, because she started to take off her clothes—almost clumsily, but deliberately, as if he weren't there. The whole time she hardly looked at him—just jerked her shirt over her head, balled it up, and tossed it over the couch. Next, her pants: a longer, more difficult process, since they were so tight, and she had to peel them away like a snake wriggling out of its skin. Only what was beneath it was so nice and small and pale, enough Steven waited much longer than he should have to say,

"Halie, wait, you're drunk."

"Nah," she said. "Check this out."

She reached into her bag and pulled out a folded pile of cloth —some kind of uniform, lumpy from the bag but still pretty nice. She sort of grinned as she held it up, like, *look at this, isn't it great?* It only took a few seconds for her to step into the skirt, another for her to throw the top over her head, and when she was done she spun in place and said, "Tadah!"

"What is it?"

"Cosplay, dummy."

"Yeah, but what are you?"

"A schoolgirl."

"I don't get it—you are a schoolgirl."

"A Japanese one."

"Ah," Steven said. "Well it looks good."

"I just bought it off the internet. I liked it a lot."

"It's—wait, shit, what's that?"

"Nothing," she said. She'd seen the direction of his eyes, so she stepped away and reached over to cover it. It had been quick, just a flash, but the scars were unmistakable.

"Christ," he said. "Your arm. Let me see it."

Halie wouldn't, at first—she sort of jerked it away and held it behind her back, but eventually she gave it to him.

"How many cuts are there?" Steven said.

"I don't know," she said.

And neither of them ever did figure out, but it was like, almost ten.

"Michael has them too," she said.

"Why?"

"So it could take the pain away."

Steven sighed, let go of her arm and said, "Fuck my life."

"You're going to get angry, right?"

"No." Steven sighed, "I just need a second."

"Good," Halie said. "I'm tired of explaining myself to people."

"Nobody has to explain anything," Steven said.

Though maybe, really, he said that to himself—because the next second he was kissing her, pressing his mouth against hers and feeling how pliable it was… and he thought, for the first time in a long time, how soft a girl's face is, but also alarmingly hard, because of the knowledge that behind her lips there were teeth, and behind the teeth there was a person—and something about that had always seemed significant to Steven, the little part in the back of his mind always thinking about these things.

Halie was a terrible kisser—she just sort of opened her mouth (Steven thought, first, of a fish, only she tasted good so it was okay, he could feel her body pressed against him and that was even better), until her tongue shot out like a drowning man reaching for sunlight. But Steven liked that too, the reminder that neither of them were very good at this, that they were lost in this life, it wasn't just him who felt terrible and confused and lost. They were suffocating, both of them; but this way at least they could suffocate together.

Her eyes were closed when he pulled back, her breath coming heavy but slow—and Steven wasn't sure how it happened next, only that a minute later she was bent over the couch, and it was good (this was something he wanted, had thought about for weeks now), maybe even exquisite—and Steven thought, here it was, that thing he was looking for... and he felt it, he really did, rising to the surface of him; he felt all the pain pushing out of him, only they didn't, they really didn't need the creature to take it away... and he really must have been out of it because his eyes were closed, he had his hands on her hips but his head was back, staring into darkness. He felt the faint wetness of her around him but it was something different, something better, to look down and see her back stretched in front of him, her skirt flung up over her hips, the way her body shook every time he thrust.

So good that, thirty seconds later, he'd already come inside her.

For a moment, just a moment, it felt very right, the burning pinprick of all that pain making its way out of him—until he realized it wasn't pain, it was just come; and it hit him how fucking dumb he'd just been, an absolute fucking idiot, and he was actually afraid to move, enough he just stood there, watching her breathe.

No part of him expected what happened next. Her back shook, he actually felt it from inside her. But it wasn't tears, like he thought first. It was laughter—she was laughing, and laughing harder as she turned around and pushed him away.

"Jesus," she said. "What a silly thing to do."

"I'm sorry," Steven said, "I didn't—"

"I wonder. Maybe the creature could keep me from getting pregnant."

"It's okay. I'll—"

"I don't want a baby, numbnuts." But then she yawned, leaning back on the couch, and said, "I'm getting really tired."

"We don't have to stop," Steven said.

"That big couch where you usually sleep. We could just share it, right?"

"If you want," Steven said.

So they both laid down on the couch (she must really be tired, since she didn't go anywhere to clean up), and Steven felt strange and tired and heavy. It was nice to have a girl shaped pillow pressed against him—only the girl pillow, he would find out soon, also snored sometimes.

"Your family," she said. "You're just a bunch of dummies."

"What?"

"Nothing," she said. "Gimme a kiss, huh?"

He did—it was a light, soft kiss, and both of them tasted like cheap wine but it was still pretty nice.

A few second later, she was asleep; but Steven laid there, alone, for half the night.

AN EARLY MORNING

STEVEN WOKE up early the next morning with a dry, dry mouth, a bit bloated in his stomach, and a terrible boner (still pressed against Halie), but one he already wanted to go away, because he needed to take a piss. At first it was distant, faint, but no, he needed to piss bad—enough he felt guilty, but knew he had to find a way to roll out from beneath her in order to get to the bathroom. Fortunately, it turned out okay. Apparently she could sleep through pretty much anything, including him getting up.

He stepped into the front room and there was Michael, sitting at the table. His hair was greasy as hell—it had been probably two, maybe three days since he showered—wearing the same wrinkled clothes as yesterday. But it wasn't like him to be up this early. Steven didn't like it. It was never good when Michael did something out of the ordinary.

"There you are," Michael said.

"I need to take a piss," Steven said.

"Not right now you don't." The look on Michael's face— Steven wasn't sure what he expected. Anger? It wasn't like Steven was afraid of him, even now. Michael had always been full of anger, the kind of person who would lash out whenever the situation was right, and sometimes when it wasn't.

Steven said, "Is this about Halie?"

"What?" Michael looked up, surprised—which is when Steven realized he'd been wrong. That wasn't anger on

Michael's face. It was fear. Which was weird, because Steven had never seen Michael afraid. None of them had been, really. Fear wasn't something real people felt. It was an emotion from movies, from stories, not something you saw on your brother's face.

But Steven didn't want to talk about that, not right now, so he said, "That wasn't cool, what you did yesterday."

"With mom?"

"Yeah."

"It's okay. You can tell her I'm sorry."

"Are you?"

"Who cares?" Michael shrugged. "It doesn't matter anymore."

"Man, you're being weird."

"Life is weird." Michael beckoned, like *come here*, but not to Steven—to the creature. It had been standing behind him this whole time and he hadn't even noticed. But wasn't that how it always was? There, but also not.

"Are you scared of it?" Michael said. "Last night, when I went back to my room, I sat and thought for a long time. I thought about a lot of things. And I remembered that normal people would be scared right now."

"No, I'm not scared."

"I am," Michael said—except he looked calm, vaguely euphoric, as the creature slithered up his arm. It was both sitting beside him and lying on him. Nothing with bones could do that. Nothing with normal skin.

"You don't look scared."

Michael shook his head. "That's not what I mean. There are others. That's part of what they want—they want to fight each other."

"That's dumb," Steven said. Only he felt it, right then, at the worst possible time—he felt that itching in his ankle, the bone deep itch. That was the reminder. That meant it was time for the creature to eat.

"But it makes sense, right? Everything has to grow up."

"Is this about you? You think you're grown up?"

Michael shrugged. "I don't know."

"Growing up is taking responsibility. That's what dad always said."

"Dad wasn't right about everything," Michael said. "I am though, I guess. I'm about to take responsibility for myself."

"Halie says you want to go away with it."

"I guess so."

"Then what are you going to do?"

"Whatever I want. It'll still be better than here."

"Life isn't so bad," Steven said, "if you do an okay job of living it."

"I don't know," Michael said. "Maybe for you. I just—I hate it here. But… shit, this is hard to say."

"Yeah?"

"I feel bad about mom, yesterday."

"Then tell her."

"I don't know, maybe. Probably not."

"Okay."

"I feel like… things are about to change."

"How do you mean?"

"I mean I can feel it." Michael thumbed one hand on his chest —an unfamiliar gesture, not like him. "The thing is, I know where to go. It's weird to put it into words, but I feel it."

"What, like you mean—"

"I know where they are," Michael said. "I felt it, last night, when I went up to my room. It actually made me feel bad. I guess we're lucky though."

"You felt what?"

"Outside," Michael said. "I mean there's one outside. But it's… shit, it's just waiting."

"There are more of them?" Steven asked. He stared at Michael, frowning—but then Michael did something almost like Halie. He started to laugh, only it was a weird, strained laughter, and it kind of made Steven angry for someone to laugh at such a serious time.

"I forgot," Michael said, finally. "You don't know, do you? I never even told you."

"You all suck. Both of you."

"It doesn't—it doesn't matter. Man. I can't believe I never told you."

"So there's one outside?" A fist clenched in Steven's stomach— for some reason he couldn't imagine another creature. But he didn't need to. He saw Ben in his head. The way the creature had eaten him. The things it could do. In some ways not seeing them actually made it more frightening.

"Yeah," Michael said, "except—"

Steven heard Halie's footsteps too, yawning and stretching as she walked out from dad's den. She was still wearing her cosplay, and no underwear beneath it, which Steven sort of liked knowing. It was the first time Steven had ever known something about her Michael didn't.

Well—maybe not the first.

"My head," she said. "Fuck."

"I take it you drank a lot?" Michael said.

Halie pointed and said, "The box is still sitting there, if you want some."

"But what are you wearing?"

"My cosplay," Halie said. "You don't remember?"

"She wanted to show me," Steven said.

"It's nice," Michael said.

"Good." Halie nodded and said, "Steven and I had sex yesterday. I think I might be pregnant."

"Jesus Christ," Steven said.

"Oh," Michael said. "Good."

Steven said, "Halie, what the—"

"He's Michael." Halie shrugged. "We talk about stuff."

"You should go to the gas station," Michael said. "There's, like—"

"I know," Steven said.

"Are you jealous?" Halie asked.

"Sure," Michael said. "Whatever."

"Guys," Steven said. "Come on."

"I really shouldn't have a baby," Halie said. "I might drop it."

"If you drink more wine," Michael said, "I think it might make your headache go away."

"Really though," Steven said, "we should probably—"

"Is that true?" Halie asked. "I've always wondered if that was true."

"No reason not to try," Michael said.

Halie squinted at the boxed wine and said, "I need to pee."

"Me too," Steven said.

"Good, we can go together."

"That's okay." Steven wasn't sure if she was joking. "I'll wait."

"Okay then." Halie sort of skipped towards the bathroom, obviously much more awake than she'd been a few minutes ago. The bathroom door shut, and Steven heard her peeing behind it but it seemed weird to listen to someone pee, so he walked in the other direction and back towards Michael.

"I need to call mom," he said.

"Now?" Michael asked.

"Later, but today. What am I supposed to tell her? That you're gone?"

"I don't know, tell her whatever you want."

"I still—I think you should tell her."

"I'll think about it later."

"But what—you said there's one outside? What are you going to do?"

"Go fight it, of course."

"That's dumb," Steven said. "This isn't a movie. You don't, like—"

"Why can't I?" Michael said.

"Because it doesn't work that way."

Steven noticed it again—his ankle itched, enough he reached over with the other foot to scratch it. Michael glanced down, and said,

"Itches, doesn't it?"

"Like hell."

Michael reached to pet the creature and said, "Hey there. You wanna eat breakfast right?"

"Shit, Michael. That's gross."

"Gotta get fueled," Michael said.

Maybe it was the morning that made all of it seem so unreal. Or maybe it was just that yesterday was so bad. Steven had thought he would yell at Michael, maybe even punch him in the face. But now he just felt sad. Sort of sad and confused.

Halie flung the door open and said, "What did I miss?"

"Steven won't stop talking about mom," Michael said. "Same as usual."

"It's more serious than that." Steven scratched his ankle again.

"They don't have them at gas stations," Halie said. "But we should go to a pharmacy."

"You two should go," Michael said.

"Fuck," Steven said. "It really does itch."

Bad enough he sat down and pulled up his jeans to scratch it, only Halie sat down too and reached out and said, "Hey, I'll get it."

"That's weird," Steven said.

"It's honestly pretty nice letting someone do it for you," Michael said.

"This is—" Steven paused, then said, "Okay, yeah that feels alright."

Only the creature was leaning over already, and it almost—strange, but Steven had never thought this about it before—it almost looked hungry.

Steven said, "Are you really going outside to fight somebody?"

"You're what?" Halie's head whipped up towards Michael. "Where?"

"Outside," Steven said. "He just told me."

"And you're not angry?"

"You people," Steven said. "I'm not a monster."

"You two should go," Michael said again.

Except Halie was frowning, a powerful, vindictive frown (a part of Steven was a bit annoyed she'd stopped scratching) and she said, "You dick."

"Halie told me you broke your leg," Steven said.

Michael said, "She what?"

"Asshole," Halie said.

"What?" Michael asked.

"I want to see it," Halie said. "Obviously."

"You both—you can't come with me."

"It's here though," Halie said. "I can't believe—"

"You two," Steven said. "You know this is dangerous, right?"

"Don't be a little girl," Halie said.

"It's not just that," Steven said, "I mean—"

"I agree with Steven for once," Michael said.

"You see?" Halie said. "You're always wrong when it counts most."

"But shit," Steven said. "If it's out there, why hasn't it attacked?

"That's what I was thinking," Michael said. "I was thinking—"

"What?" Halie said. "Come on."

"Jesus, don't interrupt me—I was saying. I think—shit."

"What?" Steven said.

"It's not alone," Michael said. "It's out there, and it's waiting for me. But there's someone with it. That's why it's waiting this time."

No one asked it, *what do we do?* Steven felt the question in the air. Both of them looked at him, probably because they expected him to ask it, but he decided not to be predictable for once.

"Ah," Halie said. "That's why you're sitting here."

"I couldn't piss," Michael said. "I got up in the morning and I tried but I couldn't piss."

"Did you sleep?" Steven asked.

"I slept fine," Halie said.

"I'm aware," Steven said. "I mean—Michael are you okay?"

Michael said, "Didn't you need to piss, Steven?"

"Yes, but—"

"If you need to take a shit, wait. I want to pee first."

"Fuck, Michael—"

"The house," Halie said. "It could just, like, tear into the house."

Steven said, "It could what?"

"They can do a lot of things," Michael said. "But you still need to go to the pharmacy."

"Shut up, Michael," Halie said. "We'll take care of it."

"I mean," Steven said, "if it happens, it's—

"You too, Steven," Halie said.

"Can you imagine the conversation with mom?" Michael said.

"I'm just saying," Steven said. "But what is this about—"

"We saw them fight," Halie said. "It's terrifying."

"But last time it just attacked," Michael said. "There was no one with it, or at least I don't think so."

"Maybe they want to talk to you," Steven said.

"I doubt it," Halie said.

"No way," Michael said.

"Damn it," Steven said, "I was just—"

"There's your dad's gun," Halie said. "We could take it out."

Silence, a sort of ringing silence after what Halie had said.

Michael shrugged like, *Not my problem,* and Halie was still looking around—first at Michael, then at Steven—but then they all looked at him. Steven didn't know why, because they weren't going to get any support.

"We aren't shooting anybody," Steven said.

"What do you think he's going outside to do?" Halie said. "Yell at them?"

"It's good idea," Michael said. "But who is going to take it?"

"Not me," Steven said. "I'm not touching a fucking gun."

"Me, obviously," Halie said. "We need somebody with some balls around here."

"You think you could do it?" Michael asked.

"Obviously," Halie said.

"Fuck," Steven said. "Fuck both of you."

A STRANGE WOMAN

MICHAEL WENT OUT FIRST, then Halie, then Steven, last. They had talked about it for quite a while afterwards, but yeah, she'd still come out carrying the gun. She held it slung casually over her shoulder in a way Steven didn't like, mostly because it made him think of that one time, just once, he'd gone to shoot it with dad. Dad wasn't a gun person, but he'd go on, sometimes, about how this was America and how it was his duty to teach his sons how to shoot a gun. So they'd gone into the forest, set up a bunch of Coke cans, and blasted them with the shotgun.

Eventually. First there had been lectures, a bunch of them, on being careful, on keeping the safety on and *never, ever pointing it at someone*. Of course dad would start that way. He was a Hanson and he was always careful about everything. He did his best to plan, not to take risks, not to do anything; which is also why watching Halie swing the gun around like a stick made Steven's stomach tie itself up in a knot. But, god damn it, it's not like he could do anything about it, except for saying "Be careful" and "Jesus, don't point it at me!" and things like that. They were about as effective as Steven might have expected. Meaning, not at all.

"Here we go," she said, as they walked through the garage, towards the deck. "Ima kill a fucker."

"Shit," Steven said. "I can't believe we're—"

"Man," Michael said. "Grow some balls, or go back inside."

"It's not that," Steven said. "I'm just—"

"It's okay," Halie said. "I'll protect you."

"Just…" Steven paused as they walked through the door ahead of him, so confident it was vaguely stupid. Nothing he said would slow these two down. They were crazy, stupid kids, and they needed someone to keep them in line—except nothing he said would do anything, he could already tell. Probably they weren't even listening as he finished what he'd meant to say, but that didn't keep him from saying it, even if it was meaningless, even if the words that came out were, "I'm just saying, alright?"

But it was okay now. He'd said it, and by saying it, somehow he felt he'd spared himself—made it no longer his responsibility, so later they'd be the ones to take the blame for whatever happened. They would be, really. Only that didn't make a lot of sense, because he was coming with them, just walking along behind them and not saying a thing to stop them, which also made him feel like he should—

"It's fine," Halie said. "Don't be such a noob."

"Okay," Steven said. "Okay, okay."

Michael stood in the center of the deck, looking around, and Steven had to step to one side to see past them, but—no, there was no one there, just the yard. The same as always: the deck, then lots of open space (which Steven had resented mowing for years because it got hot as hell out here in the summer, and when he cut the grass the pollen was so bad it turned his nose into this ridiculous mess of snot) with just the swing set and the shed in it, going back to the line of the forest in front; and, way to the left, the neighbor's yard, which was just another open field with a fence dividing the two.

All of that, only there was no one here, nothing, except—

"Jesus," Michael said. "It's still there."

The cat, he meant—Steven didn't, shit he didn't even want to look at it. Only a quick glimpse from the corner of his eye. All this time and it had finally rained once, so maybe that had thinned out the blood; but also the skin, thin and crispy, had sloughed away from the bone then gone crispy again. At least—fuck, at least there were no flies or some big glut of maggots.

"It's disgusting," Halie said. Except Steven had realized by now that she mainly said that when she liked something, which was weird as hell really, and now she was staring at it.

"Man," Steven said. "I can't believe you never cleaned it up."

"Gimme a break," Michael said. "We've got bigger things to worry about. Isn't that right, boy?"

The creature, he meant—and there it was, standing over the corpse to look down: lofty and contorted, easily the height of a person except it still had four legs, the torso jutting up and over in an impossible way, almost a jagged arch. Like a ghost coming back to look at its own body. Steven didn't know whether the creature was attached to itself, or what it had been, or if it had been in the cat at all. He didn't know anything.

"Is that you?" Steven asked.

The creature turned towards him as he asked, but no response. (He'd seen it nod, sometimes, when Michael talked to it.) And all of them looked curious, but in the midst of the creature's silence, the responsibility seemed to fall on Michael, who said,

"It doesn't matter. Let's go."

"But where?" Steven asked. "There's nobody here."

Halie pointed the gun into the woods and said, "Motherfucker, I'll shoot you."

"Christ, Halie," Steven said.

Michael said, "There's someone there. I can feel it."

"I'll just shoot this fucking gun right into the woods," Halie said.

"Can't the creature find them?" Steven said.

Silence again—the wind licked Steven's skin as it blew, and then a sound (it was hard to place, but) and he realized that, yeah —the sound was laughter. Coming from—where? It didn't belong to any of them. A woman's laughter, strong and composed, maybe even mocking. It went on for not long, only a few seconds. A voice followed it, clear and strong.

"You all can relax," it said. "I'm coming out."

It didn't come from the forest; it came from the far side of the house, near the neighbor's field, on the side near Michael's room. A woman, walking from the other side of the yard.

She wore a long coat—a tall woman in nice clothes, with brown hair down around her shoulders. And she was young, but maybe not as young as she looked—probably somewhere in her thirties. Like an office worker on vacation, except her clothes were wrinkled and dirty in a few spots, which made sense if Michael was right and she'd slept outside last night.

But of course, she wasn't alone. At her shoulder, like some mutated shadow, followed another creature—only it was so black, so tall, and it didn't look like a cat at all, it looked like a mantis, like a wraith.

Somebody gasped, maybe all of them. The woman laughed again as she slowed—almost an awkwardness, a forced stillness—until they heard her voice again, cool and authoritative.

"All this for a bunch of kids," she said. "What, are you going to shoot me?"

"Fuck you!" Halie said.

"Guys," Steven said. "There's no need for this."

"You were so easy to find," said the woman. "After what happened in the park? And you're sloppy. That man who disappeared."

"It was an accident," Michael said.

"And you're a child," said the woman. And really, it was true —it must be. Not just Michael. Steven felt like a child. Standing here, looking at this woman, he felt like all of them were children. Like they'd been playing a game this whole time, living in a little imaginary world. But now an adult was here, someone who really knew how things were. The reality of it made Steven feel absurd and small; and it didn't just feel like a question, it felt like a mockery when the woman asked,

"Do you mind if I smoke?"

"It's a free country," Michael said.

"Anyone want one?" she asked, pulling a pack of Marlboros from her front pocket. She pushed her hair back to light one and held the pack up, like a peace offering.

"Me," Halie said. "I want one."

"Fuck," Steven said. "Halie, she—"

"I want a cigarette," Halie said. "I haven't smoked in like three days."

"But what if she—"

"What do you think I am?" said the woman. "A monster?"

It was funny, kind of funny that Steven had asked that same

question fifteen minutes ago, enough he started laughing. That got him a strange look, almost a tilt of the head. Steven didn't like that. It felt strange. But of course it felt strange. This was a new feeling, a new problem of existing in the world. He'd never wondered before if he might be dead in a few minutes.

"I'm not here to hurt you," the woman said. "Why do you think I waited outside?"

"Here." Halie passed the gun to Steven, almost shoved it at him. He didn't want it, but there it was, and he wasn't going to just drop it. "I'll be back in a second."

It was so dumb, what she did next, such a stupid thing—but Halie walked forward, took a cigarette. Steven could see it in his mind's eye: the woman would grab her and put a knife to her throat, and it would be like a movie situation. It would happen in just a second, it really would. Except the woman just lit her cigarette and Halie walked back.

"Ah," she said. "It's so good to have a cigarette in the morning. I just realized—we didn't drink coffee."

"You guys," Steven said. "This is serious."

The look on the woman's face—it was hard to place. On one hand she looked friendly, sort of open (another part of Steven basically just wanted to check her out), but there was something else behind that. He didn't like them relaxing around her. He didn't even like holding the gun. But there they were, the woman's creature flattened behind her like the most terrible shadow as she stood there with one hand in her pocket, casually smoking.

"I take it this is your first fight," said the woman.

"No," Michael said—but didn't clarify. That was good, even if it was a lie.

"Ah," said the woman. "I'm Marissa, by the way."

"What the hell is this about?" Steven said. He'd cut Michael off, but he didn't care.

"It's a challenge," Marissa said—strange, meeting someone like this but her having such a normal name.

"But what the hell for?" Steven asked.

"Because it's what they want," Michael said.

"She's in our fucking yard," Steven said.

"Thanks for the cigarette though," Halie said.

"The boy with long hair is right," the woman said. "It's what they want."

"What the hell does that mean?" Steven asked.

"They make us happy," Michael said. "So we want to make them happy too."

"That's bullshit," Steven said. "Since when have you cared about anyone but yourself?"

Michael scowled—the creature crouched, coiled beside him. It looked different, almost bristling, ready to leap ahead at any second. An animal getting ready to strike. Which Steven supposed it was.

"A bunch of kids." The woman laughed again. "I swear."

"Fuck you." Michael this time—maybe Halie had mellowed out a little now that she had her cigarette.

Steven said, "So you're here to, what?"

"To fight," said the woman. "It's not personal."

"So you just, what—travel around?"

"When I have the time, yes."

"Wait." Halie was doing that thing again where she was about to laugh, but she held it in long enough to ask, "Do you have a job?"

"Of course. I'm an adult."

"This is ridiculous," Steven said.

"Then go inside," Michael said. "This is what I want."

"I guess I don't have to shoot you after all," Halie said. "Steven, you can keep the gun."

But something very important occurred to Steven then. They would think it was fussy, maybe even dumb, but it was important. This was real life after all.

"Not here," he said. "There are neighbors."

Michael said, "Stop being lame."

"No, he's right." The woman nodded—and gave Steven a sort of warm, conspiratorial look. It had been a long time since someone agreed with him, and along with that look, it almost made him like her. "No witnesses."

"Can you imagine if someone saw?" Steven asked.

"These woods," the woman said. "They go back—half an hour?"

"Something like that," Steven said.

"There's a clearing," said the woman. "I found it yesterday."

"This is stupid," Michael said. "Here is fine."

"Whatever," Halie said. "I'm not in any hurry."

"Come on then," said the woman. "Let's be responsible about this."

A PERILOUS JOURNEY

IT WASN'T A LONG WALK, not really, but it definitely felt like one to Steven. As kids, there had been a sort of path in these woods; but it had been a long time, and it was gone now. So they walked through low shrubs, pricker bushes dragging along Steven's jeans. At least he was dressed for it—Halie was still in her cosplay. She flinched a few times as protruding branches left long red marks on her legs. Steven even saw up her skirt once when they had to step over a log, which sort of turned him on. But that reminded him they'd never gone to the pharmacy, which was something he didn't even want to think about.

The walk started out silent. Which made it stranger. The feeling fluctuated, basically at random, between comfortable and antagonistic—fluctuated so quickly that Steven didn't know what to feel. Everything was just this crazy, insane mess in his head. And it made it worse that, for the first few minutes, they were silent. It was both more and less dramatic than a scene in a movie: the long, slow drudgery. What made it dramatic was the lack of drama, that flatness of it. In movies there was always music playing. But now, in real life, there was no music, no camera angles. And this walk—shit. It would probably be cut out of any decent movie.

It was awkward enough to bother all of them. Halie normally would have broken the silence, but she was so focused on not getting scratched; and Michael just walked, determined, with his head down, so Steven realized he would have to do it. But it took a while. It was hard, thinking of something to say.

"So where do you live?" he asked. It came out sounding dumb, stupid and banal and he regretted it immediately, but that's life.

"Minneapolis," said the woman. "I work in sales."

"I was thinking of doing that," Steven said. "I just graduated. A job in sales would be nice. A good company?"

"They pay me and I get time off."

"Boring," Michael said. "I can't believe you work."

"Of course I work," the woman said. "Everyone works."

Steven said, "So you just, like, travel around doing this when you can?"

"I'm careful with my vacation."

"Sales," Michael said. "Fucking boring."

Michael kept muttering, and Steven supposed he knew why—here was Michael imagining himself going on a kind of journey, then they meet someone and she's just a normal adult with a job. (Or at least she claimed to be.) Steven had seen that look on Michael's face as he talked about it, this impression like he was a hero about to set out on his journey.

It was hard to see it now, but Steven remembered, as a kid, how attached Michael had been the idea of heroism, to epic journeys. The reasons didn't matter, not really—just the knowledge of someone special, someone chosen, setting off alone, doing what they were meant to do. The thing itself didn't matter, just that sense of being special, chosen. That was the only kind of story Michael had ever liked, the only kind he had any time for.

It occurred to Steven, just now, that this was a rare opportunity. All this time, with the creature, he'd taken care hardly to ask certain questions—what it was, where it came from. They'd taken care because a certain part of him knew there were no answers; that Michael, even if he was closest to the creature, didn't understand a fucking thing about it, and it wasn't going to tell them anything. Maybe it could, but it wouldn't. Except this woman, she seemed to understand it, maybe she could finally explain it to them.

Now that the silence had fallen again, Steven waited a while before asking the question. He fell back, next to the woman—

glimpsing, for just a second, the fullness of her breasts beneath her shirt, buttoned low to show the tanned skin around her collar. She walked with her eyes forward, like someone who knew where she was going; but she seemed casual enough when she met his eyes.

"But what are they?" Steven said. "All of this and we don't even know what they are."

"Hell if I know," said the woman.

"How did yours show up?" Michael asked. "What died?"

"What do you mean?" asked the woman. "Nothing died. I found it."

"You found it?" Michael asked. "Fully grown?"

"Of course. How else would it happen?"

"I don't know," Michael said. "I was just curious."

There was a pause, another silence. Steven had wanted to say more, ask a better question, but he felt sort of flat and deflated after the last one. All of this, this walk with the blood pounding in his temples, and he thought he would at least get some answers for it—but she didn't know anything! Or if she did, she wasn't going to tell them. It was disappointing. Though he didn't feel disappointed exactly. Maybe, as he fell behind and caught a glimpse of the woman's legs, he mostly felt a bit horny, a bit like he needed to piss again.

It was hot as hell—for some reason it had taken Steven this long to notice the dense, humid press of the leaves, the way it kept the faintest trace of wind away. It was humid like it always seemed to be in Michigan in summer, and he was sweating. Hot, burning lines of it falling down across his face; more beneath his armpits and that queasy, stagnant heat where his balls stuck between his legs.

It was a mission to walk this far, an ordeal, and they kept at it in silence until Halie said, "You guys, I think I'm pregnant."

Shit. All of this and Steven had almost forgotten.

"We can turn around," Steven said. "Let them go."

"I don't know," Michael said. "Is it already too late?"

"Pregnant?" said the woman.

"It's nothing," Steven said. "I don't know—how long does it, shit. Does it actually have to be morning?"

"I think it's seventy-two-hours," Halie said.

"Are you sure?" Steven said.

"I still can't believe you two did it," Michael said.

"What?" Halie said. "Jealous now?"

"Guys," Steven said—feeling it, this weird, awkward unpleasantness in his chest every time it was mentioned, this brutal impending fear mixed, just faintly, with pride. "Stop it."

"I'm not jealous," Michael said. "It's just dumb."

"You sound jealous," Halie said.

"This is serious," Steven said. "Let's deal with this later."

"I don't understand," the woman said. "Isn't she your sister?"

That did it—it got Halie laughing hard, so much she slowed down and fell behind, but it got Michael laughing too. It was ridiculous, ridiculous enough it almost made Steven angry, but also kind of infectious. Though he couldn't—he really couldn't laugh. He couldn't.

"A sister," Michael said. "That's hilarious."

"I guess I was wrong," the woman said.

"I feel it," Halie said. "I feel pregnant."

"I don't think it works that way," Michael said.

"Why do you keep bringing this up?" Steven said.

Michael said, "Imagine if she had to get an abortion."

"Stop," Steven said. "It won't—"

"Do you actually like Steven?" Michael asked. "Seriously?"

"He's fine," Halie said.

"Wait," Steven said. "You—"

Halie said, "You're sweet, okay."

"I'm still leaving after this," Michael said. "I'm still leaving."

"I'm sweet?" Steven said. "What the hell does that mean?"

"It means I like you," Halie said. "And Michael, you can do whatever the hell you want."

"It doesn't matter," Michael said. "I could do better than you."

"You what?" Halie said.

"I don't understand any of this," the woman said. "But you—be careful, okay? If you get an abortion."

"Nobody is getting an abortion," Steven said.

"I'll get an abortion if I want," Halie said.

"That's not—" Steven caught his breath, "I don't mean—"

"It's a very serious procedure," said the woman.

"I hate kids," Halie said. "If I had a kid I would throw it off the roof."

"You would what?" Steven said. "That—"

"Just think of the health risks," said the woman. "You could consider—"

"Adoption?" Halie said. "Hell no. Then, you know—I'd have to have it."

"We're not having this conversation," Steven said. "We really aren't."

"But hon," said the woman. "It's a very serious decision."

Hon, Steven thought—the same word mom always said. He didn't like it, actually it made him uncomfortable to hear it. Like this woman was their friend. But she wasn't their friend. She was their enemy, at least, he was pretty sure she was. It didn't—

"My god," Michael said. "You aren't Christian, are you? Steven hates Christians."

"We're all adults here," Steven said.

"Are we?" Halie asked.

"I've been curious," the woman said. "Your outfit, it's—"

"Japanese," Halie said. "I'm a schoolgirl."

"But why—"

"It's a sex thing," Michael said.

"Fuck you, Michael," Halie said. "It's an anime thing."

"Like cartoons?" the woman said.

"It's these Japanese cartoons," Steven said. "They're obsessed with them."

"Because they're better than anything else," Halie said. "And they're cute."

"I know kids like them," said the woman. "But I don't know anything about them, except—they have the big eyes, right?"

"That's about all I know," Steven said.

"Because you haven't given it a chance," Halie said.

"Someday," Steven said.

"I've tried," Michael said. "He'll never give them a chance."

"It just—it just looks kind of silly."

"Take that back," Halie said.

"Shit," Steven said. "It's just—"

"But why are you wearing it now?" the woman said. "That's the first thing I wondered, when I saw all of you."

"I told you," Steven said. "I think it looks good."

"Not you," Halie said. "Michael, I even—"

"It goes well with your hair," the woman said. "The way you teenagers do it. I like it."

"Who are you supposed to be?" Michael asked.

"I already told you, numbnuts."

"Wait," Steven said. "Everybody, calm down."

"That's so weird," Michael said. "Since when have I remembered everything people said to me?"

"Since—ah, shit."

Halie must have gotten caught in the argument and stopped looking where she was going. Steven didn't see what happened (probably she caught her leg on an especially sharp branch; scratched herself, maybe even tripped), even though he'd fallen behind to wait for her. But he turned as she stumbled forward, not quite falling but close, and he reached so she could brace her arm against his.

"Careful there," he said.

"Fuck." Halie reached down to trace a long scratch on her left thigh. It was thin, barely visible, but maybe it hurt much more than Steven could see. She stopped walking and started just rubbing her hand against it like that would do something. All it did was make her leg jiggle a bit. "That hurts."

"Are you okay?" the woman asked. She slowed, came back around, bending down to look at Halie's leg.

"It's fine," Halie said. "I just scratched myself again."

"Let me see," she said. "Maybe we could—wait, what's that?"

The woman had shook, almost recoiled—but then she reached out, not for Halie's leg, but for her left arm. Her grip looked firm, almost rough, as she held out Halie's forearm and looked at it.

"What are these?" she asked. "Do you—I don't get it."

"It's fine," Halie said. "I'm not—I'm not depressed. It's just—"

"The creature," Michael said. "I've been doing it too. Look." Michael held out his arm, but very quickly. Next he rolled up his shorts, showing a bunch of cuts (more than Halie) up his thigh.

"Why would you do this?" the woman asked.

Michael said, "I thought here was better. I don't like wearing long sleeve shirts."

"I stopped a while ago," Halie said. "Actually. But the marks, I was hoping they would go away."

The woman turned towards Steven and said, "You. Did you know about this?"

"It's not my choice what they do."

The woman looked up, looked back, and her voice wasn't relaxed anymore as she said, "What's wrong with all of you?"

"Nothing," Michael said. "It's just, the creature. It takes the pain away."

"What are you talking about?"

"When you get hurt," Michael said. "Or when you feel bad. It makes us feel better."

"Where is yours at?" Halie gestured towards her ankle. "Where the black pellets come out?"

The woman said, "I don't know what you're talking about."

"There's nothing wrong with us," Michael said. "It was just to take the pain away."

The woman's eyes were wide—somewhere between repulsion and anger—her voice tense as she said, "That's disgusting."

"It's just what it's for," Michael said. "Right?"

"It's natural," Halie said.

"A bunch of kids," the woman said. And this one was aimed at Steven. "You too. You don't know what's good for you."

"That's not fair," Steven said. "I didn't—"

"It's sick," she said. "All of you are sick."

"Why should we listen to some old woman?" Halie said.

"Stop it," Steven said. "We don't have to—"

"It's disgusting." The woman was stepping away now. "I can't believe it."

"Come on," Steven said. "It's not—"

"What does she know?" Halie said. "Why would she know what's best for us."

"I don't understand," Michael said. "What's the problem?"

The woman's face hardened as she looked at them—from Steven, to Halie, stopping at Michael. Her features settled into a mask of resolve, the face of someone making a decision, who believed what they were about to do was right; and she would have it for the rest of the walk, the sense of someone who had discovered a new purpose, not just the one she'd come for.

"Let's go," the woman said, her shadow setting off behind her. "It's not far now."

THE BATTLEFIELD

THE CLEARING WAS a bit too small—maybe thirty feet at most—but it was better than nothing. Steven wasn't sure why nothing had grown. Over on one side there was a place that had been a dry, stagnant pond, next to the trunk of one tree that had been cut down. But it felt liberating, stepping out of the trees and into the light; even if the sun was too hot, it was cooking his skin and making it all scratchy.

The woman squinted as she walked into the light, and said, "This is as good a place as any."

And that look on her face. Even after what had happened, Steven had forgotten. It had been so easy to forget. They'd come out here for a reason—not as friends, but to fight. It was a dim reminder, for better or worse, of the gun he still had slung over his shoulder, its barrel covered with sweat from his hand; but the sun was heating it up and soon it might even burn.

"Bitch," Halie said.

"I'm ready," Michael said.

Steven looked back and forth between them—two groups, them standing near the line of trees, and the woman further out. But it wasn't the group that mattered. It was their shadows, their creatures, spreading out like they fed off the light.

"Over there," the woman said. "Let's stand back. Give them some space."

"We don't have to do this," Steven said.

That got him a lot of looks, like he knew it would—but it wasn't right. It wasn't right now that none of them, not a single one, was agreeing with him.

Michael said, "Shut up, Steven."

"So we just watch?" Halie asked.

"Nothing we do matters," said the woman. "This is all about them."

The stillness took solid form as they stepped away—so far they were actually back inside the trees. Though not too far, since they wanted to see after all. It felt good to be out of the sun, but it also felt wrong. Everything about this was wrong. Like always: it felt wrong, everything in the world was infused with that same sense of *wrongness*, but Steven didn't know how to make it right.

"How many times?" Steven asked. "How many times have you done this?"

"Enough," the woman said.

A limb lashed across the clearing, so quick Steven couldn't begin to follow it—it left nothing to follow, no kind of movement that made sense, just the awareness of a thing begun. Neither creature had lunged forward; they still stood right where they'd started, even as their limbs streaked out across the clearing, enmeshed with each other, whipping faster than anyone could ever see.

It was a little, Steven thought, like two people with twenty arms, having twenty sword fights at the same time, from twenty feet away—which was a ridiculous, stupid comparison to make. Only it was impossible to describe it right, the ferocity as the two creatures hurled their bodies at each other; and somewhere beneath them, inside the unraveled black mass, maybe, were their original bodies.

Steven didn't know how it worked. He didn't know if the creatures had organs, or circulatory systems—but he saw them bleed. Half of the fight, maybe more, wasn't them going for the main bodies. They were trying to sever limbs.

It only took a second for the first to fall, but more came afterwards—they shot off into the undergrowth, severed but still maintaining all their momentum. The first landed on the ground ten feet ahead of them; the next few embedded themselves in trees. Others went over the treeline like accidental home runs;

they would fly however far (Steven really had no idea) until they leapt into the ground somewhere, maybe even got caught in the branches.

The limbs were sharp at the end—slightly different for each creature. One had limbs that spread out, hooked like clawed hands; the others' were curved blades. Whenever they hit, they would stay solid, but just for a few seconds. Then they deflated, spurting long lines of blood where they'd been severed, until what remained of the limbs looked like flimsy black balloons, melting in the grass.

"Fuck," Steven said. "We should move back."

"Don't be a pussy," Michael said.

Except, half a second later, Halie keeled over, grasping at the same thigh as earlier—only now there was a huge gash in it (lower, maybe six inches above the knee), spurting blood that seeped between her closed fingers. It must've be deep for there to be that much blood, but Steven didn't see the limb. It must have gone through and landed somewhere behind them.

Halie didn't scream, just looked down at her leg, puzzled like she didn't understand what she was seeing. It wasn't just Steven. All of them were looking at her, but none of them were saying anything; and it was the normal feeling, what Steven felt next. The feeling of being the only one willing to do what needed to be done.

"The trees," he said. "Get back!"

There were two larger trees—one closer on the left, and another back to the right. They split up, almost as a matter of principle. Steven wanted to look back (it seemed idiotic, like a huge waste), actually to just stand there and watch the fight; but instead he grabbed Halie's arm and dragged her.

She took the first step fine, but she stumbled on the second. Steven had to drag her the last little bit. He tried to sit her down, but she sort of stumbled and maybe hit her head on the tree. She didn't seem to notice, just clasped her hands against the wound, staring at the blood that seeped between her closed fingers.

"It's disgusting." She raised her hands, the red so pronounced it hid the lines on her palms, and said, "Steven, look!"

"Michael!" Steven said. "Come on."

But Michael wasn't going anywhere. He'd taken a few steps

back, but now he was still just standing there. And the look on his face—Steven recognized it. He was in awe. Sometimes, years ago, when they'd gone to see big Hollywood movies with dad, Steven had looked over and seen a look like that on Michael's face.

An explosion—or something that sounded like one. Steven flinched; he felt the aftershock, actually reverberating in his body. And it was like—it was hard to describe—like something in his body just let go. The whole immensity of the world pressed down around him, and he just wanted to flatten himself to the ground until all of this *just stopped.* The only thing he wanted more was to punch Michael in the face and say *I told you so.*

Steven looked over, sticking his head just faintly beyond the tree—but there was nothing, just so many scarred markings in the grass. So many limbs—these hanging black satchels of flesh scattered all through the trees and the grass. Everything, all the leaves and grass, had been covered with splashes of black blood, something that seemed it didn't belong in the day. Maybe didn't belong in the universe.

All of it ravaged, all of it destroyed—except Michael.

Or that's what Steven thought at first, because Michael was still standing. Only maybe something had happened, maybe after so long he was immune to pain. Because all he did was reach down one hand, as if bracing himself after a long day—but that wound in his abdomen, it was huge. So big it had also torn away a big flap of his shirt.

It was big enough—god damn, it was so big it must have taken a chunk of his ribcage. But he hardly seemed to notice.

Michael didn't look down, just stared out. But when he turned to Steven he was crying. The tears, they ran all across his face; but they weren't the right kind of tears. They weren't tears for himself.

He didn't know, Steven realized. They were the other kind of tears.

"It's losing!" Michael's voice was choked, frantic—Steven didn't know how much of that was from internal damage. "Fuck, Steven, it's losing!"

Steven couldn't see anymore—he still heard the fighting somewhere off in the forest. But he didn't care. He just looked at Michael, with a hole so big it seemed like his stomach ought to fall out of it; then back to Halie. Halie stared up, her eyes wide, and the blood on her hands. It was a lot, but now it seemed like nothing.

"Michael," she said. "Fuck."

"It's losing," Michael said again. "God damn it."

Michael leaned over—and coughed blood. A lot. Enough it spewed from his mouth like vomit. Like Steven at dad's funeral.

It only came once, like Michael was clearing his throat, so close it might have hit Steven as he walked closer.

But he wasn't alone—the woman, too. She staggered out with this wide, horrified look in her eyes. They were big, beautiful eyes. Looking close, Steven could even see it—the long, individual lines of her eyelashes, accented by makeup.

"You're hurt," she said. Again and again: "You're hurt."

"Make it stop!" Michael turned towards Steven. "Make her stop!"

"There's nothing we can do," said the woman, walking closer. "It's up to them now."

Michael stumbled forward onto Steven. Steven caught him, he knew he had to—only Michael didn't reach out for Steven's shoulders.

Michael reached out for the gun, and even then—even though he could barely stand—

"A doctor," the woman said, "We need to get him to a doctor."

Years ago, Steven remembered, dad had started off by saying that in real life, you don't shoot from the hip—you have to take careful aim. But Michael couldn't. He just held the gun, falling back onto Steven, half on his feet, in shaking hands, and pulled the trigger.

That's why the first shot whizzed off to one side; maybe it was low, so the soil leapt at her feet. And the expression on the woman's face—it was mostly just confusion, not understanding what had just happened. The rest happened so quick her expression barely had time to change; even as the second shot shattered her hip, or maybe her pelvis, so that she kneeled down and stumbled, not even knowing where to grasp.

The third got her above one eye, and took off the better part of her skull.

A roar. Steven's whole body jerked, but he wasn't sure—was

he imagining it, that vicious, agonized sound that seemed like it could come from no living body? Or was it in his head? All he knew was he didn't want to have seen it, though he had—the way the woman (her name had been Marissa, he reminded himself) had gone limp and fallen so quickly, like it was nothing. A head-shot, Michael would have called it.

Only it was so loud, the rush of a hurricane in the trees, and when Steven looked out across the clearing, he saw it: the tremors that shook the bulbous mass of her creature's contorting black body. Its head shot towards Michael on a long, long neck, a head tangled amidst a writhing mass of arms, and somewhere in the pit were its eyes, burning with immense, unbelievable pain—fueled by the pain, by the torrid gasps of its body, it lashed out, and became rage, and the rage would become death.

In just a second, each of those limbs would puncture Michael's body. They would thrust through his torso, his pelvis, his skull; they would rip the arms from his shoulders; they would impale his organs in the air, and all of that, all of him, it would explode in this terrible bloody mist, so quick—and the shower, it would fall on all of them, but probably they would be next, or even first, both Steven and Halie. And there was nothing, nothing they could do. Nothing anyone could do in the face of such terrible inhuman pain.

But behind it, behind that body, there was something else. Like a mouth, an immense mouth, with teeth, fifteen, twenty feet high —and the mouth arced downward, extending its top jaw high, the bottom braced with its unbelievable sharp teeth. Above and below; like a guillotine closing on that long neck.

If it had been a race, Steven thought, the mouth would have lost.

But all the mouth needed to do was close.

THE MAW

IT LOOKED, Steven thought afterwards, like a tumor—a twenty-foot long, black tumor. Only, now that all the threads of the severed limbs had grown together, it also looked like an arm with the skin peeled, so you could see the threads of the muscle beneath it; except there were no joints in that limb, no fist at the end. And at the far end, where the neck had been severed, so much—gallons and gallons of black blood, just spurting off into the earth.

Michael was down—he'd fallen as soon as he took the last shot. Only a few feet from the woman, but Steven didn't want to look at her. He didn't want to look at anything. Now there was nothing, no movement. Just the aching, terrible sound of Michael's breath.

He was still lying there, even though he kept trying to get up —to prop up his head even though he couldn't anymore. The persistence of it. It was so stupid, just like Michael. That was no surprise. Of course Michael would be stupid even while he was dying.

"Did we win?" he asked. At last he gave up, just setting his head back, and there was a sort of hazy, distant smile on his face. His voice didn't sound right. He barely sounded like a person.

"Michael," Halie said. "What the fuck?"

Halie had propped herself up on the tree. At least she could stand. Maybe not walk.

"You idiot," she said. "Look at all of this."

"I'm sorry," Michael said. "But we won, right?"

"Yes," Steven said. "Fuck, Michael. You won."

"You killed somebody," Halie said.

"Told you I could do it." Then Michael—he started laughing. God but even listening to him laugh hurt. At least it didn't last long. Maybe he was immune to pain, or maybe not, but Steven could tell. He didn't have much laughter in him. There was nothing much in him anymore.

"You guys," Michael said. "Don't have a baby."

"Fuck you," Halie said. "I'm not an idiot."

"That woman," Steven said. "She—"

"Let it eat me," Michael said. "Her too."

"That's—"

"You have to," Michael said. "I know you think I'm an idiot, but I wrote a note. It's in my room. It says—I'm running away, in my handwriting. Except they'll never find me."

He laughed again, that terrible, painful laughter.

"That—" Steven stopped, started, felt the words in his mouth. "It's not—"

"It's what I want," Michael said.

"You fucking idiot," Steven said. "This is all your fault."

"It's coming," Michael said. "I can feel it."

And Steven too, he could hear—the creature. It was putting itself back together, slithering towards them in a brutalized, shapeless body, spurting black blood. Steven saw pain when he looked at it. This is what the black pellets became, after the creature ate them; when they became a part of it. Every bit of it, that terrible, inhuman black, it all came from them. The whole, terrible mass of it was full of uncontainable pain.

"You don't have to stay," Michael said. "I know—it would suck to watch."

"Michael," Halie said again. "God."

"Don't worry about what to tell mom," Michael said. "But I'm—"

"You killed somebody," Steven said. "You deserve this."

"Steven," Halie said. "Let him—"

"No," Steven said. "I mean it."

"He's dying, Steven."

"He's an adult," Steven said. "He's getting what deserves."

Michael didn't respond. The creature was close, so close, all nine feet of it dragging along the ground, a thing without shape or meaning or any trace of humanity—but, Steven knew just looking at it, it would survive. It would survive and he had no idea what to do with it. He never had. He didn't know if it was natural, or good, or bad, whether it had a place in their lives, or even in the world. He didn't know any of those things.

But he also didn't know if he'd be able go on without it, when the pain came back—the real pain. The kind of pain no one, nobody can deal with. The kind of pain that is everywhere, in everything. Just a part of life.

It was hideous, and it was terrible, but also beautiful, as it leaned over Michael, leaning down with this mouth made of absence and darkness and everything a person was not.

And Michael—Michael saw it too, he must have. He saw inside that mouth, saw how it would free him from himself, from everything; and, as the creature lowered its jaws, he wasn't crying, he was laughing, even if the laughter had tears mixed in, amidst the blood and emptiness and the pain. Michael looked from Steven to Halie, but he looked the longest at the creature; and the expression on his face, Steven would never forget it. It was terrible, the most awful thing—how even at the end, Michael was still smiling.

ACKNOWLEDGMENTS

My thanks to Eddy Rathke, who has been the first reader of all my work for over a decade now and an invaluable sounding-board for ideas; also, to Kevin Muntz and Jiayu Wu, for their early enthusiasm and support. This book never would have happened without Matt Pelkey, who gave a small suggestion that later changed everything, and Valerie Sayers, who may have been the person I most wanted to impress. And finally, my endless gratitude to Leza Cantoral and Christoph Paul for believing in this book, and to Matthew Revert for an amazing cover.

ABOUT THE AUTHOR

Kyle Muntz is the author of Scary People (Eraserhead Press), and winner of the Sparks Prize for short fiction. In 2016 he received an MFA in fiction from the University of Notre Dame. Currently he teaches literature and writing at the Guangdong University of Foreign Studies in Guangzhou, China.

ALSO BY CLASH BOOKS

ANYBODY HOME?

Michael Seidlinger

I'M FROM NOWHERE

Lindsay Lerman

NIGHTMARES IN ECSTACY

Brendan Vidito

DIMENTIA

Russell Coy

SILVERFISH

Rone Shavers

HEXIS

Charlene Elsby

COMAVILLE

Kevin Bigley

CHARCOAL

Garrett Cook

PEST

Michael Cisco

HIGH SCHOOL ROMANCE

Marston Hefner

GAG REFLEX

Elle Nash

WE PUT THE LIT IN LITERARY

CLASHBOOKS.COM

FOLLOW US
TWITTER
IG
FB
@clashbooks